Nicole's Black Cherry Burgundy Pie

1 cup water
1/4 cup sugar
1 pkg. cherry gelatin (3 oz)
2 cups fresh dark sweet cherries, pitted
1 pint vanilla ice cream
3 tbsp burgundy
1 tsp lemon juice
1 baked pie shell (9-inch)

Bring water to boil and dissolve sugar and gelatin. Stir in cherries. Add ice cream a spoonful at a time until melted. Blend in burgundy and lemon juice. Pour into pie shell and chill until set. May use maraschino cherry juice instead of water, or use blackberry ice cream instead of vanilla. Almond or vanilla extract may be used instead of burgundy, and pie can be topped with whipped cream and cherries.

SUSAN MALLERY

Sweet Spot

HQN™

ISBN-13: 978-0-373-77314-5
ISBN-10:   0-373-77314-5

SWEET SPOT

Copyright © 2008 by Susan Macias Redmond

This edition published by arrangement with Harlequin Books S.A.

® and TM are trademarks of the publisher. Trademarks indicated with ® are registered in the United States Patent and Trademark Office, the Canadian Trade Marks Office and in other countries.

www.HQNBooks.com

Printed in U.S.A.

To my editor, Tara Parsons. Because we both love this book! Because working with you is a delight. Because you make my books so much better. A thousand thanks.

Sweet Spot

CHAPTER ONE

NICOLE KEYES had always believed that when life gives you lemons, stick them in a bowl on the counter, then go get a Danish and a coffee to get you through to better times. Which explained why the time cards were sticky and she had a very effective caffeine buzz going on.

She eyed the display case, where a cherry-cheese Danish softly whispered her name over and over again, then glanced down at the brace on her knee and cane by her side. She was still healing from her recent surgery, which meant not a whole lot of physical activity. If she didn't want to risk making her jeans even tighter, she was going to have pass on that second Danish.

"Better to be tempted by a pastry than a man," she reminded herself. Baked goods could make a woman fat, but a man could rip out her heart and leave her broken and bleeding. While the cure for the former—diet and exercise—wasn't pleasant, it was something she could handle. But a cure for the latter was iffy at best. Distance, distractions, great sex. At present, she didn't have any of those in her life.

The front door to the bakery opened, causing the bell above it to tinkle. Nicole barely glanced up as a high school kid walked to the case and asked for five dozen doughnuts. She licked her fingers, wiped them on a paper napkin, then began initialing the time cards so they could be dropped off at her accountant's that afternoon.

Maggie, working behind the display case, put three big boxes on the counter, then started to ring up the order. Just then, the phone rang. Maggie turned to get it.

Nicole couldn't say what it was that made her look up at that moment. A sixth sense? Luck? The way the teenager's fidgeting caught her attention?

She saw the kid stick a cell phone back into his shorts' front pocket, grab the boxes of doughnuts and head for the door. Without paying.

Nicole accepted that she was, by nature, a crabby person. She rarely saw the bright side of any situation and she was known to overreact from time to time. But nothing, absolutely nothing, pissed her off more than someone playing her for a fool. She'd had a lot of that in her life lately, and there was no way this kid was going to add himself to the list.

Without really planning her actions, she stuck out her cane, tripped him, then shoved the cane in the center of his back.

"I don't think so," she told him. "Maggie, call the cops."

She half expected the kid to jump up and run away. She couldn't have stopped him, but he didn't move. Ten minutes later the door opened again, but instead of one of Seattle's finest walking in, she looked up and saw someone who could easily pass for an underwear model/action hero.

The guy was tall, tanned and serious about working out. She could tell about the working-out bit because he wore red shorts and a gray T-shirt from Pacific High School ripped off just above his waistband. Muscles she hadn't even known existed on the human body twisted and bunched as he moved.

Reflective sunglasses covered his eyes. He looked down at the kid still held in place with her cane, the doughnuts scattered across the floor, then whipped off the glasses and smiled at her.

She'd seen that smile before.

Oh, not from him specifically. It was the one Pierce Brosnan, playing James Bond, used to get information from slightly-out-of-breath secretaries. It was the one her ex-husband had used, more than once, to get out of trouble. Nicole couldn't be more immune if she'd invented the vaccine herself.

"Hi," the guy said. "I'm Eric Hawkins. You can call me Hawk."

"How delightful for me. I'm Nicole Keyes. You can call me Ms. Keyes. Are you with the police?" She looked him over, trying not to be impressed by so much male perfection in such a tiny space. "Is your uniform at the dry cleaner's?"

His smile widened. "I'm the football coach at Pacific High School. One of my buddies at the station took the call and phoned me."

People thought of Seattle as a big city, but it was made up of a lot of small neighborhoods. Mostly Nicole liked that about her hometown. Just not today.

Disgusted, Nicole looked at the woman behind the counter. "Maggie, would you call the police again?"

"Maggie, hold that thought," Hawk said. He nudged Nicole's cane aside so the kid could scramble to his feet. "Raoul, are you okay?"

Nicole rolled her eyes. "Oh, please. What could possibly have happened to him?"

"He's my star quarterback. I'm not taking any chances. Raoul?"

The kid shuffled and ducked his head. "I'm good, Coach."

Hawk took the kid aside and had a whispered conversation with him. Nicole watched warily.

Washington State might not be Texas, but high school football was still a big deal here. Being the winning quarterback of a high school team was nearly as good as being Paris Hilton. Hawk probably expected her to succumb to his questionable charm and let the kid off with nothing more than a shrug over the misunderstanding. Which was *so* not happening.

"Look," she said, her voice as stern as she could make it. "He stole five dozen doughnuts. In your world, that might be perfectly fine, but it's not okay to me. I'm calling the police."

"It's not his fault," Hawk told her. "It's mine."

She was sorry she'd rolled her eyes before—it meant she couldn't do it now. "Because you told him to steal?"

"Raoul, wait for me in my truck," Hawk said.

"Raoul, don't even think about moving," Nicole snapped.

She watched as Hawk's good humor faded. He pulled up a chair next to hers, sat down and leaned toward her.

He was one of those guys who took up too much space, she thought, fighting the need to scoot back. Still, she held her ground, even though he was so close, she could see the various shades of brown, green and gold that made up his irises.

"You don't understand," he said, his voice low. His breath smelled minty. "Raoul is cocaptain. Every Friday the captain brings in doughnuts for the guys."

His hands were massive, she thought, distracted by their size. Big and strong looking.

She forced her attention back on the conversation. "Then he should have paid for them."

"He can't," Hawk told her, still speaking softly. "Raoul's a good kid. He lives in foster care. Normally he holds down a job, but during training, he can't. Our deal is I give him a few bucks for the doughnuts, but I forgot yesterday and he was too proud to ask. It's Friday. He had to provide doughnuts. He made a bad choice. Haven't you ever made a mistake, Nicole?"

He'd almost had her. The sad story of poor Raoul had actually touched her cynical heart. Then Hawk had dropped his voice to an intimate tone and drawn out her name in a way that really annoyed her.

"Don't play me," she snapped.

"I'm not—"

"And don't treat me like I'm stupid."

Hawk held up both hands. "I'm not—"

She cut him off with a glare.

She could just bet he was used to getting his way, especially with women. One flick of that killer smile and anyone with an X set of chromosomes melted like butter in the sun. Well, not her.

She stood, then grabbed her cane to support herself. "That kid is going down."

Hawk sprang to his feet. "Dammit, that's not fair."

She pointed to the doughnuts still scattered all over the floor. "Tell it to the judge."

Hawk moved toward her, but Raoul stepped between them. "Coach, it's okay. I was wrong. I knew it was wrong to steal and I did it anyway. You're always saying we have to learn to accept the consequences of our actions. This is one of them."

The kid turned to her, then dropped his gaze to

the floor. "Not having the money isn't an excuse. I shouldn't have done it. I was afraid of being embarrassed in front of the team." He shrugged. "I'm sorry, Ms. Keyes."

Nicole hated that she wanted to believe him. There was something so defeated about Raoul's posture. She told herself he could be playing her, too, that the two of them made a real great team, but somehow she sensed the kid was telling the truth. He *had* been embarrassed and he *was* sorry.

She debated what to do. While stealing was wrong, she didn't want to punish Raoul just to get back at Mr. High and Mighty. The fact that his coach was a womanizer/possible former underwear model/jock wasn't Raoul's fault.

Knowing she was going to be hating herself come morning when the kid didn't show up, she said, "I'll make you a deal. You can work off what you stole. Be here at six tomorrow morning."

For the first time since she'd tripped him, Raoul looked at her. Something very much like hope brightened his dark eyes. "For real?"

"Yes. But if you don't show up, I'll hunt you down like a dog and make you regret the day you were born. Do we have a deal?"

Raoul grinned. She sighed. Give it a couple more years and he would be just as deadly as his coach. How fair was that?

"I'll be here," he promised. "I'll be early."

"I won't."

Hawk turned to her. "*Now* can he wait for me in the truck?"

"Sure." Although if it were up to her, Coach Hawkins could go, too. They had nothing to say to each other.

She looked at him then wanted to rub her eyes. Maybe it was just a trick of the light, but she would swear he'd just gotten better looking. Talk about annoying.

HAWK GLANCED OVER at the woman glaring at him. She reminded him of a stray cat his daughter had brought home years ago. All spit and attitude.

Nicole was sensible. He could tell from her exactly-to-the-knee skirt in dark denim, her plain T-shirt, the lack of makeup and the way she hadn't bothered to do more with her long blond hair than pull it back in a ponytail. She wasn't the kind of woman who impressed easily. Not that he was worried.

"Thanks," he said. "You didn't have to do that."

"You're right. I didn't. I also know I'm going to regret letting him off like that."

There was temper in her blue eyes. She looked like she wanted to hit someone. He thought about offering—it wasn't as if she could hurt him—but sensed she would think he was mocking her. Which he was…a little.

"You won't. He's a good kid. He has a lot of talent—he can go all the way."

"You see yourself in him, don't you?"

Hawk grinned. "Yeah."

"That is just so typical." She glanced at her watch. "Don't you have to be somewhere?"

"Practice. The guys are waiting." He pulled out his wallet. "How much do I owe you for the doughnuts?"

She frowned. "Weren't you listening? Raoul is going to pay them off with hard labor. At least that's my fantasy."

"Then I still need five dozen for the team."

Nicole looked at the women behind the counter. "Maggie, would you get the coach his doughnuts so he can get out of here."

Hawk bent down and picked up the doughnuts on the floor. "You're trying to get rid of me."

"You think?"

"But I'm the best part of your day."

"Maybe I'll get a splinter later and that can be my highlight."

He laughed. "You're not easy."

"That's the first smart thing you've said."

He put the crumpled boxes and doughnuts on one of the tables. "I'm plenty smart, Nicole."

"Keep telling yourself that and one day it might be true."

He stared at her, his gaze steady, until she began to squirm. "Why are you trying so hard not to like me?" he asked. "Do I intimidate you?"

"I… You… Just go away."

With that, she braced herself on her cane and moved toward the back of the bakery.

"No snarky comeback?" he called after her. "Does that mean I win?"

She turned and glared at him. "Not everything in life is about winning and losing."

"Sure it is."

Her jaw clenched. "Go away."

"I will because I have guys waiting. But I'll be back."

"Don't bother."

"It's not a bother. It'll be fun."

He left the bakery, whistling as he walked to his truck parked out in front.

Hawk could tell Nicole disliked not having the last word. She was obviously used to being in control and getting her way. Football had taught him a whole lot about life. Sometimes teams got too cocky about being really good at one thing. If you could take that away from them, they were left scrambling. The same with women. Especially women.

It was going to be a good day, he thought as he handed Raoul the doughnuts and started the engine. Suddenly there were a whole lot of possibilities.

"WHAT DO YOU THINK?" Claire asked.

Nicole continued to flip through the shirts on the rack. "No."

"Come on. It's pink."

"Uh-huh."

"You're not even looking."

Nicole held in a smile. "I don't have to look. No. It doesn't fit."

"How do you know?"

"Because you're maybe three months pregnant and you've gained all of five pounds. You don't need maternity clothes."

"But I want to buy something."

"Get a receiving blanket."

"I want something I can wear."

Nicole glanced up and groaned as she saw her sister standing in front of a mirror wearing a bright pink T-shirt with a sequined arrow pointing toward her stomach and the word Baby in case anyone was confused.

"You're kidding," Nicole muttered.

"Maybe not this one, but I want people to know I'm pregnant."

"Have cards printed. You could hand them out to everyone you see."

"You're not helping."

"You don't need help being insane. You do great all on your own."

Claire flipped her long blond hair over her shoulder. "You're not a very good sister."

Nicole smiled. "I'm the best sister you have and your favorite twin."

"My only twin and I haven't decided if you're my favorite sister. Maybe one with ducks?"

"No."

"Bunnies?"

"The baby is the size of a pencil eraser, Claire. Maybe a grape. You don't need special clothes because you're carrying a grape."

"But I'm pregnant."

"In a couple of months, when you've gained all of eight pounds, we'll talk. Until then, wearing anything maternity is going to make you look like you're in a potato sack."

"But I'm excited."

"I know, and you should be. This is very cool news."

Claire beamed.

Nicole considered her own genuine excitement at her sister's pregnancy a testament to her good character. She could find happiness for Claire even knowing the odds of her ever having a kid of her own were as great as her winning the lotto…not that she ever bought a ticket. Pregnancy, unless one wanted to get science involved, generally meant having a man around. She'd given up on men. Permanently.

"Are you okay?" Claire asked. "You're thinking of Drew, aren't you?"

Nicole flinched and leaned more weight on her cane. "How do you *do* that? Know what I'm thinking?"

"We're twins."

"Fraternal."

"Still. I know you."

It was borderline creepy, Nicole thought. And

annoying. She didn't know what Claire was thinking all the time.

"I'm not thinking of Drew," Nicole told her. She refused to waste any mental time or energy on her soon-to-be ex-husband. "I was thinking about men in general."

"You'll find someone," Claire promised, sounding irritatingly pitying.

"I don't want anyone. I'm barely separated and I'm perfectly content to be on my own." Or she would be if everyone in her life stopped assuming she was crumbling from the emotional devastation of walking in on her baby sister in bed with her husband.

Yes, it had been horrible and degrading and maybe even heartbreaking. But she was dealing.

"I need to get used to being alone," Nicole said.

"Why? You were alone before, when you were married to Drew."

"Ouch."

Claire sighed. "Sorry. I didn't mean for that to come out that way."

"It's fine." Nicole wouldn't show heartache. Not even to her sister.

Claire gave her a gentle smile. One that spoke about compassion and an internal decision to bring this up later. When Claire felt Nicole was stronger, emotionally.

Oh, great. *Now* she could read her twin's mind? How delightful.

Nicole glanced at her watch. "We need to go meet Wyatt."

"Oh! The time. I'll hurry."

Claire darted back into the dressing room. Nicole wondered if she should scold herself for tricking her sister into forgetting to talk about Nicole's tragic life, but then decided she'd earned the reprieve. After all, here it was, a Friday night and she was at the mall, an obvious extra party in what should have been a twosome. But they'd asked and she hadn't wanted to spend the evening by herself.

"I'll meet you out front," Nicole called toward the dressing room.

"I'll just be a sec," Claire promised.

Nicole walked out of the maternity store and found Wyatt waiting by the front window display. He looked uncomfortable as he studied an obviously pregnant mannequin.

"Hey," she said. "You owe me. I just kept your fiancée from buying something hideous."

"You did it for yourself," Wyatt told her. "You'd care more than I would."

Nicole knew that was true, so she ignored the statement. She glanced at the bag in Wyatt's hand. It was from the bookstore.

"Another instruction manual on pregnancy," she teased. "Is there one left you don't have already?"

"We want to do it right," Wyatt told her. "Like you'd be any different."

Nicole knew she wouldn't, but that wasn't the point. She was about to suggest they take in a movie when Wyatt said, "How are you doing?"

She blinked at him. "Excuse me?"

"We haven't talked in a while. You okay? You know. With stuff?"

"Stuff" being man-talk for anything emotional.

Wyatt had been her friend and brother-in-law long before he'd fallen for Claire. He knew way too many of her secrets. He'd offered to beat the crap out of Drew when he'd learned about the cheating. She loved him like a brother—except for right now when she wanted to slap him upside the head.

"Have you and Claire been talking about me?" she demanded. "Am I the subject of one of those horrible 'what are we going to do about poor Nicole?' conversations? Because if I am, you need to stop right now. I don't need help from either of you. I'm fine. Better than fine."

Wyatt was unimpressed by her outburst. "You're mostly staying home, you're not seeing anyone. You're crabbier than usual, which is a trick."

"I'm not in the mood to date. I know that's a surprise, but there we are."

"Don't judge everyone by Drew, okay? There are great guys out there. You need to get back on the horse again."

"Tell me you didn't just say that. Back on the horse? I didn't fall off my bike. My husband cheated on me with my little sister. In *my* house. That is not a 'back on the horse' moment. It's the kind of thing that makes someone rethink her sexual preference, okay?"

Her chest felt tight. Was it just her, or was it hot in here? "Look, I have to go. Thanks for letting me tag along for dinner. I'll talk to you later."

She turned and moved away.

"Nicole, wait."

She kept walking. When she saw the sign, she hurried—as best she could—toward the parking structure, incredibly grateful she'd met them at the mall. At least she had her own car.

Thirty minutes later she was home where it was quiet and familiar and there was no one to ask her stupid questions or feel sorry for her. There were also too many memories and an emptiness that made her flip channels until she found a sitcom. She stared at the screen and vowed she wouldn't cry over Drew. Not now and not ever again.

CHAPTER TWO

SATURDAY MORNING Nicole arrived at the bakery about ten minutes before Raoul was due for his shift. Not that she was actually expecting the teenager. She'd reacted to the moment—she'd been nice. And she was a firm believer that no good deed went unpunished. So he wouldn't show and she would be pissed, mostly at herself.

She walked toward the rear door of the bakery, only to be joined by a tall, dark-haired kid who fell into step with her.

"Good morning," Raoul said politely.

She glanced at him. "You're early."

"I didn't want to be late."

"I'm impressed you're here at all."

"You didn't expect me?"

"No."

"I gave my word."

"You stole doughnuts. That makes your word questionable."

She wasn't exactly looking at him as she spoke, so she couldn't be sure, but she caught what looked like a flinch out of the corner of her eyes. Because she doubted him? Because she mentioned the stealing? Great. Every morning should start with a hypersensitive pastry thief.

"You're also a jock," she added, not sure why she felt compelled to make him feel better. "I have this thing against jocks. It dates back to high school, when all the guys I had crushes on ignored me."

"I don't believe that."

She sighed. "Are you trying to be charming?"

"Only a little. I'm practicing."

She could guess who the master he'd learned from was. "Save it for someone who's more easily impressed. I'm immune."

"I noticed. You didn't like Coach Hawkins much."

"I wouldn't say that," Nicole murmured, even though it was true. She thought Hawk was gorgeous and had an amazing body more than capable of making her entire being go up in flames, but that didn't mean she had to like the man. There was no way she was going to be taken in by his practiced smile and sexual heat that sizzled so much it probably contributed to global warming.

Raoul held open the door to the bakery. Nicole went in and waved at Phil.

"Morning," she called.

Phil, an older man dressed all in white, including his apron, hurried toward them.

"Morning," he said, looking Raoul over. "You ready to do work?"

"Yes, sir."

Phil didn't look convinced. "This isn't going to be easy and I'm not interested in complaints. You hear me? No whining."

Raoul straightened. "I don't whine."

"We'll see."

Phil led him away.

Nicole watched them go. Raoul would work off what he owed her by scrubbing massive mixing bowls used to make bread dough. That would be followed by an assortment of tasks designed to make Raoul think twice about stealing rather than buying. She wondered if the lesson would be learned or simply endured.

FOUR HOURS LATER Nicole had gone through the pile in her in-basket, a task she always dreaded. But she'd wanted to stay through Raoul's shift and working in the bakery itself wasn't going to happen until she was cane-free. She dropped the invoices into a folder and labeled it to go to her accountant. Phil knocked on the open door and stepped in front of her desk.

"How's it going?" she asked.

"Good. Better than I expected. The kid can work. He does what he's told, no attitude, no slacking off. I like him."

Nicole raised her eyebrows. "That's unusual."

"Tell me about it. I think you should offer him a job. We need somebody like him in the off-hours.

He goes to school and plays football, so he'd be available then. That's when I could use him."

"Okay. I'll talk to him."

Nicole stood and stretched. The ache in her knee was manageable and getting better.

Raoul was in the back, stacking sacks of flour. He set each one squarely on the bag below, making sure the piles wouldn't lean and eventually topple.

"Nice work," she said. "You impressed Phil and that's not easy."

"Thanks."

"You want a real job? Part-time. We'd work around your school schedule and football. The pay isn't bad." She named an hourly rate slightly above what he would get working retail or even at a restaurant.

Raoul put the last bag in place, then wiped his hands on the apron Phil had found for him.

"I can't," he said, not looking at her.

"Okay."

"I need the money. It's not that."

"Then what? It's casting season for the new TV shows and your agent is going to want you to fly to L.A.?"

That earned her a slight smile that faded quickly. He seemed to collect his courage before looking at her. "You won't want to hire me. Not yet. I'm going to be eighteen in a couple of weeks. When I'm an adult, I can petition to get my juvenile records sealed. Until then, I have a criminal record."

She was a little surprised and disappointed. "What did you do?"

"I stole a car when I was twelve. To impress my friends. It was stupid and I got caught five minutes later. I didn't do anything else before or since. Except the doughnuts and you know about that. I learned my lesson." He dropped his gaze to the floor. "There's no reason for you to believe me."

There was one, she thought. Checking out his story would be easy, so he'd be an idiot to lie. And Raoul didn't strike her as stupid.

"Starting your criminal life by stealing a car is pretty impressive. Most people just shoplift. You headed right into the big league."

That earned her a slight smile. "I was a kid. I didn't know any better."

He was still a kid, she thought. Did he know better now?

"The job offer still stands. It's not easy work, but it's honest. And you'll get all the leftover baked goods you can stomach."

"I can stomach a lot."

"Then this is a great deal for you."

He looked into her eyes. "Why would you trust me?"

"Everybody gets to screw up once." She thought of her baby sister. Jesse had been given four or five hundred chances and still managed to blow every one.

"Then I'll take the job," he said. "I have football

practice every afternoon, so maybe I could work in the morning, before school."

"Talk to Phil about that. He'll be your boss. If you're interested in more hours once the season is over, let him know."

Raoul nodded. "Thanks. You didn't have to do any of this. You could have called the police."

She didn't bother pointing out that she'd tried. Instead of Seattle's finest, Hawk had shown up.

"What is it with men and football?" she asked. "Why do you play? For the glory?"

"I love the game," Raoul told her. "I want to go to college. I can't afford it, so I'm hoping for a football scholarship."

"Then you'll turn pro and make millions?"

"Maybe. The odds are against it. Coach says I have talent."

"Is he in a position to judge?"

Raoul frowned. "He's my coach."

Which didn't answer the question, Nicole thought. How would a high school coach know if any one player would make it all the way to the pros? How could anyone?

"You don't know who he is," Raoul said, sounding shocked. "You have no idea."

Nicole shifted uncomfortably. "He's your coach." And totally hot, but that was beside the point.

"He's Eric Hawkins. He played pro for eight years and retired at the top of his game. He's a legend."

She found that hard to believe. "Lucky him."

"He's the best. He doesn't have to work for the money. He's teaching high school football because he loves the game and he wants to give back."

Nicole resisted the urge to yawn. Raoul was reciting what sounded very much like a canned speech. Probably one the kid had heard dozens of times from the legend himself.

"Good to know," she said and pulled forty dollars out of her back pocket. "Here."

He didn't take the money. "You can't pay me."

"Sure I can. You won't be an official employee until you fill out the paperwork. So take this for now. You'll punch a time clock and get a real paycheck soon enough."

He actually tucked his hands behind his back. "I was working to pay off the doughnuts I stole."

"Technically you didn't even get them out the door. You're not very good at the whole stealing thing." She sighed when he didn't smile. "Look, you worked hard today. I appreciate that. You earned this. Take it or I'll get really crabby and trust me, you don't want to see that."

He reached for the money. "You think you're really tough, but you don't scare me."

That almost made her laugh. "Give it time, kid. Give it time."

NICOLE LED RAOUL to the front of the bakery, where she filled a couple of bags with day-old pastries and baked goods.

"You don't have to do this," he said, even as he stared longingly at the half-dozen cookies she scooped up.

"You can handle the calories. Like I said—it's a perk."

"Are there other perks?"

That question didn't come from Raoul. Nicole didn't have to turn around or even think to know who'd been speaking. And in case there was any confusion in her brain, her entire body flushed a welcome.

She straightened, braced herself for impact, then turned. Sure enough, Hawk stood behind the case, smiling that sexy, you-know-you-want-me smile of his.

He was slightly more dressed than he had been the previous day. Today his shorts were longer and his T-shirt covered all of his chest and stomach, which was both good and bad. In theory she should be able to think more easily. In reality, she was just a little disappointed.

"What do you want?" she asked, not caring that she sounded snappish.

"Interesting question," he murmured, then winked at Raoul. "I came to see how my star player worked out. He impressed the hell out of you, didn't he?"

Nicole found herself neatly trapped. She actually liked Raoul and had been happy to offer him a job. But with Hawk there, she felt the need to say nothing had gone well and she was happy to be rid of him.

"He was fine," she said and handed the bags to Raoul. Afraid she would see disappointment in the kid's eyes, she added, "Better than fine. He did great."

"I knew it."

"This isn't actually about you. I know that's an amazing concept, so I should probably give you a minute to wrap your mind around it."

Hawk chuckled. "Raoul, you don't have to stick around here. I'll see you at practice in a couple of hours."

The kid nodded and left. Nicole watched him go because it was easier than trying not to look at Hawk. The man was like catnip.

When they were alone, Nicole suddenly didn't know what to do with any part of her body. She wanted to back up…or move much, much closer. Her arms felt funny just hanging at her sides. But crossing them seemed too hostile.

She hated this. The man had the power to make her feel awkward in her own skin.

"You don't still need to be here," she told him.

"I want to thank you for giving Raoul a chance," Hawk told her, easing closer without seeming to move.

Quite the trick, she thought grimly.

"He worked hard. That happens a whole lot less than I would like. I gave him a job."

Hawk raised one eyebrow. "He *did* impress you."

"He needs the work, I need the help. Don't make it more than it is."

Dark eyes seemed to stare into her very being. "You want people to think you're tough."

"I am tough."

"You're a marshmallow inside."

She stiffened. "I could have had your player's ass thrown in jail. Don't think I wouldn't have done it if he hadn't shown up today. I've been running this place for years. I know what I'm doing."

"Do you like what you're doing?"

"Of course," she said automatically because it was always what she answered. She'd known she would run the bakery from the time she was eight or nine years old. It had been understood...expected. Hers wasn't to be a life of many surprises. Lately there sure hadn't been any good ones.

Wait. There had been Claire. Reuniting with her sister had been good. Watching Claire fall madly in love, get pregnant, get engaged and find total happiness had stretched her good nature a little, but she was dealing. Because what choice did she have?

"Earth to Nicole."

She blinked and saw Hawk standing a little too close.

"I lost you there," he said.

"That must be a first," she said without thinking. "A woman focusing on something other than you for an eighth of a second."

"Because I'm so hard to resist?"

"Not for me."

"I don't believe that. You're interested."

If she'd been able to look at him for more than five seconds at a time without wanting to make moany noises, she might have picked up something heavy and clocked him on the head. As it was, he was telling the truth and she was too embarrassed to figure out a quick way to verbally eviscerate him. Which left her with the humiliating comeback of, "I'm not interested."

He grinned. "That was convincing."

"I don't care what it is, it's the truth." Almost. Annoyance pushed her to honesty. "You know you've got a great body and you obviously enjoy flashing it at the world. Which means what? You're well into your thirties. Shouldn't you be over that by now? Shouldn't you spend about a third as much time developing your mind as your body? You can't be a football coach forever."

Too late, she remembered that, yes, he could be a coach forever and that Raoul had mentioned something about him being a professional football player. Which probably meant he was rich.

"You're assuming I'm stupid?" he asked in a tone that was both amused and outraged. "Is that because I have muscles or because I play football? Isn't that the same as me assuming you're an idiot because you're a natural blonde?"

Maybe. Yes. She ignored the question. "How do you know I'm a natural blonde?"

"My excellent powers of observation."

"I run a successful business. I'm obviously more than capable," she said primly.

HAWK LIKED how Nicole got all pinchy when she was annoyed. He liked how every time he moved closer, she got flustered and didn't know where to look. If she hadn't been interested, she would have told him to back off and get away, but she hadn't said a word. He liked that, too.

"Obviously," he teased, as he moved closer.

"Don't you have any respect for personal space?"

"No."

She raised her head and glared, but before she could speak, he said, "You have beautiful eyes."

Her mouth opened and closed. "What do you think you're doing?"

"Flirting."

"Why?"

"It's fun."

"Not for me."

"Everyone enjoys attention."

"Speak for yourself."

"You don't think your eyes are beautiful?"

"They're fine. Functional. I don't care about the color."

"Sure you do. You have to know they're pretty. You're pretty."

Nicole blushed.

He didn't see it at first. She turned away and muttered something under her breath. All he caught were a couple of words, including "unbelievably arrogant" and "ego." So he wasn't paying attention until he saw her press her fingers to her cheeks as if trying to cool the skin.

Why would someone so together blush because he noticed she was pretty? Unless no one else bothered to look. He had a feeling she was the kind of woman who scared off men and then wondered why she was lonely.

He could fix that.

"You like me flirting with you," he said. "It's the best part of your day."

"You're amazing."

"I know."

She groaned. "I don't mean that in a good way. You are delusional. Nothing about you is the best part of my day."

"Liar."

She made a sound of frustration low in her throat. It was almost a growl. He wondered what she sounded like right before she lost control in bed. He had a feeling she would scream.

"Save the flirting for someone who's interested," she muttered, holding on to her cane so hard her knuckles turned white.

"You're interested."

She shook her head. "Don't you have somewhere you need to be?"

"Sure, but this is more fun."

"No, it's not."

He was getting to her. The blush deepened and she couldn't decide if she wanted to throw herself at him or punch him. Frustration was good. It meant she was interested and annoyed with herself at the same time.

"We should go out," he said, knowing the invitation would push her further off balance.

"What? No."

"Dinner. We'll go to dinner."

"I'm not going to dinner with you."

"Why not?"

"It's not a good idea."

And the first round went to him. If she really hadn't been interested, she would have told him directly.

"Sure it is." He moved so close that she had to tilt her head back to continue to meet his gaze. "It's an excellent idea."

"I'm not going."

"Yes, you are."

"I'm not and you can't make me."

He walked to the door of the bakery and paused. "Want to bet?" he said, and then he left.

As he crossed to his truck, he could practically hear her sputtering. That had gone well. It was early in the first quarter, and he was already deep in enemy territory and poised to score.

"AMY'S THERAPY is going really well," Claire said as she chopped more mushrooms, then scooped them into a bowl. "She's young, which helps. Her brain is still open to change. Unlike those of us who have closed brains."

Nicole shredded lettuce into a bowl. "I have no idea where my brain stands on the whole open-closed issue."

Amy was Wyatt's daughter and Claire's soon-to-be stepdaughter. She'd been born deaf and had recently asked for a cochlear implant to help her hear. While the surgery put in the required hardware, special therapy was required to train her to recognize sound in a new way and process it.

"Amy's so excited about the implant," Claire said. "She asks me to play for her every night."

"Which you love."

"I do. She's my biggest fan."

Given that Claire was a world-class concert pianist, with Grammy-winning CDs and more concert dates than she could fill in two lifetimes, that was saying something.

"I thought Wyatt was your biggest fan," Nicole teased.

"He is. In other ways."

Her sister laughed and Nicole smiled. She was happy for Claire. Seriously. She didn't want Wyatt for herself. She tried telling herself she didn't want any man for herself, but she knew she would be lying. She wanted someone special. Someone who would love her and always be there for her. Unfortunately she'd picked Drew.

Instantly she flashed back to that night when she'd walked in on Drew and Jesse in bed together. They'd been kissing, or about to. Jesse'd been topless. Nicole had—

She reminded herself not to go there. She had to stop torturing herself with the past. She'd put Drew behind her; she had to move on. She should think about something more pleasant.

Immediately images of Hawk filled her brain. The man might make her crazy, but he had a body to die for. She'd never been all that into appearance, but in his case, she was willing to make an exception.

Time for a mental change of subject, Nicole told herself.

She finished with the lettuce and passed the bowl to her sister. "So have you figured out your fall traveling schedule?"

Claire shrugged. "Nearly. Lisa gave me a list of places and I'm narrowing them down. I don't want to be gone too much. Not just because of missing Wyatt and Amy, but I don't want to get exhausted for the baby."

"Are you checking with your doctor?" Nicole asked, trusting the medical profession with Claire's health a lot more than she trusted Lisa, Claire's manager.

Claire nodded. "She wants me to keep travel to a minimum during the last couple weeks of my first trimester. Then I'll travel a lot during the second. Less during the third. Lisa mentioned something about a holiday concert series in Hawaii, but I don't think I'll be up for it."

Nicole reached for an avocado. "Why not? Can't you take Amy?"

"Oh, sure. We'd have a nice beach house to use, but it's so far and not really a time when I want to be traveling. You know. Away from family."

Nicole was about to point out that most of Claire's family—her fiancé and his daughter—would be with her. Then she got it. Claire didn't want to be gone from her. She didn't want to leave Nicole alone for Christmas.

"I'll be fine," she said quickly. "You should go."

"This isn't about you," Claire said, but she didn't sound convincing. "This is our first chance to be together at the holidays since we were six. I'm not going to Hawaii. I don't want to."

"I don't believe you."

"I can't help that," Claire told her.

"You worry about me."

"Sure, but I'll get over it."

Nicole tried to smile, but couldn't quite make her lips move. She appreciated that people cared, but disliked the need for sympathy. Normally she managed her life such that she was the capable one. The one others looked to for guidance. She wasn't usually the one they pitied.

"Speaking of getting over things," Claire said casually. "Have you talked to Jesse lately?"

"You know I haven't."

"You have to eventually."

"Why?" If Nicole had her way, she wouldn't deal with Jesse ever again. "Bad enough she slept with my husband. Then she stole the secret family recipe and sold our famous Keyes Chocolate Cake on the Internet."

Just thinking about it made her crazy. Drew was one thing, but screwing with the business, too?

"It's just like her," Nicole muttered. "I bet you anything that if I talked to her, she'd have a million excuses. She never takes responsibility."

"You threw her out," Claire said quietly. "She had to make a living."

"Exactly. She had to get a job. There are dozens of jobs out there, but did she even try to find one? No. She stole. First Drew, then the cake." Nicole's stomach started to hurt. "I don't want to talk about this anymore."

"It's not going away until you figure out how to reconcile with her."

"Maybe I don't want to have anything to do with her." Nicole fought anger and hurt. "There was this kid who came into the bakery last week. He stole a bunch of doughnuts, or at least he tried. When I confronted him, he took responsibility for what he'd done. He felt guilty and knew he was wrong. He worked off the amount he'd stolen. He did such a good job that he's an employee now. Why can't Jesse be like that? Why can't she take any responsibility for what she's done?"

"I know she hurt you."

"More than hurt," Nicole muttered. "A lot more than hurt."

"You two have to figure this out."

"I know," Nicole muttered. "I will. Eventually. I think about it but then I get so mad I don't even want to see her, let alone talk to her."

"It makes me sad that you're not getting along," Claire told her. "You're family."

"Not any family I'd want."

"I don't believe you." Claire looked at her. "You have every right to be angry and hurt, but I think it's time to ask yourself how much of your behavior is about teaching your sister a lesson and how much of it is about getting revenge."

CHAPTER THREE

NICOLE FELT STUPID and obvious as she leaned on her cane and walked toward the high school football stadium. She was too old to be at a Friday-night game…or too young. She wasn't a student and she didn't have a kid in high school. So what exactly was she doing here?

"It's what I get for talking to my employees," she grumbled to herself. She should have just waved and kept on walking. But no. She had to stop and talk to Raoul at the end of his first week working for her. She'd asked how things were going, because she was an idiot. And when he'd mentioned the football game tonight, she'd pretended that she was interested.

"You could have said no," she reminded herself. When Raoul had asked her to come, she could have easily said she was busy. Only she wasn't and she didn't lie all that well. In a spiritual sense, that was probably a good thing, but as to how it affected where she would be spending her evening, it sucked.

She looked up at the rows of benches that passed as seats. She didn't know anyone here. Still, given the choice between the high school kids and the parents, she would pick the parents. At least she had a chance of talking to one of them.

"Nicole!"

She turned toward the field and saw one of the football players running toward her. He was suited up in his gear and it took her a second to recognize Raoul.

"Hi," she said as she walked toward the railing separating the field from the stands. "Impressive. You look mean and burly."

Raoul grinned. "Yeah?"

She nodded. He looked different. Older. Dangerous. The urge to tell him not to get hurt welled up inside of her. Apparently maternal instincts didn't need much to kick in.

"Are you playing a tough team?" she asked.

"They're okay. We're gonna kick their butts, though."

"I look forward to that."

He grinned. "Thanks for coming tonight. I don't usually have anyone at the games. Except for my friends, you know. Not an adult."

That was her. Adult. "I'll cheer a lot and try to embarrass you," she teased.

"Good."

A pretty blond girl in a cheerleader uniform ran up. "Hi," she said with a big smile. "I'm Brittany."

The teenager was even more lovely close-up. She looked perfect and popular. Nicole thought about hating her on general principle.

"Nicole," she said.

"My boss," Raoul said. "I told you about her. Brittany's my girlfriend."

"Nice to meet you," Nicole said.

"You, too. I hope you enjoy the game. We're going to have a great year."

Someone blew a whistle on the field.

"I gotta go," Raoul said. "I'll see you after the game."

He ran off before Nicole could explain that she wouldn't be staying. Then she reminded herself it wasn't as if she had a full social calendar. So what if she spent the whole evening there?

"Couldn't stay away, could you?"

Nicole heard the voice, felt the rush of heat and despised both him for causing it and herself for reacting.

She looked over the railing to where Hawk stood on the grass.

For once he was dressed…khakis, polo shirt in school colors. He looked good. Better than good. Talk about annoying.

"Raoul asked me to come watch him play."

Hawk looked unconvinced.

"I'm telling the truth," she insisted. "He says he doesn't have any adults come watch him. Why is that?"

"He's in foster care. Has been for a long time. It's nice that you could take an interest."

He sounded sincere, which made her feel guilty about complaining about coming.

"It's no big deal," she mumbled.

"It is to him. I gotta go. Enjoy the game."

Hawk ran off. Nicole tried not to stare at his butt as he moved, although it was difficult to ignore any part of him. Weird, because she'd never been that superficial before. She was always far more interested in a guy's mind.

It was because of where she was in her life, she told herself as she turned back to the bleacher seats and started to climb, using her cane for balance. Under any other circumstances, she would barely be able to remember Hawk's name.

"He's damn pretty," a woman said.

Nicole looked at her.

"The coach. He's the best part of the game, although my two boys would be humiliated if they heard me say that." She smiled. "I'm Barbara."

The woman scooted over to make room.

Nicole sat next to her. "Hi. I'm Nicole."

"You're a little young to be a mom," Barbara said. "You here for Hawk?"

"No," Nicole said quickly. "I own a bakery. One of the guys on the team works for me. He asked me to come."

"That's nice of you. I'm not sure I'd be here if I didn't have to be. Of course I've been sitting on hard seats for years now. My boys are twins and they're into sports. We've done it all. Little League, soccer, football, baseball. My husband travels a lot so it's up to me to show up at the games."

"It's great that you want to see them. I'm sure they appreciate the support."

Barbara wrinkled her nose. "They never say anything unless I can't make a game. Then they won't stop complaining. But I'm used to it by now."

Family, Nicole thought sadly. That's what people did for each other in a family.

"So," Barbara said, her voice low. "How do you know Hawk?"

"I, ah, met him through Raoul."

"Dating him?"

"No."

"Tempted?"

"No."

"Because you're dating someone amazing?"

"Not really."

Barbara smiled. "So you're either into girls or you're lying."

Nicole laughed. "How are those my only choices?"

"I don't believe any woman can be around Hawk and not wonder what it would be like to have her way with him. He's got that body of his. Plus, he's actually nice. I know it seems unfair, but there we are. He's single and he likes to play. Rumor has it he's a real gentleman out in public and a wild animal in the bedroom. They say he can go for hours."

Barbara fanned herself. "Not that I have any personal experience. He doesn't get involved with married women and I wouldn't cheat. At least I don't think I would. No one's ever asked."

Nicole didn't know what to say. This definitely fell in the category of too much information.

"He used to play professionally," Barbara continued.

"I'd heard that."

"It's an amazing story. He got his high school girlfriend pregnant. Everyone said they wouldn't make it, but they got married anyway. They lived on macaroni and cheese while he was in college on a scholarship. Had the baby, were blissfully happy. Then Hawk got drafted into the NFL and started making big money. Instead of living on a golf course somewhere, they bought an average house in a regular neighborhood here, in Seattle. Raised their daughter."

This was the expanded version of what Raoul had told her, Nicole thought. Although she hadn't known about a child. Hawk was a father? He seemed too flashy and sexually charged for that.

"Then Serena, that's the wife, got cancer. It was maybe six or seven years ago. Hawk quit the NFL to stay home with her. She died and he became a single dad. He took the high school coaching job because he wanted to give back. He sure doesn't need the money."

Barbara pointed to the pretty blonde Raoul had introduced Nicole to earlier. "That's his daughter."

"Brittany?"

Barbara looked at her. "You know her?"

"We met earlier. She's dating Raoul, my employee."

"That's her. She's absolutely perfect. Good grades, head cheerleader, interested in saving the planet. Loves her dad. I console myself that even if I was single and Hawk was desperately in love with me, Brittany would be a challenge to any relationship. She's a real daddy's girl. But who can blame her?"

Nicole studied the teenager urging the crowd to cheer, then turned her attention to Hawk. He paced along the sidelines, a clipboard in his hands.

"So he's not a jerk," she murmured.

"Not even close. You still not interested?"

"He's just someone I know," she said. "Nothing more."

Not that she wanted more. He was the kind of trouble she didn't have time for.

She watched him point to a couple of kids and send them into the game. He was totally focused and intense, and he never once glanced in her direction, damn him.

NICOLE SPENT the rest of the game watching the plays and trying to figure out what was going on while listening to Barbara fill her in on everything from which teachers might have a drinking problem to which parents were divorcing. It was an information dump that made her head spin.

When the game ended, Pacific High School had beaten the other team 38 to 14. Even her untrained eye had told her that Raoul was an outstanding quarterback with an arm that never seemed to get tired.

She stood and thanked Barbara for sharing her section of bench, then rubbed her numb butt as she made her way to the railing. Raoul and Brittany stood close together, talking intently. The blonde reached up and touched his face. Then Raoul saw Nicole and hurried over to the railing.

"What did you think?" he asked.

"You're great," she said honestly. "I was incredibly impressed. Even knowing nothing about the game, I could tell you did really well. How far can you throw a football anyway?"

Raoul grinned. "We were awesome tonight. The whole team really pulled together. No one player can make or break a game."

"I see you're already training for your sports interviews," she teased.

Hawk joined Raoul and gave him a high five. "Great job," he said, then turned to Nicole. "Our boy's going all the way."

She ignored the implied connection. "I'm happy to hear it."

"So how many can you take in your car?" Hawk asked.

"What?"

"Kids. How many can you take in your car?"

"I have no idea what you're talking about," she said.

"She drives a Lexus Hybrid," Raoul said. "So four, but the three in the back can't be huge. They won't fit."

Hawk nodded. "I'll have them meet you in the parking lot."

She made a T with her hands. "Who are they and why are they meeting me anywhere?"

"Pizza," he said. "We get pizza after the game. The players, their girlfriends, a few kids from school. It's a tradition. I like to keep them busy while the adrenaline is still pumping. Hanging out at a pizza place is safer than just cutting them loose where they could do something stupid and hurt themselves. Not all the kids drive, so we need rides."

She was aware of Raoul standing right there. For some reason she wasn't comfortable refusing in front of him. Maybe it was because she knew he didn't have anyone on his side. But if she agreed, she knew she would feel as if she'd been manipulated into doing something she didn't want to do. Worse, Hawk would probably assume she was only hanging out on the off chance she got to spend time with him.

Why did everything have to be a complication?

"I'll be waiting in the parking lot," she said, her teeth clenched.

"I'll have the guys look for you. They know where we're going. I'll see you there."

"Not if I can help it," she muttered.

JOE'S HOUSE OF PIZZA was one of those great neighborhood places with plenty of tables, a jukebox and delicious smells of fresh garlic, peppers and tomato sauce.

Nicole hadn't eaten dinner before the game but didn't think she was starved until she walked into the building and took a breath. Suddenly she was weak with hunger and desperate for the recipe.

The four boys she'd brought with her drifted away as soon as they arrived. They'd been polite, but obviously terrified that she would want to join them for the evening. She'd thought about explaining that she wasn't interested in interfering with their good time when she realized she didn't really know anyone here. The only parent she knew was Barbara, who hadn't come. The only other adult of her acquaintance was Hawk and she was confident he would be holding court with his players. Not that she wanted to sit with him.

It would probably be best if she just left, she told herself. Maybe she could order a pizza to go.

She was already in line at the counter, leaning on her cane, when something large and warm settled on the small of her back. She'd never felt the touch before, but she recognized it. Recognized it and melted from the inside out.

How was it possible for her body to react so strongly to one man? What combination of chemistry and cosmic humor made her want to turn around, pull Hawk close and demand that he prove all the things Barbara had said about him weren't just cheap talk?

She carefully sidestepped his touch. Instead of taking the hint, he grabbed her hand.

Just like that. Palm against palm, fingers lacing. As if he owned her. As if they belonged together. Worse, he wasn't even looking at her. He was talking to some father.

She wanted to pull her hand free and demand that he stop touching her. She wanted to tell him that they weren't together, they would never be together, and ask him what the hell was he thinking. She wanted to see if that bench seat in his truck was big enough for the two of them.

The father walked away and Hawk turned to her. "You don't have to order," he said. "They know we're coming. I called ahead to let them know when the game was over. Technically you can get a beer, but I'd rather you didn't. I don't like anyone drinking in front of the kids on game night. It's probably dumb, but there it is."

His eyes were dark, as if they could absorb all the light in the room. She had the weirdest feeling she could get lost in his eyes, which just went to show that she'd moved past being hungry and was well into low blood sugar delusions.

"You're holding my hand."

One corner of his mouth turned up. "It's all I can do in a crowd, but once we're alone I'll crank up the heat."

She jerked free of him. "I have no idea what you're talking about, but let me be clear. You and I are never—"

"Hey, Coach, did you order salads?" one of the cheerleaders asked. "You know some of us don't want pizza."

"I ordered salads," he said, sounding tired, then he turned back to her and grabbed her hand again. "What is it about women and their damn weight? Okay, yeah, carrying around an extra thirty or forty pounds is bad. But women today are obsessed with every fat cell and teenagers are the worst."

"She's a cheerleader. What did you expect?"

"That she should be happy she's healthy and athletic and get off me about salad."

"Doesn't your daughter worry about her weight?"

One eyebrow raised. "You've been talking about me."

"Not on purpose. The mothers are all too willing to chat about you. I'm confident you totally love their interest and do whatever you can to fan the flames."

It was as if he didn't hear anything she'd said. "You were asking questions."

"Did you listen at all? I didn't ask. It wasn't necessary. Information was offered."

He smiled, a slow, sexy, self-confident smile that made her both want to hit him and crawl inside of him. "I'm getting to you. I can tell."

"Someone just shoot me now," she muttered.

One of his players came up and asked him a question about the game. As Hawk answered, Nicole tried to pull away, but he didn't let go. Short of a tugging match, she seemed trapped and couldn't decide if that was good or bad.

She glanced around the place and saw several mothers glaring at her. When she caught their eyes, they turned away and whispered to each other.

"The fan club isn't happy," she murmured to Hawk. "I don't know you well enough to be risking life and limb."

"I'm worth it."

"You know, if we could harness your ego, we could solve the energy crisis."

Just then several servers walked out carrying massive pizzas. All the kids milling around dove for tables. Hawk kept hold of her hand as he moved to a large booth in the corner, one apparently reserved for him.

At his urging, she slid in. He followed. She found herself shifting closer and closer to make room for players and their girlfriends. Despite her efforts to keep at least six inches between them, they ended up touching from hip to knee. She tried to find a good place for her cane, but there wasn't one.

"I'll take that," Hawk said, pulling it out from

under the table and placing it along the back of the booth. "What happened to your knee?"

"I fell and tore it up."

"Are you getting better?"

"It's a slow process."

"I had knee surgery," he told her. "We should compare scars."

A simple statement, but the way he said it, the words sounded dirty.

"Maybe another time," she murmured as three pizzas were placed on the table. Plates were passed out and pitchers of soda poured.

"Coach, whatcha think of that last play in the first quarter?" one of the guys asked. "That block came out of nowhere."

"You handled him," Hawk said. "Good job with the footwork. The extra practice is paying off."

The kid, at least six feet three inches of solid muscle, beamed.

Nicole reached for a piece of pizza as Hawk was bombarded with question after question. The players didn't just want to talk about the game—they wanted to make sure their coach knew they'd worked hard and done well.

It was probably a very healthy dynamic, one responsible for immature teenagers blossoming into responsible, productive citizens. She should be listening attentively, or at least taking notes, but all she could think about was how she and Hawk were touching.

His skin was hot against hers, as if he had a higher body temperature than mere mortals. She was aware of the muscles bunching and releasing—amazing, rock-hard muscles. Hawk was a big guy. Drew, her cheating bastard of an almost ex-husband, had only been a few inches taller than her and not much heavier. Hawk had massive hands, which made her think about old wives' tales and possibilities.

"Earth to self," she muttered. "Stay focused on reality."

Hawk looked at her. "Did you say something?"

"Not me."

The football recap continued. In an effort to distract herself from Hawk, Nicole glanced around the restaurant. There were a few parents sitting at one of the tables. Raoul and Brittany cuddled together in a booth across the room.

The kid had set himself up with a serious challenge, she thought. Dating his coach's daughter. She wasn't sure if she should admire Raoul for being willing to take on the task or question his sanity. Either way, she liked him.

As the pizza disappeared, conversation slowed. The kids drifted away until she and Hawk were the only ones left at their table. She eased back, putting some distance between them.

"Thanks for coming," he said.

"You're welcome. I'm still not sure how it happened. One minute I was minding my own business, the next I was here." She picked up her paper napkin and began folding it. Anything to avoid staring at Hawk.

She hated how *aware* she was of him, how she missed the heat of his body next to hers. She was only twenty-eight so she couldn't blame her reaction on swinging hormones. Maybe it was just the recent string of disasters in her life. Maybe it was cosmic humor.

"You wanted to be here," he told her.

Which might be right, but she wasn't going to admit it. "You don't actually know that."

"Yeah, I do."

Time for a subject change. "Your daughter is lovely."

Pride brightened Hawk's dark eyes. "Brittany turned out great. I want to take all the credit, but a lot of it was her mom."

"You must have been pretty young when she was born."

"Eighteen."

"That's not an easy life choice."

He shrugged. "We managed. There were some long, scary nights. Serena's family didn't want anything to do with us once we decided to get married and keep the baby. My mom was supportive but sick, and she didn't have any money. We made it on our own."

"You were lucky."

"Maybe."

"How long have she and Raoul been dating?"

"A few months. Despite what happened in the bakery, he's a good kid."

"I know."

"I trust him with my daughter." He hesitated. "I'm *trying* to trust him. What can I say? She's my baby girl. Of all the guys around, he's the one I'd choose for her." He looked at her. "Do you trust me?"

"No."

"You should," he told her. "I'm very trustworthy."

"Not even for money."

Nicole looked so serious as she spoke, Hawk thought, holding in a grin. He liked that about her. He liked the way her long, blond hair swung as she moved, and the way she always seemed to be on the verge of glaring at him. He liked that he made her nervous.

"You look nice tonight," he said.

She blinked. "Why would you say that?"

"Because it's true."

She didn't believe him. He expected that. He was going to have to work for her and he planned to enjoy every second of the hunt.

"We should go out."

She pressed her lips together. "No."

"Why not? You like me."

He watched the battle raging in her eyes. On the one hand, she wanted to tell him that she didn't like him, wouldn't ever like him, and yell at him for assuming she did. But she wouldn't want to hurt his feelings, because despite how she pretended to be tough, he knew she was a total girl on the inside.

"I'm amazed you need to date at all," she finally said. "Doesn't your ego give you enough company?"

"It doesn't keep me warm at night."

"Perhaps a heated blow-up doll."

"I'd rather have you."

She muttered something under her breath, then slid out of the booth. "I need to get home."

He grabbed her cane. "I'll walk you out."

"Not necessary." She took back the cane and started moving. She probably thought paying for the pizza would slow him down. She didn't know that Joe billed him.

When they were outside, Hawk slowed his steps to match hers. The parking lot was mostly deserted.

"No kids to take home?" she asked.

"The ones that don't drive get picked up here by their parents. Or friends take them home. You don't have any responsibilities, Nicole. Want to rethink that date?"

"No."

They were by her car, a Lexus 400 Hybrid. A girl car, he thought with a grin. Cute and curvy, with attitude. Just like her.

He touched her cheek with his fingers, lightly brushing her skin. Her quick intake of air told him she wasn't as immune as she pretended.

"Want to skip the preliminaries and go right to bed?" he asked.

She held up her cane. "How about if I just beat you with this."

"I'm not into pain. Are you? Should I be offering to spank you?"

Even in the dim light of the parking lot, he saw her blush.

"No," she sputtered. "I can't believe you said that."

"Just trying to figure out what you like and how I can provide it."

"You think you're really smooth, but you're not."

"Sure I am."

"Go away."

"You don't mean that."

"Yes, I do," she told him.

"Prove it. This is your chance. I'm going to kiss you. I'm warning you so you have plenty of time to get in your car and drive away. I'll even count to ten if you want. To give you a head start." He touched her face again, rubbing his thumb across her bottom lip.

"I don't have a problem admitting you get to me," he murmured. "I like that you get to me."

Indecision flickered in her eyes. He could feel the battle raging inside of her. Pride versus need. He knew which side he wanted to win.

CHAPTER FOUR

NICOLE KNEW that the sensible choice was to bolt for the safety of her car. Instead she gave in to temptation, put her hand on Hawk's shoulder and asked, "Are you ever going to stop talking?"

"Right now," he said, just before he kissed her.

She didn't know what to expect. A strong, demanding kiss that made her feel practically unnecessary to the process? Feeling completely weirded out because she hadn't kissed a strange man in years? Icky? Excited? Ra—

His mouth brushed against hers with a tender, erotic brush that took her breath away. Hawk didn't just kiss—he invited, teased, aroused and promised, all with barely more than a chaste whisper of skin on skin.

Her brain shrieked, sighed, then completely shut down. Her body went from "fight or flight" to "take me now" in an eighth of a second. Heat poured through her, making her weak and shaky, something she usually disliked, but not right this second.

He put one hand on her waist, tilted his head and pressed more firmly on her mouth.

The moment was amazing. Sparking jolts of desire exploded all around them, landing on her skin and practically burning through her clothes. Without meaning to, she eased forward until they were almost touching. Almost...but not quite.

She told herself she should break the kiss—pull back, act mature, or at least indignant. Instead she stayed there, taking in the warmth radiating from him, and the promise of so much more.

He licked her lower lip, the tip of his tongue barely caressing her sensitized skin. She did her best not to jump, wanting to act casual and sophisticated. It was tough, considering the liquid desire that began to pour through her.

What was up with that? Until a couple of months ago, she'd been married and living with her husband. It wasn't as if she was a sex-starved matron who hadn't gotten any in years. Yet that was how it felt. As if she'd never really known what it was like to be with a man.

She told herself Hawk wasn't all that different. That there was something chemical making her react this way, but it was meaningless. He wasn't special. Which sounded great, but didn't stop her from parting for him, or nearly gasping in pleasure when his tongue touched hers.

He moved inside, taking her with a sureness that made the trembling worse. He kissed her deeply, thoroughly, as if he had all the time in the world and planned to use every second to please her.

He explored and stroked, withdrawing, then plunging inside. He kept one hand on her waist and settled the other on her hip. Slowly, achingly slowly, he moved it down, over her rear, cupping the curve, then squeezing. Instinctively she arched against him, thighs touching, her breasts nestling against the rock-hard muscles of his chest.

Then her belly came into contact with something big and thick and…

She pulled back and stared into his fiery dark eyes. He was aroused. She'd felt his erection. Which meant he was excited by what they were doing.

Nicole liked to think she had herself pretty together. That she was confident and capable and finding her husband having sex with her baby sister hadn't totally destroyed her self-worth. Still, it was something of a shock to realize that a few minutes of kissing had turned on a sex machine like Hawk. A good shock.

"Kiss me again," she told him.

"You're demanding."

"Is that a problem?"

"Hell no."

He pulled her hard against him, then claimed her with a kiss that made her insides clench. She rubbed her stomach against his erection, which turned out to be a bit of a mistake as it made her think about his offer to take her to bed. He moved his hands up and down her back, but didn't shift them anywhere interesting.

Probably because they were outside in a parking

lot, she told herself, wondering how tacky it would be to do it on the hood of her SUV.

He slipped his fingers through her hair and tugged slightly. They stared at each other. He smiled.

"You want me."

"I'll get over it."

She said the words automatically, not sure she meant them. She *did* want him, and wasn't that good? Except the last thing she needed right now was a relationship. Even one based on an explosive sexual connection.

He leaned in and nipped on her earlobe. She gasped and trembled.

"You're wet right now," he whispered. "If I were to touch you, you'd come for me."

He was probably right, she thought, pulling back and suddenly feeling as if she were going to cry. The emotional outburst had nothing to do with Hawk and everything to do with her recent past. The body was willing but the spirit and the heart were too fragile.

"I can't play that game," she told him.

"Is that what they told you about me? That I play games?"

"It was implied."

"What if they're wrong?"

Meaning what? "I can't take the chance."

HAWK WAITED UNTIL TEN in the morning to knock on his daughter's door. "Hey, sleepyhead," he said as he pushed into the dark room and walked to the window. After opening the blinds, he faced the bed. "Do I have to tickle you?"

Brittany rolled onto her back and yawned. "Daddy, it's Saturday."

"You know, the calendar said that, but I wasn't sure. Saturday. Huh. Thanks for the clarification."

"I get to sleep in on Saturday."

"It's ten and I'm making blueberry pancakes."

Brittany sat up. "I can't eat those. They'll make me—"

He held up his hands. "You know the rule. The 'F' word is not allowed."

"I wasn't going to say fat."

"Yes, you were. Do you want pancakes or not?"

"I want them."

"Then get your girly butt up, kiddo."

Brittany grinned at him. "I love you, Daddy."

"I love you, too."

She scrambled out of bed. "Give me five minutes."

"Sure thing."

Her bathroom door slammed shut.

He returned to the kitchen where he heated the griddle, then stirred the batter. Brittany was growing up. She was a senior this year and even if she went to the University of Washington, she would be living in a dorm, so this was her last year at home. The time had gone by too fast.

Brittany walked into the kitchen just as he slid

the cooked pancakes onto a plate. She kissed his cheek, then settled into a chair.

"The game was great last night," she said. "The team is pulling it together. You're going to have a kick-ass season, Dad."

He eyed her. "Ass" was one of those borderline words. He decided not to start the morning with a fight.

"We'll see how it goes. We're focused on each game as it comes."

"All you have to do is win the next game and the play-offs take care of themselves," she said, repeating what he'd said a hundred times.

He laughed. "What are you doing today?"

"A bunch of us are meeting up around eleven-thirty. We're going to lunch and an early movie. Then back here to finish up the homework I didn't get done before the game yesterday." She wrinkled her nose. "I have two more pages on my paper. It's not due for another week, but I want it done. There's a party at Michelle's house, which you already know about. You talked to her mother on Thursday."

"I remember."

"So we'll go to that. Tomorrow I want to work on my college admission essays."

Hawk listened as she detailed her plan. As the words washed over him, he found himself thinking more about how much she'd changed in the past few years.

She was everything he could have wanted. Popular, a good student, caring, responsible. He wanted to take all the credit, but he knew Serena had laid the foundation. She'd been the perfect mother. After she'd died, he'd done his best to fill in the gaps. Apparently he'd managed to do a pretty good job.

"Things okay with Raoul?" he asked.

She chewed a mouthful of pancakes, then swallowed. "Sure. We're fine."

"You seemed pretty tight last night after the game. You're not taking things too far, are you?"

Brittany ducked her head. "Daddy, jeez. Get personal much?"

"You're my daughter. I worry about you. You're nearly eighteen. You've been dating Raoul for a while now. Do I have to kill him or not?"

"Not!" She shuddered. "This is humiliating. I won't talk about this with you, mostly because there's nothing to talk about. We're not doing…that. It's too soon."

"Okay." He kept his voice casual, but inside he was doing the happy dance. She'd said exactly what he wanted to hear.

If he had his way, his daughter wouldn't have sex until she got married…around age thirty-five. But that wasn't realistic. While he liked Raoul, he was wary. It wasn't personal—he wouldn't totally trust any teenage kid with his daughter. So he would do what he could to keep her safe and hope for the best.

He ate his own pancakes, remembering that

when he'd been Brittany's age, he and Serena had been doing it for nearly a year. They'd tried to be careful, but passion had often overridden common sense. Brittany had been the result. What had seemed like a disaster had turned out to be the best thing that ever happened to him. He'd been lucky and he knew it.

Speaking of luck… He remembered the previous evening and kissing Nicole. There was an activity he could get behind in a big way. She wasn't going to be easy, which was fine with him. He was more than up for the challenge.

NICOLE CONFIRMED the deliveries for the upcoming week, then shut down her computer. Once the rush for Saturday-morning pastries was over, there was a lull until the cake order pickups started. They were usually done by lunchtime. The bakery closed in the afternoon. She was often done by noon. Today she'd finished early because she'd forced herself to only think about work. It was either that or endlessly relive kissing Hawk. While it might seem like a great way to waste time, she knew he was nothing but trouble and she would be smart to avoid him, even in her thoughts.

Maggie knocked on her open door. "There's a bunch of high school kids out front."

"What do you mean?"

"Just what I said. They came in a few minutes ago, ordered coffee and pastries. Now they're just sitting there, talking. Like we're a hangout. We've never been a hangout."

"Are they causing any trouble?"

"No. They're real polite. It's just weird."

Nicole had to agree with her. "Let me see what's going on," she said.

She walked to the front of the store. Sure enough most of the tables were full of teenagers laughing and talking. They were a little loud, but not doing anything she could object to. She was about to turn away, when she recognized one of the girls. A pretty blonde in shorts and a T-shirt who smiled and waved.

"Hi," the girl said. "I'm Brittany. We met last night."

"Raoul's girlfriend." Hawk's daughter—a fact that was still hard to believe.

"Right. We're waiting until he gets off work, then we're all going to lunch and a movie."

"Sounds like fun." Nicole glanced at the clock. It was quarter to twelve. "I'll go tell him you're here so he can finish up. It should only be a couple of minutes."

"Thanks, but he doesn't have to hurry. We're having fun. Your Danish are incredible."

Nicole patted her hip. "Tell me about it."

She returned behind the counter where Maggie waited. "You know them?" her employee asked.

"I met a couple of them last night at the football game."

Maggie had worked at the bakery for years. She and Nicole were friends, so a simple questioning look got the point across.

"I don't know what I was doing at a high school football game," Nicole admitted. "Raoul plays. He asked me to go. I wanted to be supportive. He introduced me to Brittany, his girlfriend. She's a cheerleader."

Maggie started laughing.

Nicole glanced at the kids. "Stop it. Nothing about this is funny."

"It is to me. You're popular."

"Great. It only took ten years of being out of high school for that to happen."

Nicole went in the back and told Raoul he could leave early. According to Sid and Phil, he was doing a great job. She appreciated having her instincts validated. She was about to leave herself when Maggie found her.

"You have a gentleman caller waiting out front."

Nicole winced, even as her heart started thundering in her chest. Hawk? Was it Hawk? She hated how much she wanted it to be him. "No one talks like that."

"I do and he's gorgeous."

Definitely Hawk.

"Thanks," Nicole said. "I'll go see what he wants."

Maggie patted her hairnet. "If you're not interested, ask him if he's into older women. He's what, in his mid-thirties? That's only twenty years."

Nicole grinned. "You're happily married."

"Don't remind me."

Nicole returned to the front of the bakery. The teenagers were gone. Hawk stood by the counter, looking more tempting than anything in the bakery. She would take him over chocolate lava cake any day.

Without wanting to, she remembered their kiss from the previous night. How he'd left her both wanting and afraid. Maybe she'd exaggerated the fear. If they kissed again, she would know for sure.

"Hey," he said, giving her a slow, sexy smile that sent her heart into a healthy aerobic state.

"Hey, yourself."

Low blood sugar, she told herself. It was low blood sugar. Or the flu. It couldn't be the man. She refused to be nothing more than a quivering mass of nerves over a guy.

"I wanted to stop by and thank you for last night."

Nicole heard a snort behind her and knew that Maggie was listening. She ignored her friend.

"Thank me?" He couldn't mean the kiss, could he?

"For taking those kids to the pizza place and hanging around. For listening. You're a great role model. Older than the students, but not a parent. You're successful, together, someone they can look up to."

Which all sounded nice but couldn't she be his

sex slave instead? No, wait. She *wanted* to be successful and together. Sex slave wasn't her most comfortable role. She'd always been the girl-next-door type. Something told her that wasn't Hawk's style.

"You didn't come out here to thank me," she said, wondering if he was playing her and how long it would be before she trusted a man again.

"That's part of why I came by."

"And the other part?"

"Dessert."

She flashed to a very big bed with rumpled sheets, naked bodies and someone—hopefully her—moaning with pleasure. That was a dessert she could get into.

He pulled a sheet of paper out of his back pocket. "We're talking about thirty-five guys, a couple of parents, some friends. So say fifty people. Nothing fancy."

She blinked. "You're here to order dessert for fifty?"

"Uh-huh. Sunday afternoon we review the films from the game Friday night. It keeps them focused on the prize. I like them wired up on sugar. That way no one falls asleep. I've been using another bakery, but I like yours better. So what have you got?"

Disappointment made her want to snap at him, but she didn't. No point in letting him know how pathetic she was.

"You won't want a cake," she said, stepping

behind the counter and reviewing the contents of the case. "I would say cupcakes and cookies. I can put a selection together."

"That would be great."

"Any flavor requests?"

One of Hawk's eyebrows raised slightly. "What do you suggest?"

No way she was falling for that, she told herself. "The usual cookies. Chocolate and vanilla cupcakes. They're frosted but not decorated. Probably better that way."

"You're resisting."

"What?" she asked.

"My charm."

"Were you being charming?"

"You know I was." He handed her a card.

She glanced at it. There was a logo for the high school, the address, his name and a phone number with an extension.

"This is?" she asked.

"Where I need everything delivered. About two-thirty tomorrow. The meeting room by the gym. I wrote the directions on the back."

"I'm not delivering this stuff."

"I have nowhere to store it. Or a way to get it there."

She looked past him to the big truck parked in front of the bakery. "That would hold a lot."

"Probably, but if you brought the dessert, you could stick around for the films."

"I already saw the game once."

"Not with me explaining what happened."

Why on earth would he want her there? "It's Sunday."

"Do you have plans?"

"No, but that's not the point."

"Sure it is. Come on. You'll have fun."

She was confused, and not being in control always annoyed her. "Why are you doing this?"

"Because if you spend time with me, you'll like me."

"And that matters why?"

"You need to like me so you'll want to sleep with me."

Nicole was grateful for the cane. It helped keep her upright. "This is all about getting me into bed?"

"Naked," Hawk added in a mock whisper. "Don't leave out the best part."

She totally understood her attraction to him. He was amazing looking and kind of funny and maybe nice, even if he was a playboy. Obviously there was a chemical thing going on, but that only explained her end of things. She wasn't making it easy, which begged the question…

"Why me?"

"You intrigue me. You're not easy."

That was it? He couldn't say he thought she was pretty or interesting or sexy? Intriguing was as good as it was going to get?

"I'm not sure about your standards," she muttered, feeling slightly sick to her stomach.

She turned away. He grabbed her arm and pulled her back so they were facing each other and suddenly much closer than they had been.

"I can't stop thinking about you," he said, staring directly into her eyes. "I want to see you again. Naked would be my first choice, but I'll deal with clothes if I have to. Despite what those women you were talking to might have said, I don't do this a whole lot. There's something about you, Nicole. I can't figure it out, but I will."

And then what? He would be over her?

She didn't know what to say, what to think. What was he asking? To date her? To have sex? Both?

She wanted to say yes, but the fear returned. The chilling emotion that warned her that, while she might be over Drew, she wasn't over being hurt and she wasn't ready to get involved or even play. Not that she'd ever been much of a player.

"Say yes," he told her.

"I can't."

He leaned in and kissed her. It was hard and hot, his tongue pushing into her mouth. He took what he wanted and left her breathless. She kissed him back, feeling her blood heat. It was a battle of wills. Based on the way they were both breathing hard when they pulled apart, there was no clear winner.

"Say yes," he repeated.

If only she could.

He sighed. "Bring dessert."

"Okay."

He released her and was gone. When her head stopped spinning, she saw he'd left a hundred-dollar bill on the counter, which would cover a whole lot of cookies and cupcakes.

Maggie walked in from the back.

"That was interesting," she said. "He's very clear about what he wants. I like that in a man. You should go out with him."

"I can't. I'm not ready to have a relationship."

"Who said anything about a relationship?" Maggie's smile faded. "Oh, right. Sorry. I forgot about what happened."

Nicole bristled at the pity she saw in her friend's eyes. She wanted to defend herself, to say she was doing fine. Based on how she couldn't handle Hawk's playful invitation, that wasn't true.

"I'll get the order together," Maggie said. "You head home."

"Okay. I'll be in to pick it up tomorrow."

Nicole left.

On the drive home, she tried to talk herself into a better mood. She should be grateful she had friends who cared. And she was. Sort of. But she really, really hated anyone feeling sorry for her. She prided herself on managing. Whatever happened in her life, she managed.

It was her own fault, she reminded herself. She'd wanted to go out with Drew. She'd accepted when he'd proposed. She'd known she wasn't madly in love with him, but she'd begun to think no one would ever care about her enough to want to marry her. A stupid reason to get involved. There was nothing like a little hindsight to make everything clear. Unfortunately, knowing what she should have done didn't change the past.

So now what? How did she get over what had happened? She wasn't missing her bastard of an ex-husband, but she sure wanted her pride and self-respect back. If only she could buy them online.

She was still smiling at the thought when she pulled up in front of her house. A familiar car was parked on the street. The guy leaning against the car straightened as she drove by.

Speak of the devil, she thought grimly.

Drew waved as she circled around to the garage in back. She ignored him and parked, but he was waiting when she walked to the door and she had a bad feeling that ignoring him wasn't going to make him go away.

CHAPTER FIVE

"Go away," Nicole said by way of greeting.

"You don't mean that."

"Amazingly I do."

She thought about standing on the porch and refusing to go in the house, but wasn't excited about providing entertainment for her neighbors.

She went inside, knowing he would follow, walked to the center of the room, then faced him.

"Say what you have to say and get out."

"That's not very friendly."

"What a surprise."

She was pleased to see that the gouge on his cheek wasn't healing all that fast. The last time Drew had come calling, it had been the middle of the night. Claire had still been staying there. She'd attacked him with a high-heeled shoe that had done an impressive amount of damage.

Drew didn't seem bothered by her lack of welcome. He smiled at her. "I've missed you, babe, and I know you've missed me."

He still had the ability to leave her speechless,

she thought, stunned by his arrogance. "What am I supposed to miss? You sleeping with my sister?"

He threw up his hands. "When are you going to let that go?"

"I'm not sure. Maybe when I feel as if either of you are the least bit remorseful about what you did. You've never apologized or admitted you did anything wrong."

Jesse hadn't. She kept complaining that Nicole wouldn't believe her. So far she hadn't heard anything that would excuse their actions.

"It wasn't what you think," Drew grumbled. "You're taking it all wrong."

That made Nicole wish she knew how to throw a knife. Or hit really, really hard. "You were in my sister's bedroom, on her bed, kissing her. Her shirt was off and your hand was on her bare breast. What about that isn't what I think?"

Drew shifted uncomfortably. "I made a mistake. I'm sorry."

"Sorry isn't good enough."

"This is so typical," he said, his voice getting angry. "You take everything so seriously. Yeah, I made a mistake. People do that. Even you. I told you Jesse shouldn't be here after we were married."

"After you moved into my house and no longer had to pay rent, you mean."

"Don't do this, Nicole. Don't be hard."

What was she supposed to be? Happy?

"If Jesse hadn't been here…" he began.

"So you're saying it's my fault you were tempted and gave in to that temptation. That you have no responsibility for what you did?"

"You're twisting my words. You always do that."

She looked at the man she'd married. He was reasonably good-looking, but he didn't make her heart beat faster. He'd been a mistake—one she would be recovering from for a while.

"You need to take me back," he told her.

She shook her head. "There's no way you just said that."

"It's true. I love you. No one is going to love you like me."

He was trying to hurt her. Or maybe just scare her. "People in love don't cheat."

"Sure they do."

"I don't." She shook her head. "You can't make this right. I can't trust you, Drew, and I don't want to try."

His expression hardened. "You're going to be alone forever. Is that what you want?"

She knew she shouldn't listen to him. The fact that he was speaking her deepest fears didn't make them the truth.

"I don't believe that," she said with a conviction she didn't feel. "You're a loser, Drew. My mistake was hooking up with you in the first place."

"My mistake was trying to make it work. No one's surprised I cheated on you, Nicole. You're not easy to love. You're closed off and distant and you can be a real bitch, but I'm trying here."

She felt as if he'd slapped her. Knowing he was trying to hurt her didn't make the words any less painful.

"Aren't you magnanimous," she murmured. "How did I get so lucky? Tell you what, Drew. You stop trying to win me back with your own peculiar brand of charm and I'll do my best to get over you."

"You don't *want* to get over me. That's your problem."

"Get out," she said as she walked to the door and held it open. "Don't bother coming back."

He hesitated, as if he had more to say, then he left. She shut the door behind him and locked it, then told herself she wouldn't cry.

When she was alone, she crossed to the sofa and sank onto a cushion. She had no idea what Drew's visit had been about. Did he just want to punish her? Did he actually think they could make their marriage work and that insulting her was the best way to win her back? No one was that stupid.

So why didn't he want to let her go? Pride? The fact that she was a great meal ticket? She doubted he still loved her. Maybe he never had.

Doubts crowded in on her. She hated how they made her feel. She needed a distraction.

Just then the phone rang. She jumped up and ran into the kitchen.

"Hello?"

"Hi. How's it going?"

While hearing from Claire wasn't as exciting as

an inappropriate sexual advance from Hawk, it was still better than thinking about Drew.

"Okay. How are you?"

"Still waiting to look pregnant. Do you want to come over for dinner tonight?"

Nicole hesitated. Did she want to spend the evening with her sister and Wyatt, watching them coo over each other as the waves of their love filled the room with more hormones than should be allowed by any state agency?

"Thanks, but I'm going to pass."

Claire sighed. "You're spending too much time alone."

"No, I'm not. I was just at the bakery."

"Work doesn't count. Don't be crabby. I'm worried because I love you. That's a good thing."

Nicole didn't want to remember Drew telling her she wasn't easy to love, but the words popped into her brain.

"You've been dealing with a lot of crap," Claire said. "Come over and have fun."

There it was—just like with Maggie. Pity. Nicole hated being pitied.

"You're sweet to worry," she said, trying not to clench her teeth. "But I'm great. Better than great. Another time."

"You need to get out."

"With a guy, right? You'd stop worrying about me if I showed up with a fabulous guy, wouldn't you?"

Claire laughed. "Actually, I would."

That made Nicole smile. "So you don't actually care about how I feel. This is all about you."

"Well, maybe. But you're a part of it."

"And I appreciate that. Look, I'm fine. I swear. I've gotta run. Talk to you later."

She hung up and grabbed her purse. As she opened the front door and stepped out, the phone was already ringing again. She ignored it, even as she wished she had somewhere to go.

HAWK STACKED the DVDs he'd made of the raw footage from the game. He'd already been over the material and knew the points he wanted to emphasize. Normally he would use the few minutes he had before the guys started arriving to make notes, but on this Sunday, he kept checking his watch and wondering when Nicole was going to show.

He knew he was acting like a kid around her. And even when he wasn't around her. He couldn't seem to stop thinking about her. Okay—thinking was a stretch. Fantasizing would be better. He kept picturing her naked and begging. In his fantasy he was always happy to oblige. It was just the kind of man he was.

He didn't know why she got to him, but he was enjoying the ride. She was funny and sarcastic. She challenged him. She had attitude. He liked attitude in a woman.

He heard footsteps in the hallway outside the meeting room. Light footsteps that didn't belong to any of his players. His gut clenched in anticipation. Sure enough, Nicole entered the room.

"I have about six boxes of desserts in my car," she said. "Want to help me carry them?"

"Sure," he said, wondering if there was time to kiss her before his students started arriving. He moved toward her, stopping when he saw something dark and painful flicker in her eyes. "What's wrong?"

"Nothing."

"I don't believe you," he told her. "Something happened."

Now that he studied her, he could see it in the slight slump of her shoulders and the paleness of her skin. "Someone hurt you."

"I'm fine," she told him, then shrugged. "It's nothing."

"I was married for twelve years. 'Nothing' in this context is female code for 'you're going to have to keep asking to prove you're seriously interested.' What's wrong?"

"I'm fine."

"I'm not letting this go." He wouldn't until he knew who or what had upset her.

She sighed. "I'm… I'm having a little trouble with my ex."

What kind of trouble? "You're divorced?"

"I'm in the process. The papers have been filed and the terms agreed to. I'm waiting out the time."

"You still miss him?" Hawk asked, not wanting to know the answer. What if she said yes?

"Not even a little. He came by yesterday. He wants me back. His way of convincing me is to be insulting and mean."

Hawk bristled. "Did he hurt you."

She managed a smile. "Not really."

"I can beat him up for you."

Her smile widened. "I'm sure you'd do so with amazing efficiency, but no."

He really wanted to. "I don't mind. I'm always looking for new ways to stay in shape."

"It wouldn't be much of a workout for you."

"You think?"

"I'm sure of it. You're nice to offer, though. Thanks."

There was more. He could read it in her eyes. The problem with an ex was that person knew the best way to hurt. He or she knew the weak spots, the soft underbelly. Apparently her ex wasn't afraid to attack there.

He touched her cheek. "He's wrong."

"About what?"

"Whatever he said."

"You don't know that."

"Yeah, I do."

Hawk's expression was kind, his touch comforting and just a little sexy. He was exactly what she needed, Nicole thought.

His gaze dropped from her eyes to her mouth.

Her body reacted with tingles and little sighs, and the man wasn't even kissing her. How did he do that?

Before she could find out, there was the sound of several teenagers in the hallway. She stepped back.

"Reinforcements," he said lightly. "I'll get them to bring in the boxes."

Which meant it could be done in a single trip, leaving her no excuse to stay and, for some reason, she wanted to stay.

"I have your change." She dug in her jeans pocket and pulled out the money.

"Keep that for next time," he said. "I'll be ordering in a week."

"Okay."

"You're going to stay for the meeting, aren't you?"

"I, ah, sure." Because the alternative was going home and avoiding her friends who all currently felt sorry for her.

Hawk sent several of the guys out to get the desserts she'd brought. Raoul returned with them and called out a greeting. She moved over to help with the setup.

"Am I freaking you out by being here?" she asked. "Is it too much like your boss being around in your personal life?"

He smiled. "No one says freaking anymore."

"Sure they do."

"Because you're so hip?"

"No one says hip. I know that much."

The teenager laughed. "It's fine if you stay."

"Good. Maybe I can give you a few pointers."

"Maybe. Coach says women are a mysterious island and a smart man always knows the limits of his abilities."

It was an interesting mixed metaphor. She didn't doubt that Hawk had more experience than the average guy and that Raoul would be smart to listen to him.

In a matter of minutes, everyone was settled on folding chairs. Nicole found herself sitting next to Hawk, which made her happy. He was exactly the distraction she needed.

He pushed a remote. The lights went down and a grainy image of the game came on the big screen on the wall.

"You guys got lucky," he said. "The snap was sloppy. Fundamentals are everything. Wilson, you were two seconds late off the line. Green, you're supposed to be covering the quarterback. Their guys get through, we don't score. It's that simple."

He dissected every second of the game, offering praise where it was deserved—which didn't seem that often—and giving constructive criticism. He explained things simply. Even Nicole was able to follow what he was saying…at least for the first ten minutes or so. Then she felt a hand lightly brush her arm.

The unexpected contact nearly made her jump. She managed to stay in her seat and casually glanced down to see him running his fingers across the inside of her wrist. Slowly, gently, without once looking at her.

In theory there was nothing sexual about the contact. It shouldn't have been meaningful. But there was something about the heat of his skin, the way he brushed his thumb across the inside of her palm, that made her want to squirm. She had to consciously control her breathing. After about ten minutes, she had to tell herself that throwing herself into his arms was completely inappropriate.

They took a break at halftime. The guys dove into the cupcakes and brownies, consuming everything she'd brought in a matter of seconds. Hawk leaned back in his chair.

"You enjoying the game?" he asked.

He sounds so damn casual, she thought, more than a little annoyed. With the lights on, they weren't touching. He was acting like nothing had happened. Like they were little more than people who'd run into each other at the grocery store. She felt all squishy and swollen inside and desperately hungry for more than a light brush against her arm.

"I'm learning a lot," she told him, determined not to let him know how he got to her. "I've never been into sports. It's a lot more complicated than I'd realized."

"Most things are. Want to get something to eat after this? Or head back to your place?"

"You're very comfortable just going for it, aren't you?" she asked, keeping her voice low and checking to make sure no one could hear them.

"I know what I want."

Her? She shifted on the seat, then wished she hadn't as her insides whimpered.

"Hawk, I…" What? Did she want to say yes?

Scratch that. Of course she wanted to say yes, but there were a thousand reasons why she shouldn't. Sleeping with Hawk might be a momentary distraction, but she'd never been into easy. Or casual sex. She wasn't sure reacting to Drew's scathing comments by jumping into bed with someone else was smart.

"I should go."

His dark gaze settled on her face. "How long are you going to run from me?"

"I don't know."

"Admitting you have a problem is the first step in solving it."

"How very bumper sticker of you."

She stood. He grabbed her hand and pulled her close.

"At least admit you're tempted," he murmured.

"More than you know."

"HELLO?" Nicole said Monday afternoon as she answered the phone. She'd just left work and was looking forward to a little lounging time.

"Nicole? It's Martin Bashear."

Her lawyer. "Hi, Martin. How's it going?"

"Well. I have a few things I want to talk to you about."

"Am I going to like hearing them?"

"Probably not."

She mentally braced herself. "Okay. What?"

"We're at a crossroads with the Jesse situation. We either have to pursue prosecution or let it go."

"You know what I want."

"I do, but as your lawyer, it's my job to give you advice. I'm going to advise you to drop the charges."

She tightened her grip on the phone. "She stole the family recipe. A world-famous recipe. She baked Keyes chocolate cakes and sold them on the Internet. I can't let her get away with that."

"I agree that her behavior was reprehensible."

That almost made her smile. Martin always talked like he had a stick up his butt. Usually she was the stuffy one in any relationship but with him she was, by comparison, the free spirit.

"She stole, Martin," she repeated, feeling the outrage swell up inside of her.

It wasn't enough that Jesse had screwed Drew. No. She had to go and steal the Keyes chocolate cake, too.

"I want her punished."

"Rightfully so. But, Nicole, consider the consequences. This will be an expensive and drawn-out process. Family drama never plays well in court. Jesse could get the jury's sympathy vote. We can do our best to paint her as the bad guy, but that doesn't always work. She lost her parents when she was very young—"

"So did I," Nicole snapped.

"Yes, but you're the older sister. People may blame you for her behavior."

"That's hardly news."

"Other matters might come to light."

Translation—the defense could bring up Jesse sleeping with Drew. While that should help Nicole, in truth it might make some members of the jury think the case was about revenge.

"There's also the matter of her being pregnant. We don't want that to be an issue, but by the time this got to court, she would be close to her due date. That would be in her favor."

Nicole was fairly sure that Martin kept talking, but she couldn't hear him. Not with the ringing in her ears.

"Did you say pregnant?" she asked, barely able to say the words.

There was a pause. "I'm sorry," Martin told her. "I thought you knew."

Knew? That Jesse was pregnant? Nicole stood. For once, she didn't need her cane. "How far along?"

"I'm not exactly sure. Four months. Maybe a little more."

Nicole swore. Jesse was having Drew's baby.

Heat climbed her cheeks. Humiliation? she wondered. Or good, old-fashioned rage? Pregnant. She shouldn't even be surprised.

She felt as if she was going to throw up. The room seemed to tilt.

"I have to go," she managed.

"Nicole, I'm sorry. Is there anything I can do?"

"Drop the charges."

"Are you sure?"

She nodded then remembered he couldn't see her. "Drop them. You're right. This is a losing battle."

She hung up without saying goodbye, then closed her eyes and let the pain wash over her.

There'd been too much betrayal, she thought, trying to breathe through the ache in her chest. Too much loss. She'd given her baby sister everything, had sacrificed for her, loved her, dreamed for her, wanted only the best. And this was her reward.

A baby. Jesse was having a baby.

Nicole touched her own flat, empty stomach, then sank back into her chair. It wasn't that she wanted a child with Drew, but a family…she'd always wanted a family. And someone to love, who loved her best. What she got instead was stabbed in the back.

How fair was—

The doorbell rang. She crossed to the front of the house and opened the door. A middle-aged woman with dark hair stood on the porch.

"Hello," the woman said. "I'm looking for Jesse Keyes."

"And you are?" Nicole asked.

"Paula Fenner. Jesse is dating my son, Matt. I need to speak with her. I've left several messages, but she won't return my calls."

"She doesn't live here anymore," Nicole said, knowing if Jesse was still in the house, she would kick her out all over again.

Paula frowned. "Where is she? She's not living with Matt."

"I have no idea." Nicole refused to care. Jesse was twenty-two. She could take care of herself.

"May I ask why she moved out?" Paula's expression was curious and determined.

Nicole hesitated. Her first instinct was to protect her sister, to not tell the truth. Then she remembered all Jesse had done to her, how Nicole had taken care of her, worried about her, loved her, and Jesse's way of repaying her had been to sleep with Drew and get pregnant.

The anger always lurking under the surface exploded into something hot and demanding.

"I found her in bed with my husband," Nicole said flatly. "I kicked her out."

Paula's face paled. "I'm sorry. I'm not surprised, but I'm sorry."

"I'm sorry, too," Nicole said. She stepped back into the house and shut the door. She was sorry

about a lot of things. Mostly caring about someone who had never thought about anyone but
herself.

NICOLE WAITED impatiently on Wyatt's front porch,
then rang the bell again. Claire answered the door.

"Did you know?" Nicole demanded.

Claire frowned. "Know what?"

"That Jesse's pregnant?"

Claire went pale. "Oh my God. Are you sure?"

"Reasonably. I heard it from my lawyer."

"I didn't know. I swear."

Nicole believed her. Claire was talented in many
ways, but she was a lousy liar. It was a good quality
in a sister. Jesse, on the other hand, was an expert
at avoiding the truth.

Claire stepped back to let her in. "I can't believe
it. Pregnant. Is it…"

Nicole entered the living room, wanting to hit
something with her cane. "Drew's? Based on the
timing, it seems likely. I guess the boyfriend could
be a possibility, along with whoever else she was
sleeping with. But with my luck, the baby's Drew's.
I know when I caught them together but who knows
how long they'd been sleeping together before that."

In her house. Making a fool of her. Lying to her.
Pretending they both loved her while they were
sneaking around and laughing at her.

She swallowed hard and vowed she wouldn't

cry. That was her new rule—no tears wasted on people who didn't matter.

"I don't know what to say," Claire admitted. "This is awful. Have you talked to her?"

"No. There's nothing to say. She'll deny the whole thing. It's what she's good at."

"But maybe—"

Nicole cut her off with a look. "This is not a good time to play the middle child." She sank onto the sofa. "I just don't get it. What went wrong? Why would she do this to me?"

"I don't think it was totally about you. I think it just happened."

Nicole rolled her eyes. "Is that what she told you? And you believe her?"

"You can't know she was trying to hurt you."

"Maybe not, but I have a good idea. She was angry with me. She hated that her half of the bakery was tied up in a trust until she was twenty-five. She was bugging me to buy her out now so she could go do who knows what."

Claire sat next to her and touched her hand. "I know she was difficult and you did your best. She got into a lot of trouble, but to do something like this? And what about Matt? Didn't she care about him?"

Nicole no longer had an answer. Jesse changed guys as easily as most other women changed shoes. But Matt had been different, or so she'd thought. Jesse had dated him for a few months and really seemed to care about him.

"Maybe she was playing him, too," she said slowly. "She swore she loved him, that he was the one. It was all a big game to her."

"I'm sorry." Claire hugged her. "I'm so sorry."

Sympathy was a little too close to pity for Nicole's taste. She accepted the hug, reminded herself she wasn't crying ever again, then stood.

"I should go."

"No. You shouldn't be alone."

"I'm fine," Nicole insisted. Suddenly the large room seemed too small. "I haven't told Drew. I'm not going to. That's Jesse's job."

"I won't say anything and Wyatt won't, either."

Because Claire would tell her fiancé, who just happened to be Drew's stepbrother. Talk about a mess.

Claire walked her to the door. "What can I do to help?"

"Knowing you're here helps."

"Are you sure?"

Nicole nodded. "I'll call if I need anything else."

She walked to her SUV and got inside. After starting the engine, she stared out the windshield. Where was she supposed to go now? What was she supposed to do? Her sister was pregnant by her soon-to-be ex-husband. Nicole was a cliché. She could be a character in a soap.

Jesse was unlikely to keep this kind of information to herself which meant soon everyone would know. Talk about humiliating.

She reached into her purse for a tissue and fumbled with a business card instead. She pulled it out and stared at the printing on the front, then reached for her cell phone and dialed.

When the phone was answered, she asked for the extension on the card.

"Hawkins."

"It's Nicole," she said, doing her best to keep her voice from shaking. This was *not* a good idea but it was the only one she could come up with.

"You're an unexpected surprise."

"Is that good or bad?"

"I like surprises."

His voice was teasing. That gave her courage. "Can you talk for a second?"

"Sure. Is this a regular conversation or should I close my door?"

"You might want to close it."

There was a moment of silence, followed by a chuckle. "Okay. I wouldn't have figured you were into phone sex. I'll admit I've never done it, but I'm a fast learner."

She squeezed the cell phone so tight, her fingers hurt. "I have to ask you a question. Did you mean what you said before? What you've been hinting at? Do you want to sleep with me or is it all a game?"

"Nicole, what's going on?"

"Just answer the question."

"Of course I'm interested."

Thank God. She sucked in a breath. "Then here's

the deal. I'll be your personal sex kitten. I'll be available when, where and how you want."

"That's a hell of an offer."

"There's a catch."

"I almost don't care what it is."

Now came the scary part. "I want you to pretend to be my adoring boyfriend. I want us to be seen in public. I want you to be all over me. You'll be faithful, you won't flirt with anyone else. I get to show you off to all my friends and in a few weeks, I want to publicly dump you."

He was going to say no, she told herself. She was asking for too much. Worse, he was going to know she'd asked and that would be a whole new level of humiliation.

The silence stretched between them. She closed her eyes and held her breath. He was going to say no. Why wouldn't he?

"Why?" he asked.

"I have something to prove." And her pride to salvage.

"Is this about your ex-husband?"

"A little."

"Are you still in love with him?"

"No."

"You sure?"

"More than sure. He cheated and I'm angry, but I'm not hurt. He wants to get back together. I don't. I'm just tired of how everyone's acting. The pity is the worst. The knowing looks. I want to prove I'm totally fine."

It was as close to the truth as she could get and not start sobbing.

"I don't do relationships," he said. "Not serious ones. I like serial monogamy, but I don't do permanent."

"Me, either." Wait a second. Did that mean he was saying yes?

"Brittany would have to be told that we weren't serious. I don't want her worrying."

"Just don't tell her the specifics of the deal and I'm good with that."

"Not a problem. I don't discuss my sex life with her and I don't need her knowing I had to make a deal to get you into bed."

Her heart thudded in her chest. "So you agree?"

"Yes. When do you turn into my…what was it you said? Oh, yeah. When do you turn into my personal sex kitten?"

Relief tasted sweet. It was immediately followed by sexual anticipation and an ache between her legs.

"Whenever you want."

"I can be at your place in twenty minutes," he said.

"I'll be waiting."

"Can you be waiting naked?"

"If it's important to you."

"It is."

CHAPTER SIX

NICOLE RACED HOME and ran into the house. Actually she moved as quickly as she could considering her knee was still stiff, but it was almost like running.

She looked around downstairs, decided it was clean enough, then moved up the stairs.

Her bedroom was fairly tidy. She smoothed the covers on the bed, tossed all the clothes lying around into the closet and shut the door, brushed her teeth, then stared at herself in the mirror.

Naked. Hawk had very specifically said naked. She fingered the hem of her T-shirt and knew there was no way she could meet him downstairs not wearing anything. It would be easier to learn to fly.

She turned back to her closet, pulled open the door and stared at the contents. Okay, what would be a good compromise?

She spotted a spaghetti-strapped sundress in pink. She didn't like to go braless, so she'd never worn it. But the dress was pretty, feminine, and she would only be wearing panties underneath, so that was something.

She quickly ripped off her T-shirt and stepped out of her jeans, then tossed her bra aside. She shimmied into the dress, then closed the closet behind her. After giving herself a quick once-over, she made her way downstairs just as the doorbell rang.

Until that moment, she hadn't had time to panic. She'd had too much to do. But now, as she walked toward the front door, terror gripped her. What on earth was she doing? This was crazy. Casual sex with a man she barely knew? She'd never done that before.

She opened the door. Hawk stood on her front porch, six feet three inches of gorgeous male.

He wore a polo shirt with the high school logo on one side, khakis and athletic shoes. He looked dangerous and sexy and there was an air of controlled expectation that nearly made her faint.

"Hi," he said, then smiled. "I had to make a stop."

He held up a small plastic bag from a local drugstore.

She peered at it. "You stopped to run errands on your way over?"

"You don't do this much, do you?"

"What?"

"The sex-kitten thing."

She felt herself blushing. "No. Why?"

"I didn't run errands. I bought condoms."

She swallowed. "Uh, good idea." Then she stepped back to let him in, mostly because leaving him on the porch would require more conversation and she wasn't sure she was capable of speaking just now.

The reality of what she'd offered crashed into her. Was she insane? Sex with Hawk? Like that would ever work. He was amazing. No doubt the five or six hundred women he'd been with had also been amazing. How was she supposed to measure up? She'd only been with a couple of guys before Drew. Make that one other guy. What if she'd been doing it wrong all this time?

"Second thoughts?" Hawk asked.

"And a pressing need to vomit."

"Want to talk about it?"

Did she have a choice? She squeezed her eyes shut, then looked at him. "I'm not that experienced. Before I was married, I didn't play around a lot." Ever. The word she was looking for was ever. "I'm not sure I can measure up."

He moved closer. "Is that all?"

"Isn't it enough?"

He dropped the bag onto the coffee table and cupped her face in his hands. "I was married for twelve years. Serena was the only woman I'd been with. Since then, there have been a couple."

"Hundred?"

He chuckled. "Less than ten."

"That's not possible."

He leaned in and brushed his mouth against hers. "I get a lot of offers, but I'm picky. I know my reputation. Most of it is cheap talk. I will admit you're the first woman I had to negotiate to get."

Was he telling the truth? She hoped so. It made her feel better, except… "Don't expect too much. I can't handle the pressure right now. This isn't going to be miraculous or anything."

"Of course it is."

He wrapped his arms around her and pulled her close. She held on to him as he tilted his head and kissed her. His mouth was warm and sure, firm without being demanding. She parted for him immediately and welcomed him inside.

The tingles began the second his tongue touched hers. They raced through her body, making her toes curl and her thighs tremble. She felt both weak and incredibly powerful. Even more exciting, she found herself wanting this more than she'd thought possible.

They pressed together from shoulder to thigh. They were close enough that she felt the exact second he got hard. His erection pressed into her belly, making her want to squirm closer. She circled his tongue with hers, then closed her lips around him and sucked. His arousal flexed against her.

It was as if someone had flipped a switch. Maybe it was knowing that this man wanted her. Maybe it was the emotional roller coaster she'd been on for the past couple of months. Maybe it was chemistry. But whatever the cause, she found herself aching with need. Her body burned in anticipation. Passion swept through her, stealing her breath and making her bold.

When he pulled back slightly and began to kiss her cheeks, then her jaw, she tugged his shirt from his khakis. As he kissed his way down her neck, making her break out in goose bumps, she slipped her hands under his shirt to his warm sides and felt the skin and the muscles bunching below.

He licked the curve of her neck and made her shudder. She explored his broad chest and ran her fingertips across his nipples and felt him stiffen.

The air was charged with sexual need. They reached for each other, bumping arms and hands. They kissed, tongues plunging. He ran his hands up and down her back, then to her rear, where he cupped and squeezed. She grabbed his shirt in both her hands.

"Take this off," she demanded.

He obliged with a quick tug, leaving him bare to the waist.

He was more perfect than she'd imagined. Solid muscle, sculpted in ways she'd never seen outside of a magazine.

She put her hand on his arm and felt the strength there, the definition. She moved her fingers across his shoulders, down his chest. He was like a statue come to life. She'd never been into guys who worked out, but suddenly saw the possibilities.

"You're amazing," she breathed.

"Now who's looking for miracles."

That made her smile. She looked at him and saw the need in his eyes. Sexual need…for her. It was possibly his best quality.

He reached for the strap of her dress and tugged it over her shoulder, then bent down and kissed where it had been. He nibbled her bare skin, which made her whole body tighten. When he found the side zipper without even fumbling, then undid it, she knew she was in over her head.

Too late to turn back, she told herself. And why would she want to? Sex with Hawk could be an incredible experience. Wasn't she due one of those right about now?

He pulled her dress over her head, leaving her in nothing but panties. Before she had time to get embarrassed, he cupped her breasts in his large hands and kissed her.

Even as they strained toward each other, even as his fingers explored her curves and teased her nipples, he was moving her backward. She felt the sofa and, at his urging, sank down.

He dropped to his knees and leaned in, taking her right nipple into his mouth. He used his fingers on her left breast, touching, rubbing, circling. His tongue stroked, sucked, then licked, all the while sending sensations of liquid desire coursing through her body.

She couldn't think and that was a miracle. She closed her eyes and got lost in the pleasure he gave her. A voice in the back of her head mumbled something about heading upstairs so they could do this on the bed, but that meant stopping and there was no way she wanted that to happen.

He straightened enough to kiss her mouth. As she touched his face, his shoulders, his arms, he pulled off her panties, leaving her completely naked. As he'd asked before. What a smart man.

He ran his fingers up and down her thighs, then pulled back slightly. "How much do you hurt?"

Hurt? She was wet, swollen, trembling and more than ready for the fireworks. What could possibly hurt?

"Your knee?" he asked.

"It's fine. Totally fine. I don't even know it's there."

He smiled, then tucked a strand of hair behind her ear. "Good. So doing this would be okay."

He bent down and kissed the inside of her knee.

"That would be great."

"And this?" He moved a little higher.

"Also great."

He moved higher still, getting closer to her center, but not touching it. "Better?"

She closed her eyes and rested her head on the cushions. "Uh-huh."

He parted her with his fingers, then gave her an openmouthed kiss on her most sensitive spot.

"Perfect," she breathed.

He used his lips and tongue, exploring her then returning to that one special place. He licked and sucked, every movement making her tense and push. She squirmed in her seat, wanting more. Wanting her release. She might have started this deal to save her pride but suddenly the only thing that mattered was the way her body burned and the need building inside of her.

He moved a little faster. She found it more difficult to breathe as every cell in her body focused on that nerve center and what he was doing to it. Over and over he licked. Back and forth, circling, then pressing a little harder. She wanted to scream. She wanted to beg. She wanted to—

Her orgasm caught her by surprise. One second she was rocking her hips in a desperate attempt to speed up the process, the next she was shattering in perfect pleasure as waves of release swept through her. She gave herself over to the sensations, crying out as her body contracted again and again.

Hawk continued to touch her, but with less and less pressure. He drew every ounce of her release from her until she was limp and practically boneless.

She could have stayed there for hours, her eyes closed, reliving the most amazing orgasm of her life, but muttered cursing caught her attention. She opened her eyes and saw Hawk kicking off his shoes while he tried to pull off his khakis. His movements were frantic, almost desperate. He saw her looking at him.

"What the hell were you thinking?" he demanded. "Coming like that? How am I supposed to hold it together when you moan? Do you think that's going to help me last more than five seconds? I practically lost it in my pants. I'm not a teenager anymore. I'm supposed to have some control."

It was one of those perfect moments in life she would remember forever. There was nothing he could have given her that would have been more precious. He wanted her. Desperately. She saw it in his face and his jerky movements.

He managed to push off the rest of his clothes, then stood there naked, fumbling with the condom box. He continued to mutter and swear, but she wasn't paying attention. She was too busy staring at his massive erection and wondering if he was going to go from making her moan to making her scream.

After tearing the package open, he pulled out the protection, roughly put it on himself, then knelt on the floor.

"I can't wait much longer," he told her.

"That's okay."

"This isn't going to be pretty."

"I don't judge on style. Enthusiasm counts for a lot more."

"I've got a hell of a lot of that."

She reached for him, guiding him inside.

He filled her completely. She had to stretch to take all of him and she was more than willing for that to happen.

He pushed in again, then groaned. "I have to do this. I'll go slow next time."

She smiled. "Go for it."

He grabbed her hips and pumped into her. She closed her eyes and enjoyed the ride, the steady rhythm of how he moved in and out of her. Her body began to tighten in anticipation. She parted her legs more, drawing him in.

Closer, she thought in surprise. She was getting closer. His fingers tightened, warning her he was getting closer, too. She could hear his rapid breathing, feel the tension in his body. All of that aroused her, pushing her toward the edge.

He moved one hand between them and rubbed her center. It was enough to send her over the edge.

She gave herself up to her second orgasm, reveling in the sensation of him filling her as she contracted around him. Then he groaned again and was still.

They managed to both settle on the sofa, his arm around her, her head on his shoulder. She felt good. Better than good. She felt like she could fly.

"I've never had a sex kitten before," he said. "I give it a big thumbs-up."

"Me, too."

He leaned over and kissed her. "I wish I could stay here with you but I have to get back to school soon."

"That's okay. I can relive the moment…all afternoon."

"I'll be doing that, too. When do you want to start showing me off in public?"

She hadn't thought that far ahead. "This weekend?"

"It's a date."

He kissed her again and then started untangling their limbs. She watched him dress, thinking that male perfection made for fabulous eye candy.

After he left, Nicole went upstairs and showered, then dressed back in her jeans. Despite everything that had happened, she felt much better about things. Healed even. A feeling she was going to hang on to.

"I'VE FELT REALLY GOOD, right until this second," Nicole muttered as she and Claire stood in front of a run-down apartment building.

"You need to talk to her," Claire said.

Nicole sighed. "You being the voice of reason is really getting old. Just so we're clear on that."

"I know. I'm sorry. But she's your sister."

Jesse was also a lying, cheating bitch, but Nicole didn't mention that. Bad enough that she had to be here. She didn't want to fight with Claire, too.

They took the stairs to the third-floor apartment. Nicole found herself hoping her sister was gone, but Jesse opened the door when Claire knocked.

If she was surprised to see them, she didn't show it.

"May we come in?" Claire asked.

Jesse shrugged, then stepped out of the way. Nicole followed Claire inside.

The apartment was small and dark, a studio with water-stained walls and a smell of dampness. Nicole braced herself against any feelings of sympathy. She'd tossed Jesse out when she'd discovered her in bed with Drew. If Jesse hadn't screwed up big-time, she would have still been living in the house. Her kid sister had done this to herself.

Claire looked around and tried to smile. "Everyone has to start somewhere," she said cheerfully. "This is nice."

"Sure. Whatever." Jesse folded her arms across her chest. "Why are you here?"

Her sullenness made Nicole want to leave. Unfortunately she didn't have a phone number for Jesse anymore, so she couldn't just call her.

"I'm dropping the charges," she told Jesse. "Not because I want to, but because my attorney is concerned about how our case will play in court. I've already wasted enough money on you. I don't want to keep doing that."

Despite her best intentions, her gaze slipped down to her sister's midsection. There was a slight bulge. Nicole couldn't decide if proof of the pregnancy was good or bad.

Jesse looked confused. "I don't understand."

"You're pregnant," Nicole said coldly. "That might make the jury sympathetic."

Jesse took a step back. "How do you know?"

"My attorney mentioned it."

"But I told him in confidence. He promised not to say anything. What about attorney-client privilege?"

Nicole rolled her eyes. "*I'm* his client. I pay for his service. You're the person who stole. What makes you think he'd do what you said?"

At that moment, Jesse looked painfully young and unsure of herself. "I didn't realize."

Claire stepped between them. "Jesse, I hope you appreciate the opportunity Nicole is giving you. You won't have to worry about going to court."

"For taking what's half mine?" Jesse asked, the moment of weakness gone.

"Here we go again," Nicole muttered, grateful for her encounter with Hawk yesterday. Their powerful sexual experience had made her stronger somehow. At the very least it had given her something to think about other than Jesse and Drew and being humiliated.

"Our father left half the bakery to me," Jesse said loudly.

"In trust until you're twenty-five," Nicole reminded her.

"You could buy me out. That's all I want. I didn't steal the cake recipe. I can't steal what's half mine."

Nicole felt her temper rising. "You went behind my back. You built an Internet site that looked exactly like the one we already have and you sold cakes. What would you call it?"

"Doing what I had a right to."

"And Drew? Did we share him, too?"

Jesse turned away. "I don't want to talk about that."

"Imagine how much I don't care about what you want."

"I didn't sleep with him," Jesse whispered.

Nicole wanted to throw something. "I saw him in your bed. You were naked. He was kissing you. What would you call it?"

"Don't be like that. Why can't you try to understand?"

Nicole tasted fury. "Oh, so this is *my* fault? After all I did for you?"

Claire stepped between them. "Stop. Both of you."

"She won't believe me," Jesse whined.

"She's a known liar." And worse, Nicole thought. "I don't lie."

"You leave things out. Omission is just as bad."

"Stop it." Claire glared at both of them. "We have to work this out."

"No, we don't," Nicole said quietly. "Some things can't be forgiven."

Jesse spun back to face them. "That's right. Nicole only wants me punished."

"At last you're making sense," Nicole said.

Jesse glared at her. "You know what's so funny about all this? The baby isn't Drew's. It's Matt's."

Nicole wasn't surprised Jesse would go there.

"How can you be sure? You were sleeping with both of them."

Her baby sister flushed. "That's what you think, what you'll always think. That's why you told him about Drew. You wanted to hurt me as much as you'd been hurt. Congratulations. He hates me, too."

Nicole refused to feel guilty. "As always, your flare for the dramatic overrides any need to tell the truth. I didn't tell Matt about you and Drew. I told his mother, who came over to talk to you, that you were no longer living with me."

Tears filled Jesse's eyes. "So you told her what you saw, what you believed happened with Drew and she told Matt. You ruined everything."

"The person who did that is you," Nicole said coldly.

"No, I didn't," Jesse yelled. "I didn't sleep with Drew. I didn't."

Claire looked disappointed. "Jesse, we can only make this work if we start from a place of honesty."

"I'm being honest." Jesse wiped away tears. "Why won't you believe me?"

Nicole felt more disappointed than angry. She'd seen Drew and Jesse in bed together. Jesse had been naked, at least from the waist up. Nicole had seen that much.

"I'm tired of this," she told Claire. "Let's go."

"No!" Jesse threw herself in front of the door. "You have to listen. The baby is Matt's. You have to believe me."

Claire shook her head. "I'm sorry, Jesse. You were in bed with Drew. We all know that happened. Why can't we start from there?"

Jesse straightened. "Fine," she said, tears still filling her eyes. "If that's what you want, that's what we'll talk about. I screwed his brains out for days. We couldn't get enough of each other. Is that what you want to hear? I gave him everything you never could. Is it all better now?"

Nicole pressed her hand to her stomach. "I have to go."

She pushed Jesse out of the way and left the apartment. Claire followed.

"I'm sorry," her twin told her. "I thought we could get through to her."

"That'll never happen," Nicole murmured, wondering if she was going to throw up now or wait until she got home.

JESSE SLAMMED the door shut behind them, but it didn't make her feel any better. She retreated to her sofa and curled up on the hard, smelly surface, wishing she could go back in time. Just five minutes. Maybe if she had a do-over, she could explain it to them, in a way that made sense.

It wasn't true, she thought as she cried and tried not to feel so incredibly alone. None of it. But they didn't care. They only wanted to believe the worst of her.

Somewhere deep inside, she knew that was her

fault. Nicole liked to point out how much of a screwup she was and Jesse knew she was right. She didn't mean to get in trouble…it just seemed to happen. But this. She didn't deserve this.

She was guilty of being friends with Drew, and maybe bad judgment, but nothing more. Sometimes Nicole could be difficult. Jesse and Drew had gotten into the habit of talking. Just talking. She wasn't interested in Drew and even if she'd had a crush on him, she wouldn't have done anything about it. He was Nicole's husband.

She squeezed her eyes tightly shut, but that didn't close out the memories of that last night at Nicole's house. How she, Jesse, had been upset about Matt. It had been late and she'd been in her room. Drew had come in and she'd welcomed the chance to talk.

She'd explained her fears and hopes and how she knew in her heart, Matt was the one she would love forever. Drew had hugged her.

She'd guessed he'd been offering comfort, which had been okay, if a little awkward. She'd accepted his embrace. But then he'd kissed her.

She'd been so stunned, she hadn't known what to do. He'd kissed her and started talking about how this monogamy business wasn't the real her. She was always flirting with different guys, including Drew. And then he flattered her, telling her that she was pretty and so much softer than Nicole. That she could do so much better than Matt.

It was almost instinct to respond. To agree that she wasn't a one-man kind of girl. She never had been. It was like she was watching herself from a great distance. Then he'd pushed off the T-shirt she'd worn to bed and touched her breasts. Something inside of her had snapped.

She'd tried to stop him. She'd been quiet, not wanting Nicole to find out, instinctively knowing her sister wouldn't believe that she hadn't initiated this. And that's when Nicole had walked in.

Drew had jumped up and started saying how she'd come on to him. That this had been all her idea. Nicole had looked at her with such hatred, Jesse had felt as if she'd been branded.

She'd known then that nothing she could say would matter.

Jesse pressed her hand to her stomach. She was pregnant with Matt's baby, and no one would believe her. Especially not the two people she loved most in the world. Nicole had already turned her back on her and Matt had done the same.

CHAPTER SEVEN

NICOLE DROVE HOME trying to ignore the knot in her stomach. She felt so much anger at Jesse but, despite everything, she missed having her around. Nothing about the situation was fair.

She pulled into her driveway and saw an unfamiliar car parked in front of the house. Brittany climbed out and waved.

"I have a really big favor to ask," the teenager said as she walked over. "It's Raoul's birthday. He's turning eighteen. I want to cook him something special, but I'm not sure I can pull it all together. Would it be okay if I cooked it here and you helped? Then I'll take it over to him."

Nicole didn't know what to say. While Brittany seemed like an okay kid, Nicole didn't know her. They'd only spoken a few times. So why would she...

The fake dating. Hawk had obviously told his daughter they were going out.

"I'm happy to help," Nicole told her. "But doesn't your dad cook?" He'd been a single parent for a while and he seemed the type to learn that sort of thing.

"He does, but this is different. It's for a guy." Brittany wrinkled her nose. "He understands that I date, but I don't think he likes it."

"Typical father," Nicole murmured, remembering how her dad had lacked any interest in her life. Someone being attentive would have been nice.

"I know. But he loves me." Brittany smiled as she spoke, as if she were very sure of the fact. And why wouldn't she be? "So is it okay? Helping me with dinner? I know you have a date with my dad tonight. I won't make you late."

"Sure. Come on in."

After her talk with Jesse, Nicole welcomed the distraction.

Brittany ran back to her car, then returned with a couple of grocery bags. "I wanted something special, you know. Raoul's been in foster care for a long time. Ever since his brother went to jail. Not that his home life was all that great before. He's been moving around a lot. I don't know if anyone else even remembers it's his birthday."

Brittany pulled items out of the bag as she spoke. Nicole looked over the contents.

There was beef, noodles, carrots, a small package of beef Stroganoff mix, sour cream and premade cookie dough that just had to be heated in the oven.

"Looks easy enough," Nicole said.

"Good. I brought casserole dishes and one of those insulated carriers to keep everything hot while I drive over to Raoul's."

Nicole organized Brittany's supplies, then turned on the oven to preheat and got the teenager set up with a cutting board and a knife.

"I trim the meat, right?" Brittany asked.

"Yes. Try to keep the pieces about the same size so they'll cook at the same rate."

"Okay."

Brittany cut away. "Thanks for helping with this. I didn't know where else to go. My friends' moms would probably help, but I felt weird about that."

Nicole wasn't sure why. "Have you two been going out a while?"

"Five months. Raoul is so great. He's really responsible and he loves me a lot."

An interesting combination. Nicole thought about the stolen doughnuts, then reminded herself that he'd more than made up for his actions. She was happy to have him working in the bakery.

"Do you know where my dad is taking you?" Brittany asked.

"No."

"I'm sure it will be really nice. He likes to take his girlfriends to nice places. A good quality in a boyfriend."

Nicole nodded because she didn't know what to say. She didn't actually think of Hawk as her boyfriend.

"He dates a lot," Brittany added. "Just so you know, he doesn't get serious. Not that I mean anything bad by that. I'm sure he likes you a lot."

Nicole sensed that she was being sent a message—she just wasn't sure what it was. Did Brittany want to warn her off or help her out?

Rather than deal with the question, she dug out a big pot. "This," she said, "we'll use for boiling the pasta."

AFTER BRITTANY LEFT, Nicole headed upstairs to get ready for her date with Hawk. She was more nervous than she would have expected, even reminding herself it wasn't a real date. This was him keeping his half of the bargain, nothing more.

Still, she flipped through the contents of her closet, groaning when she realized she had nothing to wear. She decided to start at the beginning and try to figure out what was appropriate for a high-profile non-date possibly taking place somewhere nice.

As it was still pretty warm, she settled on a sleeveless floral print dress with a narrow skirt. She'd been fake tanning for the past couple of days, so her legs looked decent. With dangly earrings and low-heeled sandals, she decided she wouldn't look half-bad.

Before dressing, she rolled her hair in hot curlers and put on makeup. She finished dressing, then got out the jumbo can of hairspray and prepared to spray her hair into submission.

The curlers came out, she finger-combed her curls, then sprayed until she coughed. The dangly earrings completed the outfit.

As she made her way downstairs, she found herself nervous about seeing Hawk again. The last time he'd been in this house, they'd been having hot monkey sex. She barely knew the man, but she'd already seen him naked. How strange was that?

There was a knock at the front door. Her stomach immediately plunged to her feet. She felt like she was going to throw up. This was a bad idea. What on earth had she been thinking?

Forcing herself to keep breathing, she opened the door.

"Hi," she said, trying to keep her voice from coming out in a squeak.

"Hi yourself."

The message to her brain, telling her to step back, was automatic. Which was a good thing, because she was incapable of thought.

Hawk looked amazing. He wore slacks and a long-sleeved shirt, a tie and sport coat. He looked like one of those sexy sportscasters. Or a male cover model.

He filled out his clothes perfectly—as if they'd been custom-made for him. Maybe they had. She managed to raise her gaze to his face. He smiled at her and the nerves got worse. An entire parade of butterflies began practicing their marching-band routine.

She felt weak and oddly aroused at the sight of

him. Would he consider blowing off dinner and doing her instead?

"I made reservations," Hawk told her. "The Yarrow Bay Grill. Have you been there?"

"No, but I've heard about it." That it had a stunning view, an excellent wine list and incredible food.

"I don't usually make reservations," he grumbled. "You'd better be impressed."

He could do her later, she thought as she smiled. "I *am* impressed. I'm all quivery. I'll barely be able to walk to the car. Of course I have a stiff knee so that could be part of the reason."

"You're being snarky."

"You picked up the phone and dialed and now you want a plaque?"

"It's a guy thing."

"Apparently."

"You look great."

"Thank you. You look very nice, as well."

"I did the tie especially for you. I thought you'd like it."

"I do."

She told herself not to read too much into his words. They weren't on a real date. They were partners in a bargain that would make most people who knew her shake their heads.

Forty minutes later they were seated in a booth overlooking the small marina at Yarrow Bay. Lake Washington glimmered with sunlight.

Hawk flipped through the novel-length wine

list, then ordered. When their server had left, he leaned forward.

"Brittany called me on her way to Raoul's house. She told me you helped her with his special birthday dinner. Thanks for that."

"It was fun. I was a little surprised she came to me, though."

"I would have done it, but she knows I would have given her a hard time. Teasing daughters is a father's prerogative."

"Mine was never much into that." He'd always been a distant man, more interested in what was on TV than the lives of his daughters. "Brittany is a lovely girl. She thinks the world of you. You two have a very special relationship."

He shrugged. "We do okay. I want to take all the credit, but it was mostly Serena. By the time she died, all the basics were in place."

Nicole didn't know what to make of the information. Should she ask more about Serena or change the subject? Honestly, she wasn't sure how much she wanted to know.

"Have you lived here all your life?" he asked.

She nodded. "Even during college. I went to University of Washington and lived at home. With the bakery, there wasn't much chance of doing anything else."

"Why?"

She picked up her water glass, then put it down. "My family has owned the Keyes bakery forever. I grew up knowing I would always be a part of that heritage. That I would one day take it over."

"You have sisters, don't you? Why do I think you have sisters?"

"I have two. Claire is my fraternal twin. You might have heard of her."

The server appeared with a bottle of red wine. After opening it, he poured some into a glass for Hawk to taste. Hawk sipped, then nodded. The server poured them both wine and left.

"Why would I have heard of your sister?" Hawk asked.

"Claire Keyes?"

He shook his head, then stopped. "She plays piano?"

Nicole smiled. "Concert pianist. Famous soloist. She's played all over the world, made top-selling CDs. When we were three years old, we went to a friend's house. Claire walked up to the piano and started playing. We'd never even seen one before, so everyone went crazy. Life changed. Claire started taking lessons. When she was six, she and my grandmother left so she could study in New York and Europe. Jesse, my youngest sister, was born that year. A lot of things changed."

"She was just gone? You must have missed her."

"I did. It was like someone had cut off my arm. When I was twelve, my grandmother decided Claire's schedule was too grueling for her. She came home and my mother left to travel with her."

What Nicole didn't mention, what still made her angry, was how happy her mother had been to go. She'd been excited by the opportunity to travel and see the world, live in five-star hotels and hang out with the rich and famous. Never once had she even hinted she would miss what, and who, she was leaving behind.

"The bakery was my dad's but he was never much into it," Nicole continued. "I had to handle things at home with Jesse and I started helping out in the bakery. When Claire and I were sixteen, our mom was killed in a car crash. I sort of took over after that."

She stopped talking. Was she saying too much?

"You studied business at college?" he asked.

She nodded. "So I could take over the bakery."

"What would you have done if you'd had the choice?"

No one had ever asked her that before. "I don't know," she admitted. "I have no idea. It was never an option. I knew I would inherit the bakery."

She'd accepted her fate, had never considered there might be other paths.

"You, not your baby sister?"

Nicole didn't want to think about Jesse or the fact that both her sisters were pregnant. "She never had a lot of interest."

"Do you like what you do?"

She thought about an average day, the people she worked with, the rhythm. "Most of the time. I mean hey, I'm surrounded by cupcakes. Where's the bad?"

He grinned. "Good point. I always knew I wanted to play football. I grew up north of Seattle, outside of Marysville. Small town, small high school. Football was going to be my way out."

"What about your family?"

"It was just my mom and me. My dad died when I was little. What I remember about him isn't good. Money was tight, but that was okay. My mom was so damn proud of me. She really believed in me. When things got hard, I thought about my mom." Hawk picked up his wine but didn't take a drink. "She lived to see me get to college on a scholarship, but not much longer after that. I wish she could have seen me go pro."

"Maybe she did."

He looked at her. "I like to think so. She was great when I found out Serena was pregnant. We were seniors in high school. I thought she was going to kill me, but she just said we'd handle it."

Nicole wasn't sure what her father would have said if she'd shown up pregnant. Not that it ever would have happened. Between school and working in the bakery and raising Jesse, there hadn't been a lot of time for dating. Or fun.

"How did Serena's parents take it?" she asked.

"They were angry. They told her if she didn't give up the baby for adoption and never see me again, they would have nothing to do with her."

"You're kidding."

"No. She was devastated. But I told her we'd get married and be a family. It took a hell of a leap of faith for her to believe me."

"She was in love."

"We both were. It was terrifying at first. We got married right after graduation and moved in with my mom. The coach at Oklahoma University put us in touch with some folks down in Norman and they really helped out."

Nicole didn't know much about football but she knew he'd picked the right kind of school.

"Living in a place where college football is king made a difference," she teased.

"I know. We were taken care of. We lived off campus in a great little house. I was supposed to do maintenance to pay rent, but there wasn't much to do. Serena got a job with flexible hours and decent pay. Everyone there made it easy for us. There were always babysitters so Serena could come to the games."

Nicole couldn't imagine that life. It was like hearing the plot of a movie. "You were lucky."

"We were. Even with all the help we were still a couple of teenagers raising a baby. Nights Brittany had a fever terrified me. I could take a hit with no problem, but every time she fell down, I thought I was going to lose it."

"An involved dad," she said lightly, feeling the steady ticking of her biological clock. Why was having a family such a challenge?

"I loved her and Serena. A lot of the guys on the team never understood why I was so happy being with one woman. They were out getting as much as they could and when you play ball you get a lot. But that wasn't important to me. It was the same when I went pro. For us, it was a chance to be financially secure. We wanted to go back to Seattle, so we bought the house I live in now. It's pretty ordinary. We wanted a regular life."

"An unusual dream for a pro football player."

"I don't need a lot of expensive crap to tell me who I am."

Which said a lot about him. Nicole was beginning to wonder if this dinner was a good idea. She didn't want to start to actually like Hawk. That would create a complication she didn't need.

"Why did you retire?"

"Serena got cancer. We knew she was dying. Brittany was only twelve, so it hit her hard. Serena and I talked about what was best for Brittany. Me traveling and training six or eight months out of the year wasn't it. Serena's parents finally came around, but they're in Florida now so they only see Brittany every couple of years. There wasn't anyone to take care of her but me. Retiring was the right thing to do."

He'd quit playing professional football—an occupation that practically gave him deity status—to stay home and take care of his daughter?

"I got bored in three days," he said with a grin. "That's when I thought about coaching."

"You mean you're not in it for the money?" she teased, not wanting him to be as good as he sounded.

"I don't need the paycheck, if that's what you're asking."

"Speaking of paychecks, are you going to see Raoul tomorrow?"

"I don't know. Why?"

"I have his paycheck. He didn't work yesterday and I forgot to pay him a day early." She thought about how tight money was for him. "Maybe I'll drop it off at his house tomorrow."

"I can do that."

"No, it's fine. I'm his boss."

"How's he working out for you?"

"He's great. A hard worker. I'm glad to have him."

"Aren't you happy you didn't throw him in jail?"

"I'm not going to talk about that."

"Because you don't want to admit you were wrong?"

"Something like that."

THEY TALKED all through dinner. Nicole found her entrée getting cold as she and Hawk debated everything from the Mariners' chance at making the playoffs to the best place to get coffee. As it was Seattle, there were hundreds of choices.

"You're talking flavored lattes," he grumbled. "Girl drinks."

"Oh, right. And you're just too manly."

"I am."

He looked at her and she stared back. Heat flared, making her squirm. When he reached across the table and grabbed her hand, she had the sudden wish they were somewhere else. Somewhere alone and quiet, where getting naked wouldn't upset the management.

"If you're done here," he began, "I'm thinking it's time for a little sex-kitten action."

Her stomach clenched. "I'm yours for the asking."

"One of your best qualities."

She thought about saying it was part of their deal, but after their lone sexual encounter, she found herself anticipating getting naked with Hawk again. Even without the bargain she would have been more than willing.

He released her hand and glanced at his watch, then groaned.

"What?"

"I told Brittany she had to be home by eleven, which means I have to be there to make sure that happens. It's after ten now."

Math had never been Nicole's thing, but even she could figure this out. "We don't have time to go back to my place, get busy and have you home by eleven."

Hawk looked at her. "It's your fault. I don't usually sit and talk to a woman for three hours without noticing the time. Especially when there are other ways to spend an evening."

Meaning they could have been in bed. She smiled. "Typical guy. Blaming someone else." But his words made her oddly happy. She liked knowing he'd had a good time, too. Not that she liked him or anything. Well, she *liked* him, but it was in a "we have a bargain to get through" sense. Not liked him as in any romantic way.

"We'll reschedule," she said. "After all, I'm yours to command, so to speak."

"Good." He motioned to their server and asked for the bill. "I'll call you tomorrow and we can set up a time."

To have sex. She felt her insides quiver. "Just say the word and I'm ready to purr."

HAWK SET UP THE CHAIRS in the room. It was Sunday and there would be the usual postgame film meeting in an hour.

Despite the less than satisfying ending to his date the previous evening, he was in a damn good mood. Everything was going right. The team was winning, Brittany had picked six different colleges to apply to, and he had a hot woman he not only liked to talk to but make love with at his beck and call. Oh, yeah. It was good to be him.

He heard footsteps in the hall and walked to the doorway. Nicole hurried toward him, looking intense about something. He grinned. While they wouldn't be able to do anything significant, they could probably manage some hot kisses in his office. That would—

She stopped in front of him, waving a piece of paper. "You just think you know everything, don't you?"

That didn't sound happy. "What's wrong?"

"Gee, what an interesting question. What's wrong? Hmm, how about the fact that your key player is lying to you about where he lives?"

"Raoul? What are you talking about?" He grabbed the paper from her. "What's this?"

"His paycheck. I know money's tight for him, so I decided to deliver his check. I went by his house. The address he gave me is an abandoned building. I couldn't believe it. So I went inside and someone *is* living there. I saw clothes and a sleeping bag, a couple of flashlights and this."

She fished a Pacific High School T-shirt out of her bag. "Does this look familiar?"

Hawk couldn't believe it. Raoul, living like that? How could he not know? Raoul told him everything. "He never said a word. How long has this been going on?"

"That would be my question to you, Coach. Knowing about this sort of thing would be your job, not mine."

CHAPTER EIGHT

"THAT'S NOT POSSIBLE," Hawk insisted. "There's something else going on. There's no way I wouldn't know."

"I can't wait to hear the explanation," Nicole told him, obviously still upset. "He's a kid, Hawk. I don't care that he just turned eighteen and legally he's an adult. He shouldn't have to deal with crap like this. Living alone in a run-down building?"

"He's not." Raoul couldn't be. Hawk would have known. He cared about his players. He was involved in their lives.

A few minutes later he heard the guys start to arrive. He sent several out to Nicole's car to collect the desserts she'd brought and asked Raoul to join them in his office.

Hawk watched him as he entered the room. The teen looked exactly the same. There was no hint that anything was wrong.

Maybe Nicole had overreacted, he thought. Maybe she'd misunderstood the situation.

"Have a seat," Hawk said.

Raoul looked between them. "What's going on?"

Nicole tried to smile. "Nothing too scary. Don't worry. We aren't sending you off to aliens for medical experiments."

"I wasn't thinking about that."

"It happens more than you think."

Nicole's attempt at humor didn't make Raoul seem any more comfortable.

She sighed, then held out his paycheck. "I forgot to give this to you on Thursday. You didn't work yesterday and I didn't want you to wait to have the money. So I drove by your address, thinking I'd give it to you."

Raoul stiffened slightly. Color darkened his skin and he ducked his head. He also didn't take the check.

"I can explain," he mumbled.

Hawk's gut tightened. Dammit all to hell, how had this happened? He wanted to yell at someone, but no one in the room deserved that, except maybe himself.

"We're listening," he said, doing his best to sound neutral and calm.

Raoul shifted his weight. "I got kicked out of my foster home a few weeks ago. The guy was hitting the kids and his wife. I tried to stay out of it, you know. Because I was so close to turning eighteen. But I hated it, so one day I decided to show him what it felt like to be beat up by someone."

He looked at Hawk. "I didn't hurt him, I swear. I just roughed him up."

"I know you didn't hurt him." Even if the bastard deserved to have a few bones broken.

"He threw me out. I figured they wouldn't say anything to social services if I didn't. That they'd just keep the money. They did. I have an appointment for next week with my social worker. To report the guy. But I wanted to wait until I was eighteen and out of the system."

Raoul swallowed. "I've known about that old building for a long time. No one goes there. It's pretty safe. So I set myself up there. It's okay, Coach. I'm okay."

Hawk didn't know which emotion was stronger—the desire to find the guy who'd been hitting his kids and finish what Raoul had started or pride at the young man his player had become.

Nicole glared at him. "You didn't know about any of this, did you?" She turned her fury on Raoul. "You're living alone in an abandoned building? That's so not okay. Pretty safe isn't good enough. You need to be living in a real home, with plumbing and heat and a roof that doesn't leak in forty-seven places."

"It's—" Raoul started, but stopped when Nicole glared at him.

"Don't you dare say it's fine," she yelled. "It's not fine. Nothing about this is fine."

Hawk appreciated her passion and energy on the subject and knew she was right. Raoul couldn't live like that. On a purely practical level, winter was coming. He'd freeze his ass off without heat.

"I'm not going to a shelter," Raoul said, backing up. "I mean it. I won't live there."

Something about the way he spoke told Hawk the kid had been in a shelter before. What had happened that he knew so little about his star player? He thought he knew everything about his guys. And why hadn't Raoul come to him for help?

"You're not going to a shelter," Hawk said. "We'll figure something out. In the meantime, you can come live with me."

Nicole and Raoul both stared at him.

"Not a good idea," she said.

"Coach, that's really great, but…"

Then Hawk got it. "Brittany," he muttered. Having her boyfriend living under the same roof wasn't smart.

He thought about the other parents he knew. Who would be willing to take in Raoul? He was legally an adult. Did that make the situation easier or harder? There wouldn't be any need to go through the foster system, but he was hardly some cute, little, cuddly kid.

Nicole muttered something under her breath then said, "He can live with me."

Hawk stared at her. Raoul looked stunned.

"What?" she asked them both. "I have a spare room at my house. I'm in the school district. He already works for me. Someone responsible has to keep an eye on him."

She turned to Raoul. "If we do this, there will be

rules. No parties, you keep my hours. You do your homework, you go to class. You're an adult now, so you're expected to act like one. But a responsible one. Not some jerk who comes and goes as he pleases. If that's too much for you, then you need to be somewhere else."

Hawk couldn't believe it. Nicole taking in Raoul? He held in a smile. Damn, she was better than he'd first thought.

Raoul nodded slowly. "Your rules are reasonable," he told Nicole. "I'll follow them."

"You'd better. I mean it. I run a very strict household. You'll feel trapped, I promise."

"Trapped is good," Raoul said, the corners of his mouth twitching.

Hawk felt the need to smile, too. Nicole thought she came off as so tough, but the truth was, she was completely soft on the inside.

He liked that. He liked that a lot.

JESSE STOOD on the doorstep of Matt's condo for a long time. She stared at the door, remembering how she'd first come here with him when he'd been looking for a place of his own. They'd been so happy then. So in love. She knew she'd totally blown it. What she didn't know was if she could fix it.

Her whole body hurt. She'd heard that pregnancy was supposed to be a miracle, that she should be glowing. Instead she felt beat up. She couldn't stop crying. How was it possible for one person to lose everything so quickly? And yet she had.

She rang the bell and waited. Her stomach writhed from nerves and fears. She fought back tears. He had to believe her. Somehow she would make him understand.

The door opened and Matt stood in front of her. She stared at him, feasting on seeing him for the first time in weeks.

He looked good. Tall and thin, but filling out from their regular visits to the gym. She'd been the one to introduce him to the idea of working out to build muscle and then he'd taken her to bed and rewarded her for her good ideas. He was very good at rewarding her, and telling her he loved her. He got this light in his eyes and what she called his special smile. Only he wasn't smiling now.

"I have nothing to say to you," he told her and started to close the door.

She threw herself against it and managed to squeeze inside. "We have to talk."

"You may have to talk but I don't have to listen."

God, he sounded so cold, she thought grimly. As if he hated her. Was that possible? Had hate replaced love? Didn't she matter at all to him?

She couldn't think about it because, if she did, she would fall apart. He was everything to her. She loved him. She who had vowed never to risk her heart had fallen for a geeky computer nerd with beautiful eyes and a smile that made her soul float.

"Matt, please," she whispered. "Please. Just hear me out. I love you."

His gaze narrowed. "Do you think your words mean anything to me? Do you think you do? I learn fast, Jesse. I always have. I trusted you. I gave you every part of me. I loved you. Hell, I wanted to marry you. I bought a ring. Which makes me an idiot, but it's not a mistake I'm going to make again."

She felt the tears on her cheeks and the slicing pain in her heart. "I love you, Matt."

"Bullshit. I was some fun project. Did you get a kick out of screwing the socially inept genius? Did you laugh about me with your friends?"

"It wasn't like that and you know it."

"I don't know shit about you. This was a game. You won, I lost, now get the hell away from me."

"No. I won't go until you listen. Until you understand."

"Understand what? That while you were sleeping with me, pretending to care about me, you were screwing Drew? Who else, Jess? How many other guys? I'm not asking for a total number. I doubt you can count that high. But say in the past five months. Less than a hundred? Less than twenty? Just give me a ballpark idea."

She cried harder, hating his words and the distance she saw in his eyes. "Stop. I'm not like that anymore."

"That's not what I heard."

"I didn't sleep with Drew," she screamed. "We used to talk. I could talk to him about stuff the way I could never talk to Nicole. That was it. Then one night he started kissing me and I freaked. I didn't know what to do."

"I'm not interested," Matt told her. "There's nothing you can say to make me care. Once a slut, always a slut. Everyone was right about you."

He was using her past against her, she thought in disbelief. She'd trusted him with her secrets, her shameful moments, and now he was judging her.

"Matt, stop," she said, her voice breaking on a sob. "Don't do this. Don't take us to a place where we can't get back."

"Why not? You think you matter to me anymore? Just get out. I never want to see you again."

It hurt too much, she thought, using all her strength to keep from sinking to the floor.

"I'm pregnant," she whispered.

He stared at her, then shrugged. "So what?"

She flinched as if he'd hit her. "I told you. I didn't sleep with Drew. I'm having your baby."

"No, you're not." He spoke casually, as if he'd never considered the possibility that the child might be his.

She grabbed his arm. "Matt, listen to me. This is your baby. Even if you hate me, you have to care about your child. I'm not lying. I can prove it. As soon as the baby's born, we'll take a DNA test."

He looked at her for a long time, then pulled free

of her grip and walked to the door. "You don't get it, do you? I don't care, Jess. You're nothing to me but a regret. I don't believe that baby is mine and even if it is, I don't want a child with you. I don't want anything with you. Ever. I want you to go away. I never want to see you again. No matter what."

What scared her the most was how calmly he spoke. How easily he mouthed the words that ripped her soul apart.

She looked down, half expecting to see her body torn open and bleeding, but all the pain was on the inside.

"Matt, please," she begged.

He pulled the door open and stared outside. "Just go."

Walking took all her strength. Jesse barely made it down the stairs to her car. She crawled into the front seat and cried until she couldn't breathe anymore. Until the emptiness threatened to swallow her. Until there was nothing left.

Which was the ugly truth of her life. No one she'd ever loved wanted anything to do with her. No one believed her. No one was willing to give her a chance.

NICOLE WATCHED RAOUL carry in his possessions. She eyed the black trash bags and made a mental note to buy the guy a couple of suitcases the next time she was out. No one should have to carry everything he owned in a trash bag.

"The bedrooms are upstairs," she said as she led the way. "I'm putting you in the guest room."

She'd debated putting him in Jesse's room instead, but had decided against it. Despite everything going on, she assumed that at some point her sister would be moving back. Not that Nicole could ever imagine that happening right now, but eventually…maybe.

"Thanks for doing this," Raoul said.

"You're welcome." She motioned for him to enter the guest room. "The bathroom is through there. The towels are out. There are more in the bottom drawer. In here you have a TV. I don't care what you watch, but I'd appreciate you keeping the sound down after nine. I've put a phone in. I get up early, so no late calls, okay?"

He looked uncomfortable as he nodded.

"This is weird," she said, which hadn't been part of her planned speech. "We don't know each other that well. I'm your boss. So we're both uncomfortable. But it will get easier."

"I know." He shoved his hands into his front pockets. "You can tell me what to do. It's okay. I'll listen."

Good to know. If only her sister had listened, things would have been a lot easier.

"So I can be bossy?" she asked, trying to dissipate some of the tension.

"Sure."

She smiled. "Come on downstairs. You can tell

me which of my food choices are too girly and make suggestions."

They went into the kitchen where she wrote down his requests for cereal, soda and snacks.

"You eat lunch at school?" she asked.

"Uh-huh."

"That's fine. Let me know if you're not going to be home for dinner. Oh, and if you're getting low on anything, just write it down and I'll buy more." She showed him where she kept the list.

"You don't have to be this nice," he told her.

"You can't stay in that building, Raoul. No one should live like that." She looked into his eyes. He looked both hopeful and ashamed. She wanted to tell him that none of this was his fault. That he'd been failed by a lot of people—his family, the system, who knows who else.

"This situation may create some awkward moments," she said, wishing they didn't have to discuss it, but knowing it was going to come up. "People might talk. I mean, because we're living together."

She paused and felt herself blushing. Was she going to have to spell it out for him?

His expression cleared and suddenly he looked a whole lot older than eighteen. "Because I'm living with a beautiful woman who is single?"

Smooth, she thought, fighting a smile. Very smooth. In a couple of years, he was going to be able to give Hawk a run for his money.

"Something like that."

"It's a good problem to have," he said. "I'm okay with what people say. Brittany knows I love her and that I would never do anything to hurt her."

Nicole found herself envying a high school cheerleader. Too bad Drew didn't have the same loyalty in him—it would have solved a lot of problems.

"I think that covers everything," she said. "You can park your car on the street. There's no room in the garage, but this is a pretty safe neighborhood."

Her brain went from his car, to the fact that he didn't have enough money to buy doughnuts a few weeks ago, back to his car.

"Do you have car insurance?" she asked.

His startled look told her what she needed to know. "Bad enough to do that as a minor," she said. "You're an adult now. They get crabby when you don't follow the law. Get some. I'll front you the money. You can pay me back."

He straightened. "I'm fine."

"You need insurance. If you get in an accident, you could be screwed for the rest of your life. Do you really want to have to deal with some big settlement or someone else's medical bills? Take the money, say thank you and pay me back when you're a famous football player. Got that?"

"Yes, ma'am," he said, but he was blinking fast and turned away.

"Good. I think that's everything."

He cleared his throat. "You didn't have to do this."

She thought about Jesse. She was trying to push her sister from her mind, but it was impossible. Was this her twisted way of trying to make up for messing things up with her? She wasn't sure.

"I didn't have to, but I wanted to."

"I won't make you regret it."

Nicole smiled. "Be careful with those promises, Raoul. I can be incredibly difficult and demanding."

That made him chuckle. "I'll remember."

"Go get settled, then we'll argue about what we're having for dinner tonight."

"I'd like that."

DINNER ACTUALLY ARRIVED in the form of takeout, delivered by Brittany and Hawk. Raoul lit up when his girlfriend walked into the room and Nicole was a little afraid that she got glowy, too, at the sight of Hawk strolling into her house.

She always seemed to forget how big he was, how tall and muscular. Which was dumb. She'd seen the man naked—the image of him should be burned into her brain. Not that she minded the little jolt of awareness she experienced when he moved toward her and gave her a light kiss on the mouth.

"How's it going?" he asked.

"We're getting settled. So far he hasn't left the toilet seat up so I haven't killed him."

"That's a deal breaker for you?"

"It can be."

"Good to know."

He smiled and she got all hot and flustered. Just hormones, she reminded herself, enjoying the sensation. After all she'd been through, she deserved a little fun in her life.

"We brought Chinese," Brittany said, carrying the large bag into the kitchen. "There's a ton of food, so you can have leftovers."

"They're the best part of Chinese," Nicole said.

"I know." Brittany put the bag on the counter. "I'm glad you're letting Raoul stay here. It's so much nicer than that old abandoned building. It was cold and windy in the summer. I didn't think he could stay there all winter."

Brittany stopped talking, seemed to realize what she'd said and covered her mouth with her hand.

Hawk stepped toward her. "You *knew* about Raoul being kicked out of his foster home and living on the streets?"

"Sort of, and he wasn't living on the streets."

"Close enough."

"Coach," Raoul began, but Nicole grabbed his arm and shook her head.

She had a feeling it was better for him to stay out of it. Brittany seemed like the kind of kid who was used to charming her father into getting her way. Nicole doubted Hawk would stay mad at her for long.

"I didn't want to tell you because I knew you'd

get upset," Brittany began. "Plus, if you knew, you'd have to tell someone and we didn't know where Raoul might end up. It seemed better to let him stay there until he turned eighteen and was an adult. Daddy, I'm sorry if I upset you."

Nicole waited for Hawk to figure out his daughter was apologizing for getting caught, but not for actually lying. When he nodded and gave her a hug, she tried to figure out if he hadn't noticed or simply didn't want to deal with it at that moment.

"Don't keep secrets," he told his daughter.

"I won't, Daddy."

Nicole thought about all the crap Jesse had pulled. Didn't Hawk worry about his daughter? The promise to not keep secrets aside, Raoul had been living in that building for at least a few weeks and Brittany had visited him there. Which meant they had been alone together for hours. Sex was a likely outcome.

Maybe Hawk didn't mind that. Maybe Brittany was on birth control. Not that it always worked.

Another problem for another time, she told herself.

"Why don't you two grab some plates and set the table," Hawk said. "Then pick out a couple of movies for tonight."

The teenagers did as he asked and moved out of the kitchen. The second they were gone, Hawk grabbed her and pulled her close.

"This is going to be a problem," he murmured before he kissed her.

She let herself get lost in the heat of his mouth on hers, the feel of him against her.

"You have a kid," he said between kisses. "I have a kid. So much for you being my sex kitten."

She laughed, then ran her hands up and down his chest. "We're going to have to figure something out."

One eyebrow raised. "Want a repeat of last time?"

She thought of how he'd made her feel, how he'd touched her all over and made her every cell cry out in surrender.

"Absolutely."

He grinned. "Me, too."

He kissed her again, his mouth firm against hers. When she parted, he slipped his tongue inside and aroused her with an erotic dance. She rubbed against him. He was already hard, which made her thighs tremble.

When he backed her up against the counter, she wondered if the height was right. When he eased a hand between them and cupped her breast, she decided that right or not, they could make the counter work. When she heard Brittany laugh, she swore in frustration.

"Tell me about it," Hawk grumbled, resting his forehead on hers. "Can we send them out to a movie?"

"It's a school night."

"I don't think I can wait until the weekend."

She smiled. "What's your schedule like? Got any free time this week?"

"With you as the reward, I'll find it."

CHAPTER NINE

NICOLE WALKED into her house to find it filled with teenagers. There were several girls sitting together on the sectional sofa, a group of guys sprawled on the floor. There were books lying open, papers scattered around, chips, soda, a couple of bags of cookies and the sound of conversation.

She came to a stop, not sure what to make of the invasion. Raoul had moved in so it made sense that his friends would stop by to see him...except Jesse had never brought friends around.

Nicole hadn't thought of it before, but suddenly she remembered how Jesse had always been disappearing, rather than bringing people home. When Nicole had questioned her, Jesse had said it was easier to go to her friends' houses, but had it been? Was there some reason Jesse hadn't wanted to spend time here or invite anyone she knew?

"Hi," a few of the kids called.

"Bring any cupcakes?" one of the guys asked.

She smiled. "I didn't, but I will tomorrow."

"Sweet."

Raoul scrambled to his feet and followed her into the kitchen. "Should I have asked before inviting them over?"

She had to tilt her head back to meet his gaze. He looked both excited and nervous. She doubted he'd had company visiting when he'd been in foster care, and abandoned buildings didn't provide much in the way of teen amenities.

"It's fine," she said. "The same rules apply. And no one goes upstairs or in the basement. Not even Brittany."

He grinned. "What are you worried about?"

"You know exactly what I'm worried about. It's not going to happen. No one has sex in this house."

He raised his eyebrows.

She thought about Hawk and how he'd made her feel when they were together. With Brittany in his house and Raoul in her house, getting together was going to be a scheduling nightmare.

"Not even me," she said with a sigh. "Is that clear?"

"Yes, ma'am." He was grinning as he spoke. The smile faded. "Thanks for taking me in, Nicole."

She shrugged. "We'll work it out."

She wasn't sure how. There were still details to consider. Like how long he would be staying. Through the school year? That was a serious commitment. But it was also a problem she would deal with later.

"Go back to your friends," she said. "Tell them

not to leave a mess or I'll get really annoyed. Trust me, that's nothing they'll find pretty."

He grinned. "You're the best."

"Don't I know it."

She grabbed a Diet Coke for herself and went up to her room. As she passed Jesse's room, she stepped inside.

Nothing had changed since her sister had left. Most of her stuff was still there. Jesse had only taken what she could carry.

There were stuffed animals on a shelf, posters, books, clothes piled in a corner.

She sat on the bed and looked around. What had gone wrong? How could everything have fallen apart so quickly and without warning? One minute everything had been fine and the next Drew had been cheating on her with her own sister.

Honestly, Jesse's betrayal hurt a lot more than his. She'd known Drew was a mistake shortly after they'd gotten married, but she'd been too embarrassed to admit it. She was confident there had been other women before Jesse. But her own sister?

Did Jesse hate her that much? Yes, they'd had some hard times as Jesse had grown up, but they'd been family. Didn't that count for anything?

Apparently not, Nicole thought, fighting tears. She loved Jesse, but she had a feeling she would never forgive her. Not for what she'd done, but for obviously not caring that she'd done it. Not caring who she'd hurt.

Now Jesse was pregnant. Nicole still had trouble with that one. Her baby sister having a baby. Did the promise of a child change anything? Should Nicole bring her back home?

Everything inside her screamed no. That Jesse had to grow up, learn to be responsible. Maybe a baby was the best way. But was that concern speaking or betrayal?

"Enough," Nicole said as she stood. She was done mourning the past and worrying about what couldn't be fixed. Nothing would be solved today. She had time to figure it out.

She walked into the hallway and moved to her room. A burst of laughter floated up the stairs. It was a good sound, she thought, her mood lightening. There should always be laughter in a house.

WHEN THE FRONT DOOR banged shut for the eighth time, Nicole went downstairs. She braced herself for a disaster in the great room, but it was surprisingly clean. The carpet needed vacuuming, but otherwise, all the wrappers, cans and trash were gone.

Talk about impressive, she thought as she walked into the kitchen, prepared to thank Raoul. He was turning out to be a—

She paused as she saw him drop a cooked chicken breast into a sandwich bag and then slip the bag into his jeans pocket.

Her first thought was surprise. There was plenty

to eat. He didn't have to save for later. Especially something that should be kept refrigerated. But maybe it wasn't about being hungry now. Maybe he had a strong need to hoard. She'd read an article about starving children once. How even when they were rescued, they still worried about having enough to eat. If that was his problem, maybe she should find a psychologist, because this was a problem she didn't know how to fix.

"Raoul?" She spoke softly, not wanting to startle him.

He spun toward her, the look of guilt so clear, she knew immediately this wasn't about being hungry later.

"What?" she demanded.

"Nothing."

"You have chicken in your pocket. That's not nothing. What is it?" She tried to think of possibilities and then wished she hadn't. "There's another kid, isn't there?"

She swore silently. A practically grown, legally adult teenager was one thing, but another kid? There wasn't room in the house without cleaning out Jesse's room and, despite everything, she wasn't sure she was ready for that.

"No," he said quickly. "It's not that."

"Then what?" Why would he need food?

He shifted uncomfortably. She decided to play the impatient-adult card and put her hands on her hips. "I'm waiting."

He hung his head. "There's a dog. A stray. I've been feeding her."

Nicole wasn't even surprised. A dog. Of course. Because she was a responsibility magnet.

"I couldn't just leave her to starve," he went on. "So I've been taking her food. I usually buy her dog food, but I ran out and I haven't been to the store." He pulled the chicken out of his pocket. "Should I put this back?"

What? Like she was going to tell him yes so some poor dog could go hungry?

"How big?" she asked.

"What?"

"How big is the dog?"

"About fifteen pounds. She's really friendly. I call her Sheila. That's Australian for girl." Suddenly he looked more like he was eight than eighteen.

Nicole knew there were very few choices. She could insist he take Sheila to an animal shelter and be the big bad, or she could accept that her life had taken a different kind of turn and become a dog owner. There really wasn't much of a choice.

"Go get her," she said with a sigh. "Bring her back, but know that she's going to have to stay in the garage until I can get to a vet tomorrow and get her checked out and defleaed and whatever else she needs. Also, being a pet owner means being responsible. You'll have to feed her and exercise her and clean up the yard. If I have to step in dog poop when I go outside, I'm going to be very, very annoyed. Is that clear?"

Raoul grabbed her and hugged her until he'd squeezed out all her air. Then he released her and grinned.

"You're the best!"

"That's me. Saint Nicole."

"I'll take care of everything. You won't even know she's here."

If only that were true. "Just go get her."

"I will."

"Wait." She dug in her purse and pulled out a couple of twenties. "Stop by the pet store. Get some dog food, a bed, a leash and a collar."

He grinned. "Thanks."

She waved him away. "Oh, wait. Put the chicken back."

"SHEILA IS A HEALTHY DOG," Dr. Walters, the vet in the animal clinic, said. "She's about two years old."

The vet was young, probably fresh out of veterinary school, which was fine with Nicole. She'd been grateful to get an appointment first thing in the morning.

Sheila was a scruffy pile of fur with big eyes and a friendly personality. Nicole wouldn't have thought about getting a dog, but now that she had one, even if it technically belonged to Raoul, she was getting used to the idea.

"She seems housebroken," she said. "She didn't chew on anything and she likes to play. She also eats a lot."

"Typical for a stray," the doctor told her. "You'll have to measure her food or she'll put on weight."

"More weight," Nicole muttered. Sheila might be cute, but she was also chubby.

The dog seemed to know they were talking about her. Her tail started wagging and she leaned in and swiped Nicole with her tongue.

"She's not fat," Dr. Walters said, patting the dog who sat on the examination table. "She's pregnant." He scratched the dog's back. "I would say she's due in three or four weeks."

He kept talking. Nicole could see his lips moving, but she couldn't hear the words.

Sheila was pregnant? Even the damn dog got to have a family of her own? Claire, then Jesse, and now the *dog?* Was that fair?

Nicole sucked in a sob. *She* wanted a family, too. She wanted to belong and be loved and have babies. But was that going to happen? Nooooo.

"Ms. Keyes? Nicole? Are you all right?"

Nicole started to say she was fine, then realized she couldn't speak because she was crying. Crying because a stupid stray dog got knocked up?

"I'm okay," she managed. "Ignore me."

Dr. Walters looked uncomfortable as he handed her a box of tissues. She took a couple and wiped her eyes, then tried to smile.

"It's fine," she repeated. "I'm having a meltdown that has nothing to do with you or Sheila. Go on. You were saying she's due in a few weeks."

"Ah, that's right. You'll want to be careful about what she eats. She's probably behind with her shots, but we'll wait until after the puppies are born."

"Great. Perfect. She can have a bath, though, right?" Because as cute as Sheila was, she smelled.

"Sure. We can do that here. You can leave her and pick her up later."

He seemed eager for Nicole to leave. Not that she could blame him. She gave him a watery smile, promised to read the material he sent home on doggie deliveries and left her cell number with the receptionist.

She drove to Wyatt's house and knocked on the front door. When Claire answered, Nicole started to cry again.

"What's wrong?" her sister asked, pulling her inside. "What happened?"

"N-nothing," Nicole said as she sank onto the sofa. "It's so stupid. Sheila is pregnant."

Claire sat next to her and rubbed her arm. "Who's Sheila?"

"A dog. I took her to the vet and she's pregnant." More tears fell. "Everyone's pregnant but me. I want a family. I've always wanted a family. Not with Drew, but with someone good. But that's not going to happen and now the stupid dog is pregnant. Plus the vet was really young and I think I made him uncomfortable by crying in his office."

"He'll get over it. When did you get a dog?"

"Yesterday. I cried when he told me about Sheila."

"Which will make him understand women are complex creatures. It's a lesson he has to learn eventually. Better early than late."

Nicole laughed and cried, which wasn't easy. Then she hiccupped.

"How did everything get so messed up?" she asked, knowing she sounded pitiful.

"It's not messed up."

"It's not the way I wanted it to be. Some of that is good. I'm glad you're here and with Wyatt, but what about what happened with Jesse? It's a disaster."

"So make it better."

Nicole shook her head. "She hasn't even apologized."

"Do you need to hear the words?"

"Wouldn't you?"

Claire sighed. "Probably."

"I'm upset."

"Don't be. You'll meet someone. Someone great."

Nicole realized that she'd yet to share her happy, albeit fake, good news.

"I'm dating someone," she said. "Someone really great. You don't have to feel sorry for me."

"I don't feel sorry for you." Claire looked confused. "You're dating?"

"It's possible. Men find me attractive."

"I know they do. I didn't know you were ready to start looking for someone. I think it's great."

Nicole still felt teary and upset and now defensive. "He's amazing. Handsome and funny, with a killer body. He teaches high school football and he used to play professionally. His name is Eric Hawkins. Hawk."

"You're dating?" Claire repeated. "And you didn't tell me?"

"I've been busy. I've gotten involved with the football team. I went to a couple of games and I bring dessert when they look at game films and Hawk and I have been going out." Nicole felt a little guilty for not saying anything to Claire before this. "I was going to tell you."

"When?"

"Soon."

Ironically, she'd started the relationship with Hawk in an effort to prove to the world she was doing just fine. Hard for the world to know if she didn't tell it.

"So you like him?" Claire asked.

"Uh-huh." Nicole was telling the truth. She did like Hawk. He was a good guy. She liked him best in bed, but she wasn't going to share that.

"I'm really happy for you."

"You don't sound happy," Nicole said.

"I'm just surprised. I thought we were getting close. That you would share this with me."

Nicole winced. "I didn't mean to leave you out or anything."

"I know. It's not a problem."

Claire spoke too quickly, which meant it *was* a problem.

Just what Nicole needed—another screwed-up relationship.

"I'm really sorry. Please don't be mad at me."

"I'm not. I swear."

"I'm not sure I believe you."

"You should. We'll go out," Claire said. "The four of us."

"Hawk's a little pressed for time, what with this being football season, but I'll talk to him." Was dinner with her family part of their deal? Did it matter? She didn't want to mess up her relationship with her sister.

"I'm looking forward to meeting him," Claire said.

"You and Wyatt will really like him."

Nicole wasn't pretending about that. She was sure Hawk would get along great with them. Too bad nothing about their time together was real. It was just a game and when the season was up, it would all be over.

"WHAT DO YOU THINK?" Brittany asked as she held out a spoon. She was cooking chicken and noodles, which was actually pretty good.

Nicole nodded as she swallowed. "You're getting the hang of this."

"Cooking? It's fun, but I don't have to do it every

day. I talked to my dad and said I would cook once a week if he let me stay out a half hour later."

"Interesting negotiation. What did he say?"

She scrunched up her face. "He laughed for a really long time, then said my cooking wasn't that good, but it was a nice try."

Nicole bit back a smile. "Not buying it, huh?"

"No, and that really bugs me. I thought it was a great deal." She stirred the mixture again. "You wouldn't mind us having some wine with dinner, would you? It's not like we'll be driving."

Nicole didn't even blink. "I would mind, very much. You're not even eighteen. The drinking age is twenty-one."

"Sometimes you're really parental."

"Sometimes you're really a brat."

Brittany grinned. "I know, but I had to try. It's like an honor thing."

"Is that what we're calling it?"

Nicole left the teenagers and went upstairs. She could hear the rumble of their voices, then a very long silence. The chicken and noodles had been good, but not that good.

"Are you thinking what I'm thinking?" she asked Sheila, who had followed her into her bedroom and was now curled up on the bed. When Sheila didn't answer, Nicole grabbed her phone.

"How closely am I supposed to watch them?" she asked Hawk when he answered.

"Where are you?"

"In my bedroom. They're eating downstairs but it got really quiet."

"For how long?"

"Fifteen minutes."

"I'll be right over."

He arrived thirty minutes later, carrying bags of Mexican takeout. Brittany glared at her father.

"This is my private dinner."

"Uh-huh. We'll be in the kitchen."

"I do not need a chaperone."

Hawk only made kissy noises then retreated to the kitchen where Nicole had set the small table by the window. She opened two beers.

"Nervous about what they might get up to?" she asked.

"A little. I remember being Raoul's age. I know about getting in trouble." He passed her a plate. "You got a dog."

"Sheila. She's Raoul's dog."

"She's spending a lot of time with you."

It was true. Sheila seemed to follow her all over the house. "She knows I buy the groceries and she respects that."

"I like dogs. I grew up with them. Serena never liked them, so we didn't have one."

"Sheila's going to have puppies. Help yourself."

"I like big dogs."

"We don't know the daddy. They could be huge."

He eyed Sheila. "I hope not, for her sake."

Nicole did her best to keep her attention on

the dog, when what she really wanted to look at was Hawk.

He was casually dressed in jeans and a T-shirt, but that didn't lessen his appeal. As always, he filled out his clothes and made them look good. He moved with the easy grace of an athlete, and watching him made her remember moving against him, having him move against her.

"How are things going with Raoul?" he asked. "Living with a teenager?"

"Good. He's making it easy. He's quiet, tidy, inhales my food. He works hard. He's had a tough time and he's making it. I respect that. I wish my sister had been more like him."

"The piano player?"

"No, my baby sister. Jesse. She's nothing like Raoul. I can't figure out if she was born a screwup or if it just happened."

"How old is she?"

"Twenty-two. She barely got through high school. She partied a lot, then discovered boys. I was constantly terrified she would show up pregnant. I tried lectures, bribes, tough love, forgiveness. Nothing worked. She's going to inherit half the bakery when she turns twenty-five, which is going to be a nightmare for both of us. She's not interested in the business, so I'm already saving to buy her out."

She paused and grabbed a chip. "We should change the subject."

"Why?"

"Jesse's not very fun, in life or conversation."

"Sounds like she's troubled."

In more ways than he knew.

"Where does she live now?" he asked.

"She's got a place in the university district. She's never held a job, except at the bakery and that doesn't count. If she hadn't been family, she would have been fired several times over. The thing is, I can't figure out where I went wrong or what to do about fixing things."

"Some problems can't be fixed."

She didn't want to believe that, even though she knew it might be true.

She toyed with the idea of telling him about Drew and Jesse, then decided she couldn't stand the humiliation. "She's my sister. I practically raised her. I guess I'm afraid I did a bad job."

He reached across the table and touched her hand. "I've seen you in action. Not possible."

"You've seen me on my good days. I can be a real bitch."

"You think I haven't screwed up with Brittany?"

"You're pretty smug about your relationship with her."

He laughed. "Sometimes. She's a good kid. You do your best and then you let 'em go."

"Is that a coach thing?"

"Football is life."

"Not in my world."

"In everyone's world."

That made her smile.

"Want to come back home with me?" he asked, his gaze intense.

Suddenly she wasn't hungry at all. "Sure. Is it okay to leave them alone?"

Hawk frowned, then glanced toward the great room. She could practically hear the debate going on inside his head. Which side would win? The responsible father or the guy interested in a little time with his sex kitten?

"Damn," he muttered.

She picked up her fork. "Fatherhood wins."

"This sucks."

"Tell me about it."

But she wasn't all that upset. Yes, it was frustrating to be so close to Hawk and not in a position to have her way with him. But the good news was he'd shown a side of himself that she really liked and respected. After the disaster that was Drew, she could appreciate the thrill of a good man. Of course, this being her life, the good man was only pretending to be involved with her.

CHAPTER TEN

NICOLE GRABBED frosted cupcakes and set them into a large, pink box. The special order had come in early that morning from a desperate-sounding mother whose husband had dropped the ball when it came to ordering for their three-year-old's birthday party.

Now she carefully arranged chocolate cupcakes with neon-pink frosting and sparkly sprinkles. In a few minutes the harried mother would show up for them and be relieved that at least one part of her day went right. Okay, so it wasn't rocket science. But she could still make someone feel better, at least in the moment.

She carefully taped the box shut and took it up front, then peeled off her plastic gloves and tossed them in the trash. Maggie pushed one of the swinging doors leading to the back open.

"Someone to see you," she said, not quite meeting Nicole's gaze.

"Someone I want to see?" Nicole asked, her stomach already knotting. There weren't that many people who would come in the back way.

"Probably not."

Nicole braced herself for yet another fight with Jesse. Her sister was determined to get her half of the money out of the bakery. Nicole wasn't interested in gutting the business just so Jesse could throw her future away. Legally she didn't have to do anything until Jesse was twenty-five and she planned to keep resisting until the exact day her sister came of age.

Jesse stood just inside her office. Nicole stared at her for a second, feeling anger and sadness, along with regret and resignation. Despite what Jesse thought, Nicole had always loved her and wanted the best for her. They were only six years apart in age. They should have been closer.

Nicole knew she was probably to blame for a lot of what had gone wrong. She'd been too young to be left in charge of raising Jesse, but that's what had happened.

Jesse turned and saw her. "It's not what you think," she began. "I'm not here about the bakery."

"Okay. Do you need money?"

Jesse rolled her eyes. "No. I don't need anything. That piece of information should keep you quiet for at least thirty seconds."

Nicole opened her mouth, then closed it. She was so tired of fighting and being hurt.

"I'm leaving," Jesse said before Nicole could ask why she was there. "I can't change anything here. I can't make it right. I don't want to be the bad guy anymore, so I'm going away."

"Running away," Nicole snapped, furious that Jesse would be willing to leave. "Ignoring your responsibilities."

"What responsibilities?" Jesse asked, her voice sharp. "You don't want me in your house and you sure as hell never wanted me here."

"That's not true. I do want you here. We should be partners."

"Your definition of partners means me doing everything exactly the way you say. I don't want to spend my life putting sprinkles on doughnuts."

"Then what do you want to do?"

Jesse turned away. "I don't know."

Perfect. Just perfect. "Let me guess. You're running away to find yourself. Well, guess what? Your problems are going to tag along with you. They'll slide into your suitcase and make themselves at home when you unpack. You can't escape the consequences, Jesse. You might as well stay and figure it out here."

"No. It's time for me to leave. You always complain that I'll never grow up. Maybe this will force me into doing that. I'll make it on my own or I'll fail on my own."

Nicole wanted to scream. "You can't go. You're pregnant. How will you support yourself?"

"That's not your problem."

Talk about frustrating. Did Jesse really think she could find a decent job, get medical insurance, have a baby and raise it on her own? She'd never been responsible in her life. She was awful with money, a slacker when it came to work and totally unwilling to even admit she'd been wrong for sleeping with Drew. It was a total recipe for disaster.

"It's going to be my problem when you come back, and we both know you will."

Jesse looked at her for a long time. "You think you know everything about me. You think you know who I am, but you're wrong. You don't know anything. I'm done fighting with you, Nicole. I can't disappoint you anymore. It hurts too much. You won't believe that, but it's true. I never wanted things to be like this. Please don't try to find me."

With that, she turned and walked out.

Nicole watched her go. Part of her wanted to run after Jesse and insist that she stay. Another part of her wondered if maybe being on her own for a few months would help Jesse grow up. She didn't doubt that her sister would come back—no doubt scared, desperate and broke. Not to mention pregnant. And Nicole would take her in because that's what family did. But between now and then, maybe Jesse could learn a few lessons.

So she let her go and told herself it was the right thing to do, even as she fought against feeling sick to her stomach.

AFTER THE FOOTBALL GAME, Nicole headed to the parking lot with the rest of the crowd. She felt better than she had earlier, but she couldn't seem to shake the black cloud that had surrounded her all day.

She stood by her car, knowing Hawk would send over a few kids for her to drive to the pizza place. While she was standing there, wondering if stuffing herself with Hawaiian pizza would make her feel better or worse, a tall, curvy, beautiful woman walked over.

"Excuse me," the woman said, her face perfect enough to be on a magazine. "Are you Nicole?"

"Yes."

"Really? One of the other mothers pointed you out to me."

The surprise in the woman's voice put Nicole on edge. There was only one reason anyone would be talking about her.

"You're dating Hawk?"

Nicole was so not in the mood for this. "Yes, I am."

"Really?"

There was that tone again. The one that expressed more than surprise. It was as if a law of the universe had been violated.

"I just thought Hawk had a different type," the woman murmured, more to herself than Nicole.

Nicole's temper sprang to life. She glanced at the woman's left hand and saw enough diamonds to fund the retirement of every resident in Idaho.

"You mean someone like yourself?" Nicole asked. "Sorry. He doesn't do married women. Which I have to tell you is pretty fabulous for me.

I'm single. And yes, we're dating. For what it's worth, because I know this is really what you want to know, the sex is amazing. Seriously. He's practically a god. We do things that are illegal in six states. I don't just see stars, I practically fall through a black hole and land on the planet of satisfaction. It's another plane of pleasure."

The woman swallowed hard, then pressed her lips together. "I didn't need to know that."

"I'm sure, but you were curious. Now you don't have to be."

Nicole turned away, thinking she would wait by the gate, when she ran into something tall and hard and muscled. She winced, then looked at Hawk.

"How much did you hear?"

He grinned. "I liked the god part. I'd make a great deity."

Nicole groaned, then glanced over her shoulder to make sure the other woman had moved away. "She bugged me. She was so sure I couldn't be going out with you because she's damn near perfect. I had to do something."

Hawk reached up and touched her face. "You okay?"

"I'm fine. I had a crappy day."

"Want to talk about it?"

"No."

He cupped her chin. "Want to talk about it?"

She sighed, liking him touching her. "Maybe. Just family stuff."

"I'm a family kind of guy."

"It's my younger sister, Jesse. She came to the bakery today and said she was leaving town. She's tired of always being a disappointment, so she's running away. God forbid she should ever actually try to change her behavior. That's not possible. She wants to leave and I didn't know if I should stop her. There's a part of me that says she needs to learn a lesson. Maybe being out on her own will do that."

"How old is she?"

"Twenty-two."

"She's not a kid."

"Actually, she kind of is. She's never taken responsibility for anything. And now she's pregnant." Nicole drew in a breath and looked at Hawk. "She's the reason Drew and I split up. Not that we shouldn't have broken up before. He was a total jerk. I found him in bed with Jesse."

Hawk's eyes darkened and he swore. "I'm sorry."

"Me, too. It was a hell of a shock. Drew tried to talk his way out of it, but I knew it was over. I felt worse about Jesse's betrayal than his, which is saying something."

"You're supposed to be able to trust family."

His words made her want to cry, but she was determined to be strong.

"I was so angry and hurt," she admitted. "I'd been the one to insist Jesse live with us after we got married. I wasn't going to kick out my baby sister. I guess I should have thought that through."

"You did the right thing."

"No good deed goes unpunished." She'd thought she would hate telling him the truth, but it was surprisingly easy. Maybe because he seemed to be listening without judging her. "It's even more complicated. She's pregnant and it's possible it's Drew's baby."

"Does he know?"

"I haven't a clue and I'm not going to be the one to tell him. That's her problem." She leaned against Hawk. He put his arms around her. "I worry about her being alone and pregnant. After all she's done and how she acted, I still worry."

"Because you're a good sister."

"Or a total idiot. It's a toss-up."

"No, it's not. You going to let her go?"

"For now. I know she'll be back. There's no way she can make it on her own. Not with a baby coming. Maybe a few months in the real world will help her grow up."

She closed her eyes and breathed in the scent of him. "The thing is, there's a part of me that doesn't want her to go. I can't help worrying. How crazy is that? Shouldn't I be grateful she's about to get slapped in the face by reality?"

"You love her."

"I know, but sometimes I hate her."

"Understandable. But you love her more. She's your sister."

Nicole nodded. Funny how she'd always wanted

a family of her own when she couldn't seem to handle the one she already had.

He kissed the top of her head. "What can I do to help?"

"Sex would be good."

He chuckled. "I agree, but parking lots have never been my style. How about pizza?"

"Not even a close second, but I'll take it."

"Anything else?"

"You could agree to have dinner with my other sister and her fiancé."

"Done."

She stepped back and looked at him. "Really?"

He kissed her, his mouth lingering on hers. "Really."

"I MET WYATT YEARS AGO," Nicole said as they walked up the front path to the house. "He came into the bakery to place an order and we started talking."

Hawk didn't like the sound of that. "You dated."

She laughed. "We tried. In theory, we're perfect for each other. So we went out a couple of times, but it was a disaster. We're destined to be friends. Then Claire moved here a few months ago and he fell hard for her. Which is good. He needs someone in his life."

She reached for the doorbell. "He has a daughter from a previous marriage. Amy. She's at a girl-friend's tonight. You'll meet her next time. She's a sweetie and I adore her."

The door opened before he could ask any other questions. A woman who looked a lot like Nicole smiled.

"You made it. We're barbecuing, which may not be a good idea. Men and fire. They tend to bring out the worst in each other. I'm Claire," she said, holding out her hand. "You must be Hawk."

"Nice to meet you."

"Same here."

She looked at her sister and raised her eyebrows. Hawk wasn't sure what that meant.

He followed Nicole into the house. As they walked through to the back patio, Nicole pointed out all the custom touches Wyatt—a contractor—had put into the house.

"Isn't the woodwork amazing?" she said, running her hands along a door frame. "He has the best crew. He did the remodel in my house. It's an old place so there were lots of really small rooms. He opened it up and redid the kitchen."

Until that minute, Hawk had liked Nicole's house. He'd thought it was homey and welcoming. Suddenly he never wanted to go there again.

They moved out onto the patio. It was big, with a slate floor and a wood cover. The built-in barbecue was large and stainless. Hawk had one that was bigger, not that he got to use it much. Summer was his busy time with work.

"Hawk, this is Wyatt," Nicole said.

Hawk and the other man looked at each other.

Wyatt was about Hawk's height, but maybe twenty pounds of muscle lighter. Hawk knew he could take him.

They shook hands and Wyatt offered him a beer. The women returned to the house.

"Steaks all right?" Wyatt asked, pointing to the paper-wrapped package beside the barbecue.

"Sure. Can't go wrong with a steak."

"Good. Claire was telling me you're a high school football coach."

"Been doing it about five years now."

"You like it?"

"More than I thought. Football is about more than winning. I like watching the kids grow up and head out into the real world."

Wyatt's gaze was steady, as if he were assessing Hawk. Hawk didn't blink. He wasn't afraid of what the other man might find. He had nothing to hide.

"I used to watch you play pro ball," Wyatt said at last. "You went out at the top of your game."

"My wife was diagnosed with cancer. She didn't have much time left and our daughter was only twelve. Flying around the country playing football seemed like a waste of those last weeks. After she died, I needed to be around for my daughter. She's a senior now."

"Any regrets?"

"No."

The women returned. Hawk watched Nicole walk toward him and felt a stirring inside. He liked watching her move. She wasn't aware of how beautiful she was or how sexy and she wouldn't believe him if he tried to tell her.

"We have salad and garlic bread and Claire made a pie for dessert," Nicole said. "She's constantly trying to find her inner baker."

"I have found it. Or her," Claire said. "Pie is my new thing. You're going to be impressed."

Nicole grinned. "Claire plays the piano."

"I heard," he said, liking the teasing between the sisters.

"I'll have you know I'm a very famous and very spoiled soloist who is in high demand. You're lucky I'm going to let you eat at the same table."

"When she first came to Seattle, she didn't even know how to do laundry."

Claire batted her eyes. "I must protect my hands. Housework is beneath me."

"Stop picking on her," Wyatt said. "She's not the only one with an embarrassing past."

Hawk looked at Nicole. "You have secrets?"

"No. I've told you everything."

Claire tilted her head. "Are you sure? When I was four and practicing the piano several hours a day, Nicole used to sit outside the studio and bang pots together. It was her way of accompanying me and keeping me from being lonely, all at the same time."

Nicole squirmed. "Okay, maybe I hadn't mentioned that."

Claire laughed. "I'll stop torturing you now. Come on, Hawk. Amy, Wyatt's daughter, isn't here, but we have pictures. You need to see them and listen while I brag about her."

She led him into the house. Hawk had a feeling that they weren't going to talk all that much about Amy.

Sure enough, when they reached the living room, she pointed to several photographs on what looked like a new baby grand piano, then said, "How did you and Nicole meet?"

"At the bakery." Which was how she'd met Wyatt, he thought, his good mood fading.

"You seem like a nice guy, which is great. But Nicole is special. I don't want anyone hurting her."

Which meant Claire didn't know about their deal. Was her concern one of the reasons Nicole had made her offer to him?

"I'm not going to hurt her."

Claire nodded. "I don't think you'd mean to, but she's just getting out of a difficult marriage."

"I know about Drew."

"She told you?"

"About Drew and what happened."

"Oh. Okay. Then you know why I'm worried. Wyatt feels awful about that. He never should have introduced them. But Drew's family so it was inevitable."

"Wyatt and Drew are brothers?" Nicole had left out that part of the story.

"Stepbrothers. Drew's a bit of a disaster."

Hawk tuned out the conversation. He had the sudden need to punch something, or someone. Wyatt came to mind. Not that the guy had done anything specific. He just bugged Hawk. Drew could use a good beating, too. Hawk would enjoy that.

Something wasn't right. Something—

He swore silently. That nagging, uncomfortable sensation in his gut had a name. Jealousy. He was jealous of Wyatt and maybe even Drew. What the hell was up with that? He shouldn't care enough to be jealous. And of what? Nicole was with him. Sort of.

They weren't actually dating. They had an arrangement. One that should be working for him. Still, he didn't like how well Wyatt knew her or that Drew had married her. Worse, he didn't know how to make it better.

NICOLE WALKED into the house shortly after midnight. The evening with her sister, Wyatt and Hawk had gone better than she'd hoped. Hawk had been a little quiet, but he'd still seemed to have a good time. It had been great to hang out and laugh and not worry about seeing pity in anyone's eyes.

Sheila looked up from her place on the sofa and stretched, then wagged her tail in greeting. Nicole frowned. The dog always slept with Raoul. So if she was down here, where was he?

Nicole went upstairs. The door to his bedroom stood open and the room was empty. She looked at her watch. He was late. Now what?

She'd spent plenty of nights waiting up for her sister, so she knew what to do to fill the time. What wasn't clear was how to deal with the situation. Technically Raoul was an adult. While she'd asked him to be in by eleven or let her know if he was going to be later, she wasn't sure he had to listen. She could play the "you're living under my roof" card, but that felt weird.

She went back downstairs and let Sheila out, then checked for messages. There weren't any. Great.

She considered going to bed, but knew she wouldn't sleep, so she picked a movie and loaded it in the DVD player. Sheila came back in and they curled up together on the sofa. About thirty minutes later, she heard Raoul's car pull up.

"You're late," she announced the second he walked in the door. "You're supposed to call. I don't like worrying. And don't tell me not to. You live here now. Worry comes with the room."

Which wasn't at all what she'd expected to say. She was supposed to let him talk first.

But instead of getting angry or defensive, like Jesse would have done, he smiled.

"You waited up."

"Obviously. What did you think? That I would just go to sleep, never once imagining your broken, bleeding body on the side of the road?"

"You were worried?"

"Yes, and you don't have to sound so happy about it." He couldn't seem to stop smiling, which she found really annoying.

"I'm sorry. I called."

"There's no message."

"I left one. On your cell."

On her... "Oh," she said, feeling a little foolish. "I only checked the house machine." She grabbed her purse and pulled out her cell. "It's off. I didn't think to check it." She turned it on and waited. Sure enough the message envelope flashed on the screen and the phone beeped.

"I was at a party. A couple of guys got really drunk. I didn't want them to drive, so I took them home. I'm sorry I worried you."

"No, it's my fault. I should have checked my cell. I didn't mean to yell."

"It's okay."

"It's not." She was feeling more stupid by the second. "I have a temper and I overreact." Which was probably a lot of what had gone wrong with Jesse.

"I like that you worry about me, Nicole. No one ever does."

"Don't say that."

"Why not? It's true."

It was also beyond sad. "I'd rather you didn't do anything to make me worry. Can it be enough that I'm prepared to worry at any time?"

"Yeah," he said with a grin. "That's good, too. Night."

"Night."

He started up the stairs. Sheila went after him, then followed him into his bedroom. Nicole turned off the movie and turned off the lights.

While she'd hated being concerned about Raoul, she did like having someone in her life to care about. Which made her think of Jesse, but she didn't want to go there tonight.

Families were a mess, she told herself. So why was she so determined to have one of her own?

CHAPTER ELEVEN

SUNDAY MORNING Nicole woke up early to the sound of voices. She rolled over and looked at the clock. It was barely seven. She sat up and listened, wondering what would possess Raoul to turn on his television at this time and play it so loud? He was still a teenager—sleep was precious.

She stood and grabbed her robe. As she started for the door, the voices became more distinct and recognizable. It was almost as if...

"Oh, no," she muttered.

She raced to her door and jerked it open. Raoul stood at the top of the stairs, blocking entrance to the landing. She couldn't see the man trying to pass, but she had a good idea who he was. Sheila stood beside Raoul, fifteen pounds of pregnant growling fury.

"I knew I made a mistake not changing the locks," she said, moving toward the railing and looking down at her soon-to-be ex-husband. "This isn't your house anymore, Drew. Go away."

"I'm not leaving until we talk. Although now I

know why you've been avoiding me. So this is the new boyfriend. A kid? Is that the best you could do, Nicole?"

"You know him?" Raoul asked.

"We were married."

"We're still married," Drew said.

"Separated, divorcing. It's over."

Raoul nodded, then turned his attention back to Drew. "You need to leave."

"I don't think so." Drew looked at Nicole. "Is it fun with a kid? Are you teaching him things you know?"

The slap caught her off guard and she felt herself flush. But before she could figure out what to say, Raoul grabbed Drew, hauled him up to the landing, then wrapped his arm around Drew's neck, locking him in place.

"Didn't your mother teach you any manners?" he growled. "You will not speak to Nicole that way."

Drew flailed against his attacker, waving his arms and gasping. "Nicole!"

"She deserves respect and appreciation," Raoul continued, his voice low and angry. "Something you need to learn."

While Nicole was enjoying the show, she didn't like how all the blood seemed to drain from Drew's face. The last thing Raoul needed to deal with was an assault charge.

"Thanks for looking out for me," she told Raoul.

"But you need to let him go. You can both wait for me in the kitchen."

"Do I have to?" Raoul asked, and she knew he wasn't referring to the meeting.

"Yes. It's not a fair fight."

Raoul looked disappointed as he released Drew. Drew staggered forward, gasping for air as he steadied himself on the railing.

"You bitch," he said, his voice raspy.

"I guess we won't be talking."

"No. Wait." He rubbed his throat. "I want to talk."

"Then meet me downstairs. And don't try anything. Raoul doesn't always do what I say."

There was no reason to threaten him, but it still felt good to say the words. Probably childish of her, she thought as she returned to her bedroom, but fun all the same.

She washed her face and brushed her teeth, then quickly dressed. Dealing with Drew and their relationship didn't bother her. She was over him—she'd known that from the second she'd found him in bed with her sister and had been more devastated by Jesse's betrayal than his. But there was the question of the baby. Did she tell him?

As the possible father, he probably had the right to know. But Jesse was already dealing with trying to make it on her own. Did she need to be worrying about Drew, too?

Nicole briefly debated the issue, then decided it

wasn't her call to make. If Jesse wanted him to know, she knew where to find him. As far as Nicole was concerned, she wasn't going to get involved.

She made her way to the kitchen where she found Raoul and Drew in a standoff, each on opposite sides of the kitchen, staring at each other. If there was a tree in the middle of the room, they would each be peeing on it.

She ignored Drew and crossed to Raoul. "I need to talk to him without you glaring. Would you please take Sheila for a walk."

"I don't trust him."

"I don't trust him, either, but I'm pretty sure I can take him. My leg is much better now."

That earned her a smile. "I'll be close and I'll take my cell."

"I'll call if there's trouble."

Raoul got the dog's leash from the pantry and left the kitchen. Nicole waited until she heard the front door close before turning to Drew.

"What the hell were you thinking, sneaking in here again? Didn't you learn your lesson last time?" He'd broken in before, late at night and drunk. Claire had held him at bay with a few unexpected moves and a high-heeled shoe. He still had the scar.

"I wanted to talk to you."

"So use the phone."

"Who's the guy?"

"No one you need to worry about."

"You're sleeping with him?"

"He's in high school, Drew, not that it's any of your business. He needed a place to stay so I'm letting him live here. You're the one who has inappropriate relationships, not me. I don't need to chase someone younger to make me feel better about myself."

Drew took a step toward her. "I don't want to fight anymore. It's been long enough. When are you going to let me come back?"

He couldn't be serious. "I'm not playing a game," she said. "I'm not pretending to be mad, Drew. Our marriage is over. It was a mistake from the beginning."

"Don't say that."

"It's the truth. I don't know why you're hanging on to me, but you shouldn't. We were never good together."

Just then the back door opened and Hawk walked in. He looked big and strong and sexy in his running shorts and a T-shirt. He ignored Drew, strolled over to her and kissed her on the mouth.

"I thought I'd stop by and say hi," he told her, never taking his eyes off Drew. "Who's your friend?"

"My ex-husband," she said automatically, wondering what on earth Hawk was doing here. Why would he show up like this? Then she got it. Raoul must have called.

Hawk was worried about her. Knowing that gave her a toasty feeling in the pit of her stomach.

She turned to Drew. "This is Hawk."

Hawk grinned. "The new boyfriend."

Drew bristled. "We're still married."

"I filed papers," Nicole reminded him. "We've agreed on a settlement. Right now we're just waiting out the time until the divorce is final. That's not married."

"I'm not letting you go."

"You don't have a choice, Drew. It's over."

He looked like he was going to cry. "But this isn't what I want."

She could almost feel sorry for him, until she remembered he'd slept with her baby sister. "I should have changed the locks the last time you broke in. This time I'm doing it for real. Show up here again and I'll get a restraining order. It's time to move on, Drew. It's time to grow up."

She thought he might argue or try to make his case again. Instead, he left, letting the front door slam behind him. She looked at Hawk.

"Raoul called," she said.

"Yeah. He had a feeling you would make him leave and he didn't want you alone with the guy. That's really your ex?"

She nodded. "Not my proudest moment."

"I don't want him showing up like this."

She smiled. "I like it when you get all macho."

He didn't smile back. "I'm serious, Nicole. You can't have this guy wandering around your house. He's a weasel and I don't think he'd do anything, but he shouldn't have a key."

"I know. I'll get the locks changed as soon as I can get someone out here."

He looked at his watch and swore. "I have to go have breakfast with one of my players and his parents. They're already hearing from recruiters and I'm going to talk to them about how to handle things."

He grabbed her, pulled her close and kissed her hard. She leaned into him, enjoying the feel of his lips on hers. The tingles started immediately.

When he released her, she said, "Thanks for coming to my rescue."

"Anytime. Nobody messes with my girl."

The words didn't mean anything, she told herself. They had a deal, nothing more. But that didn't stop her heart from fluttering a little and her imagination from asking what it would be like if it was real.

"IT'S HAWK," Maggie said Monday morning as she handed over the phone. "He has a very nice voice."

Nicole stepped away from the loaves of bread she'd been putting on racks to cool. "Yes, he does."

"And a great butt."

"One of his best features."

"Any chance I'll see him naked?"

Nicole laughed. "I don't think so."

"Bummer."

Nicole took the phone. "Hello?"

"I heard that," Hawk said, sounding a little rattled. "All of it."

"You have a fan."

"She's old enough to be my mother."

"So she has a lot of experience. You should enjoy her appreciation. It's flattering."

"It's uncomfortable."

"Is the big, bad football player afraid of a little old lady?"

"Maybe."

"So if I ever need you punished, I should send Maggie after you?"

"Can we change the subject?" he asked.

Nicole grinned. "Sure. Pick a topic."

"Did you call a locksmith?"

He was checking up on her. It was kind of sweet. "Yes, I did. He'll be at my place at nine-thirty tomorrow morning."

"Not until then?"

"I think Drew is sufficiently intimidated to stay away for another twenty-four hours."

"Probably."

"Is that why you called?" she asked. "To make sure I'd called a locksmith?"

"Yeah."

"Worried about me?"

"A little."

"You're sweet."

"Don't tell anyone. I have a reputation for being tough."

"Your secret is safe with me. Bye."

"Bye."

He hung up.

Nicole set down the phone and felt the fluttering start again. The sensation told her that she would have to be careful around Hawk. What had started out as a simple deal might be getting just a little more complicated.

NICOLE ARRIVED HOME to find seven very tall teenage boys sitting on her front step. Raoul wasn't with them—he would be at football practice until close to five. So who were they?

She parked in the garage, then walked around to the front. "Can I help you?"

The boys scrambled to their feet. "Yes, ma'am. Nicole. I'm Billy. Coach Hawkins asked us to stop by after school. Look around and make sure everything was all right."

Three of them held basketballs. Based on their height and the fact that they weren't on the football team, despite an impressive amount of muscle, she could guess their sport of choice.

"He's not the basketball coach," she said.

"Yes, ma'am. But we like him and we were happy to help him out."

"By coming here?"

"Yes, ma'am."

The ma'am thing was starting to get on her nerves. She couldn't believe Hawk had done this—arranged protection.

"What exactly are you supposed to do?" she

asked, trying to decide if this was funny or annoying.

"Wait for you, check out the house, stay here until Raoul gets home."

"But you don't know me."

Billy frowned. "I'm not sure why that matters."

She had a bad feeling they weren't going away until their mission had been fulfilled. It would probably be easier to simply accept their presence than fight it.

"Okay," she said and opened the front door. "Check away. I'm guessing you're all hungry, so I'll be in the kitchen, putting out food."

Billy grinned. "Thanks. We appreciate that."

Five minutes later, they'd swept the house and were clustered together in the family room. Each of the boys had introduced himself, but the names were a blur. Nicole put out chips, sodas and cookies, then retreated to her study and called the high school. A few minutes later, Hawk picked up the phone.

"I'm in the middle of practice," he told her.

"Then why are you taking my call?"

"I thought I might have to talk you down."

"Because I could be annoyed by your high-handed assumption that I need protection from the man I used to be married to? You sent me basketball players."

"They're bigger than baseball players. Drew's the type of guy to be afraid of size."

Possibly, but not the point. "You had no right to do this."

"He broke into your house."

"He used a key. I'm getting the locks changed."

"Not until tomorrow. The guys will stay until Raoul gets home. Can you be patient until then?"

"I don't know if I should hug you or hit you over the head."

"Why don't you tie me up and have your way with me?"

That made her smile. "You're pissing me off, Hawk. This wasn't part of the deal."

"It is now. I didn't like that guy showing up when he was pretty sure you'd be asleep. He wanted the advantage. That's not allowed."

"I don't need a man to protect me."

"I need to know you're safe."

Because that's the kind of guy he was. Because he would take care of anyone in need. She knew that. He didn't mean anything else by what he'd said. She would have to remember that.

"I'll let them stay."

"Good."

"It's not like I could get rid of them on my own," she muttered.

"You're always gracious. That's one of the things I like about you. Want to come over for dinner this week?"

The change in topic caught her off guard. "Dinner?"

"At my place. With Brittany. Just the three of us."

Nicole didn't know what to say. Inviting her to

his house wasn't a public date designed to further the lie that they were a real couple. It actually felt like a real date. Did she want that?

Stupid question, she told herself, remembering all the recent fluttering. "I'd love to."

"How about Wednesday night? I'll cook."

"I look forward to it." Maybe more than she should.

NICOLE ARRIVED at Hawk's house close to five-thirty. He and Brittany lived in one of the older Seattle neighborhoods with mature trees and houses with great architectural detail. The lawns were green, the porches wide, and kids' toys lined the sidewalks. Not exactly the sort of place one would expect to find a former NFL player worth millions.

She parked on the street and walked up to the front door. Hawk opened it before she knocked.

"Hi," he said, drawing her in, then kissing her.

She closed her eyes and got lost in the feel of his mouth on hers. Heat grew, wanting stirred, then she heard the sound of footsteps on the stairs and reluctantly pulled back.

"Hi, yourself," she managed, hoping she wasn't blushing. "This is not anywhere I would have pictured you."

"What do you mean?"

"A middle-class neighborhood with lots of families. Where are the gates and the fancy cars?"

He laughed. "Not my style. Serena and I bought this place when I got my first signing bonus. After the small house we lived in during college, this place seemed like a mansion. We like it here. It's home."

Brittany burst into the entryway. "Hey, Nicole. How are you? Dad said he's cooking, but it's just barbecuing, which doesn't count. He'll make us put together the salad. Want to see the house?"

If only they could harness Brittany's energy and use it to power a hospital or something, Nicole thought with a grin. "I'd love to see the house." She set down her purse on the small table in the entryway. "I like craftsman-style homes. All the details and built-ins."

Brittany wrinkled her nose. "It's old, you mean. When I'm on my own, I want a high-rise condo with a view."

"How do you plan to pay for your fancy condo?" Hawk asked.

Brittany beamed at him. "You'll buy it for me, Daddy, because you love me."

He grunted a response, but Nicole saw the humor in his eyes. Hawk wasn't just pretty—he had a great relationship with his daughter. She liked that about him.

"Here's the living room," Brittany said, leading the way. "All the moldings are original. Even the dental molding, which is unusual for the time period. We think the builder brought it from another house. Maybe one he'd owned before."

Nicole looked around at the crowded room. The

dental molding was the least of it, she thought, taking in the oversize floral-print sofas and the knickknacks dotting every surface. While she usually loved the casual hominess of country-style decorating, this was country on steroids.

There were plenty of country prints on the throw pillows and curtains, braided rugs on the hardwood floor. A porcelain goose family posed by the fireplace and silk flower arrangements filled every corner. There were colored glass dishes and little bunnies on tables, along with photographs. Lots and lots of photographs.

Nicole walked toward a display on the wall. The grouping showed a younger Hawk with a pretty young woman. Serena, Nicole guessed. There were pictures of them laughing, wedding portraits, a few from an NFL ceremony. More photos showed happy parents with a pretty toddler.

The photos on the mantel showed Brittany from birth to age ten or so.

The room felt oppressively crowded—like a museum on crack. It reminded her of her grandma's house. Too hot, with too much stuff. She wouldn't have been more surprised to find faux fur and leather handcuffs.

The dining room was more of the same. The country theme continued with floral-print wallpaper and built-in cabinets filled with old-fashioned dishes. There were several cross-stitched sayings framed and hung on the walls.

Nicole felt awkward and out of place. This wasn't a house—this was a shrine to a lifestyle lost. She would bet that nothing had changed since the day Serena died.

She turned to Hawk and Brittany and forced a smile. "It's all lovely. Did Serena make these herself?" she asked, pointing to the stitched sayings.

Brittany nodded. "She was teaching me how to cross-stitch when she died."

"Handmade projects give a house a real homey feeling," she murmured, not sure what else to say. Hadn't Hawk ever wanted to move on? Keeping Serena's memory alive was one thing, but this?

"Serena was into flowers and lots of bright colors," Hawk said. "I thought about changing a few things, but didn't see the point. This is the home she left for us."

And why would he want to change that? Nicole thought, stunned by what she was seeing. Until this second, she'd never thought of Hawk as a widower. She'd known his wife had died, but hadn't considered he was still in mourning. Or at least living his life the way Serena would have wanted it. He always seemed too powerful and take-charge. This was totally unexpected.

The house was a shrine to Serena and screamed to any guest that she shouldn't bother getting comfortable. The crowded photographs on the wall proved there wasn't room for anyone else.

The tour of the downstairs continued. The house

was large with a big family room, an equally massive eat-in kitchen, a library and a study Hawk used
as a home office. Even there Serena's touch was
visible. Silk flowers nestled up against football
trophies.

Nicole felt as if the walls were closing in on her.
When Hawk suggested they step outside, she was
grateful to be able to breathe again.

But her relief was short-lived. While Hawk fired
up the barbecue and then opened a bottle of wine,
Brittany led the way to Serena's special garden.

"She loved flowers," the teenager said. "She
planted them every year. My dad and I plant the
same ones. We want her garden to look exactly as
it did when she was alive. There's herbs, too. Every
time we use them we're reminded of her."

Nicole murmured that it was all so lovely, but on
the inside, her head was spinning. What was Hawk
trying to prove? That no one would be welcome in
his life who wasn't Serena? Did he even know what
he was doing? Telling anyone who visited that she
would never measure up to the memory of his late
wife? Had he brought her here to warn her away?

CHAPTER TWELVE

DINNER TURNED OUT to be more pleasant than Nicole had thought. Talk turned to something other than Serena, although she ate her steak with the constant need to look over her shoulder to see if someone was watching. She did her best to shake the feeling of not being welcome, telling herself that Hawk wouldn't have invited her if he hadn't wanted to spend the evening with her.

After they'd carried their plates into the kitchen, Brittany led the way into the family room.

"I want to show you something," she said, sitting on the sofa.

Nicole reluctantly settled next to her, wondering if home movies would be next.

She was close, she realized, as Brittany pulled several photo albums off built-in shelves and set them on the big coffee table in front of the couch.

"Aren't these great?" the teen asked, flipping open the first one and pointing to a high school dance picture showing a very young Hawk and a pretty brunette. "They were so in love. They're only sixteen here. Look at their smiles." She sighed.

Nicole murmured that the pictures were lovely and wondered if the problem was her. Was she over-reacting to the situation? Maybe she was just sensitive because of Drew.

No, she told herself. Remembering was one thing, but living in a shrine was totally strange.

Brittany flipped pages, pointing out ski trips and her dad after his team won the state football championship. "He was MVP," she said proudly.

"Impressive," Nicole said.

There were prom pictures, then a series showing an increasingly pregnant Serena.

"They couldn't get married when they first found out she was having me. She was only seventeen and her parents wouldn't sign anything saying it was okay. So they waited until her birthday." Brittany sighed. "My dad said he would stand by her no matter what."

A romantic version of what had to be a difficult time. "It had to be hard for her to fight with her family," Nicole said.

"I know. It's kinda sad. They never forgave her for marrying my dad. Even though they were totally in love and their lives were perfect. I don't see my grandparents much. Dad says it's their loss."

"I agree with that," Nicole told her.

Brittany gave her a quick smile, then turned the page. "That's me. I was born in Oklahoma, where

Dad played football at Oklahoma University. This is the house we lived in. It's small, but cute. My mom and dad were so lucky. They got to be together all the time, they had a baby they loved."

Which sounded a little too movie-of-the-week for reality. "I'm sure it was a struggle," Nicole said carefully. "Being that young, away from home, with a new baby. They had to have been scared."

"Maybe." Brittany dismissed her words with a shrug. "But they had each other. Dad talks about those early years all the time. How much fun they had. The boosters were really great, getting mom a job, helping with babysitting. College football is really big there and Dad was a star player."

She turned another page. "Everyone said they were too young, that it wouldn't work out, but it did. My parents were in love until the day my mom died."

Nicole ignored the reference to Serena. Being in this house made it impossible to escape her. But there were other issues. She excused herself and went into the kitchen to help Hawk with the cleanup.

"Brittany showing you pictures?" he asked as he loaded the dishwasher.

"Yes. Everything is well documented."

He laughed. "Serena liked taking pictures and having them taken. I'm not as into that. People are going to think Brittany is twelve forever."

"I doubt that." She collected glasses and carried them over to him. "She talked a lot about what it was like when you and Serena first got married. How wonderful everything was."

He looked at her expectantly, as if waiting for her point.

"It had to have been difficult at times," she said, trying to sound casual. "You were both young and away from home for the first time."

"Maybe, but we had a lot of local support. It was good."

"Brittany seems to feel it was almost magical. As if with enough love, everything is fine."

He raised his eyebrows. "And?"

"She's a seventeen-year-old girl with a steady boyfriend. Don't you want to be talking about consequences? Not every teenage pregnancy ends with little forest animals singing and dancing. Not every young marriage survives."

He leaned over and kissed her on the forehead. "You're cute when you're worried."

"And you're ignoring my point."

He gave her an indulgent smile. "I've got this covered. Brittany's a good kid. We talk. I know what's going on in her life. She and Raoul aren't having sex yet. I'd know if they were."

It wasn't his fault, Nicole thought, trying not to take any of this personally. He was a man. A father, but still a man. He saw what he wanted to see.

"Hawk, you didn't even know Raoul had been thrown out of his foster home. He'd been living in that abandoned building for weeks. Weeks in the summer, when it's warm and they were alone for who knows how long with no distractions. Are you sure about the sex thing?"

He straightened. "Nicole, I know you're trying to help, but this isn't your concern. Brittany and I are close. We talk and I trust her. You're not a parent, so you're just going to have to believe me on this one."

She ignored the dismissal. "I raised my sister from the time she was little. I would say I have experience."

"Look how that went."

She stiffened. "It was a different circumstance."

"I know my daughter a whole lot better than you do. Nothing's going on with Raoul."

Nicole was willing to bet a lot that he was wrong. "Why wouldn't it be? You've taught her that young love heals all. You've taught her that getting pregnant at seventeen is just the beginning of the adventure."

"I'm not going to talk about this anymore," he told her.

"Why? Because there's only one point of view? Because only you get to be right? I actually hope I'm wrong, Hawk, because if I'm not, both of you are going to learn a hell of a lesson."

He stared at her. "What is this really about?"

"What?"

"You have an agenda. You must. You're putting way too much energy into my daughter's personal life. What's your real problem?"

She couldn't believe it. She was just trying to

help. To be a friend. But could he see that? Of course not.

"You're my problem," she told him. "I'm going home."

She walked to the front door, half expecting him to follow her and tell her to wait. That they could talk about the situation and find common ground. But he didn't.

NICOLE CAME HOME from work in as crabby a mood as she'd left that morning. Nothing specific had gone wrong—she just felt out of sorts with the world.

She knew the cause was her stupid fight with Hawk, which bugged her. It wasn't like they'd gotten really angry with each other. They'd just disagreed. So what? People did that all the time. Why would she care more when the other party was him?

But she did care and that bugged her even more.

She walked into the house through the back door and heard the sound of voices and laughter. Raoul was there with his friends.

In her present mood she wasn't excited about a house full of teenagers, but she'd given him permission. It wasn't like any of them were doing anything wrong.

She debated a glass of wine to help her relax, but it was too early and she didn't want to drink in front of the teenagers. So she settled on chocolate, always a good soother. She poured M&Ms into a bowl and grabbed a diet soda. After all, balance was important.

The mail was on the kitchen table. She sat down with her snack and flipped through the mail, stopping to look at the cover of a magazine showing a very pregnant celebrity looking happy and radiant.

Nicole ignored the flashy headline and stared at the picture. Her mood took a turn for the sad. Was everyone on the planet pregnant but her? Was everyone in a real relationship and happy and starting a family?

Okay, Jesse probably wasn't happy or in a relationship, but she was going to have a baby and wasn't that a miracle?

Nicole touched the glossy photo and felt a deep, powerful longing inside. Nothing had turned out the way it was supposed to. Where had she gone so wrong with everything? What had she—

"Um, Nicole?"

She looked up and saw one of Raoul's friends, this one a girl, standing in the kitchen. "Hi," she said, trying to remember the kid's name.

The girl, pretty, blond and a cheerleader, smiled. "Finola. Everyone calls me Finn."

"Right. Finn. How can I help you?"

Finn had several papers in her hand. She crossed to the table and sat down. "I'm working on my college entrance essays. I wondered if maybe you could read them over and tell me what you think.

My counselor said I shouldn't use the same exact essay for every college. That I should try to match their personality, like I know what that means."

She grinned and Nicole found herself smiling back. "I don't know, either, if that's what you were hoping for."

Finn laughed. "It would be nice, but I thought maybe you could just read them and give me some suggestions on how to make them better."

Nicole was flattered, but surprised. "I'm not an expert."

"I know, but you're so together and cool and stuff. Not like my mom. She doesn't get things anymore."

Nicole felt a flash of sympathy for Finn's mother who probably tried to connect with her daughter, only to be dismissed.

"I'd be happy to." She pushed the bowl of M&Ms toward Finn. "Help yourself."

"Thanks."

Over the next hour, Nicole and Finn talked about her essays. They were variations on a theme— talking about the summer her little brother had died in a swimming accident and how that had changed her family in general and her specifically.

"I haven't done much," Nicole said when they were finished. "You did a great job with these."

Finn beamed. "Yeah? I hope so. I've been working on them a lot. I want to go to Stanford as a biochemistry major, then become a doctor."

Nicole eyed the cheerleader uniform and knew she'd been guilty of judging the teen for the wrong things. "Good luck with that. And for what it's worth, your mom probably understands a whole lot more than you give her credit for. You should try to talk to her more."

"Really?"

"Uh-huh. Give it a try."

Finn looked doubtful, but she murmured, "Okay," as she left the kitchen.

Nicole returned to her magazine and M&Ms, only to have Claire walk into the kitchen a few minutes later. Her sister stared at her.

"You have teenagers in your house," she said, sounding beyond surprised.

"I know."

"A lot of them."

"I'm a hangout. They're Raoul's friends. They seem to be fine. No one's doing drugs in the basement and they clean up after themselves."

Claire shook her head. "You have teenagers in your house."

"You said that already."

"This is very strange."

Nicole pulled out a chair. "Want anything? Water? Juice?"

"A latte with an extra shot," Claire said, then shook her head. "Sorry. Momentary caffeine urge. It'll pass." She sat down and grabbed some M&Ms. "What's going on here?"

"I told you about Raoul. How I've taken him in."

"I heard the words but I didn't actually understand them. He lives here."

"In the guest room."

"You barely know him."

"I know enough."

"How long is he staying?"

"I have no idea. Possibly through June."

Claire's eyes widened. "And you're okay with that?"

"I like having him around. He's a good kid and he deserves a break. Drew came back and Raoul protected me. Not with your style, of course."

Claire laughed. "Does Drew still have a scar?"

"Oh, yeah."

They smiled at each other.

Claire sorted her candy by colors and ate the green ones first. "Nicole, you know I love you, but you're the least easygoing person I know. You take charge of things, you're not especially patient. So how can you be so laid-back and casual about what's happening with Raoul?"

Nicole considered the question. "I don't know. I just am. Maybe I'm changing."

"Maybe this is easy because it's familiar."

Nicole's good mood retreated. "I'm not talking about Jesse. She's gone and that's a good thing." She spoke firmly, even though she wasn't sure it was a good thing at all.

"Doesn't anything about this strike you as familiar? You're raising yet another teenager."

"Raoul doesn't need raising. He needs a place to stay. That's all I'm providing."

"But there are similarities. You've traded one responsibility for another."

"Maybe." Nicole hadn't thought of it in those terms, but so what?

"You miss her," Claire said softly.

"She's my sister. I'm supposed to miss her." What she didn't say was that nothing was right with Jesse gone.

"So let's go find her and bring her back."

Nicole stood and leaned against the counter. "To what end? She needs to learn her lesson."

"Which lesson is that?"

"The one about taking responsibility. The one that forces her to grow up. She's needed to grow up for a long time. She has to learn to make it on her own."

"And if she doesn't?"

Nicole didn't have an answer for that.

HAWK STALKED through his house, unable to settle down. He felt restless, which was unusual. Normally he was comfortable in his own skin.

He went upstairs where Brittany was doing homework in her room. He paused at the door.

"How long you going to be?" he asked. "I thought we could go do something. Maybe a movie."

She looked at him. "Dad, it's a school night."

"Right." He thought about making an exception on her midweek curfew, but knew that would send the wrong message. "I'll go find something to watch on TV."

"You should call her," his daughter yelled as he walked down the hall.

That stopped him mid-stride. "I don't know what you're talking about."

"Nicole. You should call Nicole."

He walked back to his daughter's room. "Why would you say that?"

She gave him a look of long-suffering. One that said that parents were really, really stupid. "Because you've been crabby ever since you had a fight with her."

How did Brittany know about that? "What fight?"

She rolled her eyes. "The one where you both talked in really tense voices, then she left without saying goodbye." She sighed. "Don't worry. I didn't hear what the fight was about and I don't want to know. It's probably gross grown-up stuff or really boring."

He didn't know what to say to that.

"She's nice," Brittany said. "I like her. You like her. It's okay to have a girlfriend, Dad. It's not like you're going to get married."

"I don't need your permission to date."

"I know, but I'm still giving it."

She was adorable and completely irritating, he thought as he shook his head. "What am I going to do with you?"

"Worship me, like everyone else. Seriously, Dad, you like her."

"I know."

"So, go for it. Apologize."

"How do you know I'm the one who was wrong?"

"Because you're the guy. Just don't, you know, get too serious with her."

"That's not going to happen." He would never replace Serena. He couldn't. She had been the love of his life. Why would he want to fall for someone else?

"So you'll call?" Brittany asked.

"Maybe."

"You should. Nicole's great."

She was, he thought as he walked down the hall again. Thinking about it now, their argument had been pointless. He knew his daughter and trusted her completely. End of story. Nicole didn't understand that, but that was okay.

"Are you calling?" Brittany yelled.

"Get off me, kid."

She laughed and he smiled.

JESSE PULLED INTO the small parking lot to give herself a chance to try to get a grip. She was crying too hard to see the road, which made driving dangerous.

She knew she had no one to blame for her current situation but herself, which didn't make her feel better. She'd blown it totally. Everything she'd loved, everything that was important to her, had been lost.

As she brushed away tears, she told herself to get it together. She had to make a decision about what she was going to do with her life. Or at least how she was going to survive the next few months. She was broke, low on gas and three hundred miles from Seattle in Spokane. Now what?

As if answering the question, someone tapped on her window.

Great. Just what she needed. Interference.

She lowered the window a few inches, but didn't bother looking at the person. "What?" she asked sharply.

"You okay?"

It was a man's voice. He sounded concerned, which was just great for him, but wouldn't do her any good. She needed the chance to go back in time and fix all the problems in her life, which wasn't going to happen.

"I'm fine."

"You don't look fine."

She turned to look at the guy. He was old, like grandpa age, but kind-looking, which made her want to tell him everything. Except the shock of her story might give him a heart attack and she didn't need one more thing to feel guilty about.

"Go away," she told him.

"That's not very polite."

And there came the guilt. She rubbed her eyes. "I didn't mean it that way. Look, thanks for asking, but you don't want to get involved."

"How do you know?"

"Because you're not really interested in my life. No one is—not even me."

"Sounds like the first line of a country song."

Of all the insensitive things to say, she thought, willing to burn off the little gas she had left by driving away. Then part of her realized he was right and she started to laugh, only to have the tears take over again.

"Okay, that's not good," the guy said and opened her car door. "Come on, young lady, let's get you inside. You hungry? The food's not fancy, but I cook a mean burger."

Before she knew what had happened, she'd been led into a dark bar. The man flipped on lights, then pointed to the bar. "Have a seat."

She settled on a stool. He passed her several paper napkins and a glass of water.

"Start at the beginning," he said. "What's wrong?"

"Everything."

"Is that true?"

He was nice, she told herself. She should be nice back. But what she said was, "I'm pregnant. My sister thinks I slept with her husband, but I didn't, only she won't believe me. My boyfriend *is* the father of my baby and he doesn't believe it's his. He said he didn't c-care if it was his." The tears started again.

She blew her nose. "I had a big fight with my sister and with Matt and I left Seattle. I don't have any money or anywhere to go and I don't have a job or a place to stay. Is that enough for you?"

"It's a start," the old man said. "So get a job."

She glared at him. "Doing what? Do I look skilled to you?"

"You must be able to do something. Everyone can do something."

She could bake, Jesse thought grimly. She made perfect cakes and cookies that were so good, people cried when they ate them. But the recipes all belonged to the bakery and using them herself seemed wrong. Not to mention the last time she'd tried, Nicole had thrown her in jail.

"Nothing," she said at last. "I can't do anything."

"How old are you?"

She glared at him. "Excuse me?" Was he coming on to her? That was disgusting. Beyond disgusting. "I'm outta here."

He held up both hands. "Don't get all high and mighty with me, young lady. I wasn't asking for any reason you're thinking. You're young enough to be my granddaughter. Besides, I like my women with a little age on 'em. They have more to talk about and don't take crap. I like women who don't take crap."

He pointed at the sign on the wall. "Bill's Bar."

"This is my place. If you're old enough, I can offer you a job. Something temporary until you get your feet under you."

"I'm twenty-two," Jesse said, not convinced he meant what he said. "I have ID."

"I believe you."

No one believed her. No one had for a long time. "Why would you do this? Why would you offer a total stranger who's a complete mess a job?"

"Trying to talk me out of it?"

"No. I'm just curious."

"One of my girls quit on me last night. I haven't gotten around to running an ad. You'll save me the time and trouble, not to mention the money."

"But you don't know anything about me."

"It's serving drinks. It's not that hard. Besides, you're pretty enough that the customers won't care if you screw up."

She didn't feel pretty. "You know I'm pregnant, right?"

"You mentioned that. Don't worry. No one smokes in the bar."

She wasn't worried about that, although she should be. She meant that she wouldn't be appealing once she started showing. But she didn't say that. A job would give her time to think.

"I'll take the job," she said. "By the way, I'm Jesse."

"Good to meet you, Jesse. I'm Bill."

She smiled. "I got that from the sign. The alliteration is nice."

"Just lucky. You need a place to stay?"

She nodded cautiously.

"You can rent a room over at Addie's place. It's like an old-fashioned boardinghouse. Nothing fancy, but the rent is cheap and she provides two meals a day."

"Are you for real?" Jesse asked. "Is this a joke?" How could this man just show up and offer her everything she needed?

Bill stared at her for a long time. "Somebody hurt you bad, little girl, and I'm sorry for that. This isn't a joke. I'm being neighborly. That's what people do. Help each other out."

"Not in my world."

Bill nodded slowly. "A few years back, I got in some trouble. Someone helped me then. Now I'm helping you."

Was it really that simple? "My luck's not that good," she told him.

"Maybe your luck has changed."

CHAPTER THIRTEEN

"YOU'RE ACTING WEIRD," Nicole told Raoul as she stood in the middle of the family room.

He didn't look up from the textbook on his lap. "How?"

"I don't know. You keep looking at the clock."

As if to prove her point, Raoul glanced at the clock above the fireplace, then shrugged. "I want to know what time it is."

"Every fifteen seconds?"

He looked at her. "It's not that often."

"Close." She knew something was going on, but couldn't figure out what. "I'm going to start dinner," she said.

"I'm not hungry."

She put her hands on her hips. "If you're breathing, you're hungry. What's going on? You might as well tell me now. I'll find out eventually."

His attempt to look innocent failed. "Nothing." He looked at the clock again, then jumped up. "I'm going to study at Marcus's house. His parents are home. The number's on the counter in the kitchen."

"What about dinner?"

"I'll eat there." He bolted past her, heading for the kitchen. "I'll be late," he yelled over his shoulder.

And then he was gone.

"Talk about weird," Nicole muttered, wondering what he was really doing. She doubted it was anything bad, but still. Had she been this strange when she'd been his age?

Someone rang the front bell before she could decide. She crossed the great room and pulled the door open, only to find Hawk standing on her porch.

Instantly her insides sighed in appreciation. Despite their last meeting, which had ended badly, he still looked good. Better than good. He looked deliciously tempting.

"You're home," he said, not sounding surprised.

Suddenly Raoul's odd behavior made sense. "You set me up."

"In a good way," Hawk told her as he entered the house. He held up two big bags that smelled amazing. "Chinese food. You haven't had dinner. We'll eat, we'll talk, we'll be friends again."

"Is that what we are?" she asked.

"Sure." He set down the bags and cupped her face. "Hey. I'm sorry."

Despite her dancing hormones, she wasn't going to be won over by male beauty and an egg roll.

"For?" she asked.

"Maybe overreacting."

"Maybe? You plan to decide soon?"

"I overreacted. You were trying to help. I didn't see it that way." He kissed her with just enough pressure to make her lean toward him. "Did I say I was sorry?"

"Yes."

"Did you accept my apology?"

"I am now, because I'm sorry, too. I can be pushy."

"But cute. So we're good?"

She smiled. "Yes."

They went into the kitchen. While he put boxes of Chinese onto the table, she collected plates, flatware and napkins. He opened the bottle of wine she handed him, then they sat down to eat.

"Your point about Brittany is a good one," he said, which she hadn't expected. "Maybe I did make the past sound better than it was. Serena and I didn't set out to do that on purpose, we just didn't want Brittany to feel she wasn't special or that she'd gotten in the way."

Nicole was impressed he was willing to discuss this and see her side. "Maybe there's some middle ground. A casual story about how it wasn't all easy and wonderful. Unless it was."

He shook his head. "We were too young. We got lucky. I had a lot of offers from universities to play football. I'd already picked Oklahoma before we found out Serena was pregnant. Not only did they have a great coach, but the alumni support was extraordinary."

"Free everything?" she asked, knowing life was different for football gods in a football town.

"Just about. The rules weren't as strict then. We weren't handed money, but we had a lot of perks. There was always someone available to babysit when we needed it, so Serena got to come to all my games. Even the away ones. Different families took us on vacation with them. We had access to great doctors and someone was always dropping by with groceries or cooked food."

"Sounds nice."

"The guys were great, but it was the wives who kept us going. They were real nice to Serena. But it was still hard. We were away from home. Her parents never forgave or understood what we were doing. They turned their backs on their only daughter. She was sad about that until the day she died."

Nicole thought about Jesse. Would her sister say she had turned her back on her? Nicole wasn't sure. She also didn't know how she would describe the situation herself.

"The worst part for her was the loneliness," he continued. "The worst part for me was being so damn scared all the time."

"Scared of what?"

"Getting hurt, mostly. We were on a free ride because I could catch a football better than anyone and then run like the wind. But if I got busted up, it all ended. And then what? I don't think I took a deep breath and relaxed until the day the check for my NFL signing bonus cleared the bank."

In some ways she thought of Hawk as larger than life, but in truth, he was just like everyone else.

"You made it through," she said.

"We did, but I'll admit there were times when Serena and I were fighting that I wished she'd never gotten pregnant. That's what I don't want Brittany to know. About the bad times." He sipped his wine. "But I do see your point about making it all sound easy."

"I'm glad." She leaned toward him. "I wasn't trying to butt in."

"I know."

"I think you're a great dad."

"Thanks." He reached across the table and took her hand. "I'm sorry about what I said about Jesse. That was out of line."

She smiled. "That's okay."

"I guess Brittany is a sensitive topic."

"She's your daughter. You feel a real sense of responsibility toward her. Believe me, I understand that. I grew up the queen of responsibility."

His hand was warm on her forearm. He rubbed her skin.

"Your parents put too much on you. I see that with my guys. If a kid can get a job done, he gets a bigger job. Parents don't realize that it can go too far."

She appreciated the understanding. "Sometimes I didn't mind, but sometimes I hated it. In high school there were so many things I wanted to do but I couldn't, because I had to get up early to help in the bakery. Mornings are busy. So I couldn't stay out late. I wanted to go out for theater, but I had to be home after school to look after Jesse."

She stabbed her chow mein with her fork. "It was awful when my mom left. I missed her so much and I was angry with her, because I knew she wanted to be with my sister more than she wanted to be with us. She wanted to be traveling all around the world and meeting famous people. I think if she hadn't had Jesse, she would have been gone from the beginning."

Nicole glanced at Hawk. "The bakery belonged to my father's family, not hers. I don't think she ever liked the day-to-day responsibility of the place. It was a constant drain of time and energy and it was never going to make her rich. But Claire had potential."

She pressed her lips together. "I'm making her sound awful. I don't mean to."

"You're not. You're telling me what happened. How you were just a kid and you got stuck with too much."

His words were gentle, as was his tone. She found herself wanting to crawl into his arms so he could hold her and make her feel safe.

Wait a minute. Since when did she need a man to feel safe?

"Nicole?"

"What?"

"Where did you just go?"

"It doesn't matter."

"It does. You're looking fierce about something, and I'm guessing it's not going to be good if it's about me."

"It's nothing." She didn't want to go to the bad place. Not tonight. Not when she had Hawk alone in the house. "At least it could be nothing if you distracted me."

Hawk's slow, sexy smile made her quiver from the inside out. "How long will Raoul be gone?"

"He said he'd be back late."

"Good to know."

He stood and pulled her to her feet. Their half-eaten dinner still sat on the table, but she didn't care. Not only did Chinese warm up great, she suddenly wasn't hungry...at least not for food.

He pulled her close, wrapped his arms around her and kissed her. His mouth claimed hers with a heated desire that stole her breath. His hands moved up and down her back, his body warming hers. It was erotic and familiar and exciting.

"I've missed this," he murmured as he kissed her cheek, then her forehead and finally along her jaw. "I've missed touching you and being touched by you."

"Me, too."

He licked the sensitive spot below her ear, then sucked on her earlobe. He trailed kisses down her neck, making her wish her T-shirt plunged much lower.

His mouth was hot and firm. She held on to him as the world began to spin.

"I want you," he breathed in her ear, making her break out in goose bumps. "In a bed, this time."

"Conventional," she murmured, wanting that, too. "Who knew?"

He chuckled.

She took his hand in hers and led the way upstairs. Once they were in her bedroom, he stood in front of her, his hands pushing her hair off her face. He stared into her eyes for a long time, as if trying to see past the emotional barriers she always kept in place.

"You're so beautiful," he whispered.

Nicole knew that on her best day, she was pretty. While she was sure Hawk meant what he said, she had a feeling it was the sex talking. Still, it was nice to hear. So nice she suddenly felt vulnerable in a way she hadn't expected or experienced before. She wanted to look away, to hide…what? Not her body. She was more than willing to expose that. Then what? Her heart? Was her heart in danger?

She didn't want to think about that so she closed the distance between them, put her hands on his shoulders and raised herself on tiptoe to kiss him.

She pressed her mouth to his, then touched her tongue to his lower lip.

"Trying to have your way with me?" he asked, his voice teasing.

"Uh-huh. It's part of my sex-kitten duties."

"To seduce me?"

"Yes. I don't think it would be hard. What do you think?"

"That I only look easy."

There was the light of challenge in his eyes. Nicole studied him. Was he serious? Did he really think he could resist her?

She smiled. "You are so going to melt."

"Want to bet?"

"Absolutely. Winner takes all."

"I have incredible powers of concentration. I won't even know you're in the room with me."

She chuckled. "You have an erection and burning desire to make love with me. You're going to know everything I do and it's going to kill you."

He swallowed but didn't back down.

Nicole considered her possibilities. How best to seduce Hawk? He was going to be expecting a straight-on, aggressively frontal attack. That's what he would do. But she had a feeling that there were better ways to get what she wanted.

She tugged at the sleeve of his T-shirt. "You're going to have to help me with this. I'm too short to pull it over your head myself."

"Sure."

He tugged off the shirt and tossed it over a chair, then crossed his arms over his bare chest.

She moved behind him and lightly touched his back. "I keep thinking about the last time we were together," she whispered. "That was pretty incredible."

"Agreed."

She pressed her mouth to his spine and licked him. He tensed slightly, then relaxed.

"You have great hands," she continued. "Probably why you were so good at football. You know what to do with them. Where to touch me, how to touch me."

"Ah, okay."

She smiled. He sounded a little uneasy. Good. She was getting to him.

She pulled off her own T-shirt and removed her bra. Still standing behind him, she pressed herself against him, her breasts nestling against his bare back. His hands dropped to his sides.

She took advantage of that by placing her hands on his belly, just above the waistband of his shorts. She didn't move them, she just kept them there. Possibilities, she thought as heat moved through her own body. It was always about possibilities.

She rubbed her breasts back and forth. Her nipples scraped against his skin, exciting her and she hoped doing something for him.

"I like how you kiss, too," she continued. "Some guys just want to get to the good stuff. They don't bother with things like kissing. But not you. You were willing to take your time."

She moved her hands across his chest. She couldn't see what she was doing so she had to feel her way. Which was fine by her. She liked the play of muscles under skin, the coolness of his chest hair, the way his breathing hitched when she brushed his nipples.

She accompanied her exploration with little nips on his back, careful to let him feel her breath first, so he would know the bite was coming, could think about it seconds before it happened.

She dropped her hands to the waistband of his shorts and found the button. Slowly, slowly, she unfastened it, then pulled down the zipper. Working by touch, she slid her hand between his shorts and his briefs, feeling the hardness of his arousal. Instead of taking him in her hand, which he probably expected, she lightly ran her nails across his hardness, then rubbed her thumb over the tip.

He shuddered, pulled away, spun toward her and grabbed her. Fire darkened his eyes.

"You win," he growled before he kissed her. "You win."

It was the best kind of victory, she thought as his tongue plunged into her mouth. She wrapped her arms around his neck and kissed him back, savoring the teasing, stroking, claiming kiss that burned her to her toes.

He touched her everywhere, his hands moving over her back, her sides, her rear, then up to her breasts where he cupped the curves and teased her nipples.

Seducing him had already gotten her more than halfway along the path, she thought as liquid heat poured into her center. She felt swollen and ready before he'd done much of anything, which meant she was delighted when he undid her jeans and shoved them down her hips.

Her panties quickly followed. Then she was naked and he was nudging her toward the bed.

They fell together in a tangle of arms and legs. Somehow she ended up on top, looking down at him.

"Nice view," he said with a grin and put his hands on her hips. "Now just a little higher."

He was trying to move her forward, which she didn't understand until he slid down on the bed so that he was under her. At the first stroke of his tongue, she nearly fainted.

He couldn't do that with her on top of him, she thought frantically, even as waves of pleasure shot through her. She was too exposed, too vulnerable.

The second stroke of his tongue had her trying to figure out a way to keep that going while shifting position. The third had her looking for something to brace herself on so she could enjoy the ride.

She'd never done it like that, so she didn't know what to expect. Didn't know that the sensations would be more intense. He could move easily, touch her anywhere, use his fingers to rub her inner thighs or slip a finger inside.

In a matter of seconds, she was gasping. She put her hands on the wall, to hold herself in place. He flicked his tongue over her center, then sucked on that one spot. At the same time, he inserted two fingers into her, plunging and rubbing and matching the movements of his mouth.

She couldn't catch her breath. She couldn't do anything but go along for the ride and hope he never, ever stopped. Her hips were pulsing, her whole body tense. There was a rawness to the sex that almost frightened her, but in a good way. As if she could really be herself with this man.

He moved his lips against her, faster and faster. She moved with him, straining for her release. He moved in and out of her, drawing her orgasm from her.

"Come for me, baby."

The unexpected words shocked her and then she was doing as he'd asked, arching her back as the spasms rippled through her, taking her over. Perfect pleasure, again and again, riding him to the end when she was finally still.

She tried to shift off of him, but he grabbed her hips, then eased her down his body.

"Not so fast," he told her, looking very pleased with himself.

When she straddled his waist, he pulled a condom out of his shorts pocket, then pushed off the rest of his clothes. She moved aside to let him apply the protection, then got back on top.

He was hard and thick and ready, which felt exactly right to her quivering insides. She tensed in anticipation of how he was going to feel as he filled her, then she was easing down on him, stretching as he went deeper and deeper. They both groaned.

She leaned forward and put her hands on the mattress. He reached up and cupped her breasts. Her long hair tumbled down on his shoulders and chest.

"This is a really good fantasy," he told her as he rubbed her tight, sensitive nipples.

"For me, too."

"You did a hell of a job seducing me."

"You were easy."

"Part of my charm."

She clenched her muscles, tightening around him. His eyes closed as he groaned. A sense of power swept through her. "You are charming," she murmured and started to move.

"I'M NOT EATING NAKED," Nicole said nearly thirty minutes later.

Hawk set the Chinese food on the nightstand. "A little kung pao on your stomach?"

She was gorgeous. Curvy and flushed, and still very naked. Just looking at her made him want to be inside her again.

"Try it," he told her, opening one of the cartons and picking up one of the forks he'd brought upstairs. "One bite."

"You're insane," she said, but she still stretched out on the bed. "If you tell anyone about this, I'll deny it with my last breath."

"I'm not going to be telling anyone." Why would he want to share something this good?

He scooped up a piece of kung pao and placed it on her stomach, but instead of taking it, he leaned over and kissed her.

"Appetizer," he said.

"Yummy."

"It gets better."

He bent down and took the piece of chicken in his mouth. After biting it in half, he gave her part, chewed his, then licked her belly clean.

She raised herself on one elbow. "It's not an efficient way of eating."

"Agreed."

"It wasn't horrible."

He laughed. "Is that your way of saying you liked it?"

"Maybe. Let's try it again."

Nearly an hour later, he was dressed and walking out the front door. They'd never gotten to finish dinner beyond those couple of bites in her room. Not that he was complaining. What they'd done instead was much more interesting.

He whistled softly as he closed the door behind him, then came to a stop as he saw Raoul walking up the front steps.

Hawk nodded at the younger man, telling

himself there was no reason to feel guilty. Raoul had helped him set up the evening with Nicole. Still, he felt… uncomfortable and couldn't say why.

"You're here late," Raoul said, his expression unreadable in the darkness of the night.

"I am."

The teenager was in his way. Hawk wasn't about to move forward until the kid moved aside and Raoul didn't seem to be in a hurry to do that.

They stared at each other.

"She's special," Raoul said, jerking his head toward the house.

"I know. I'm the one going out with her."

"She doesn't deserve to get hurt."

Hawk couldn't believe it. Raoul was *his* player. Hawk had always supported him, been there for him. Now Raoul was going to choose Nicole over him?

"You're out of line," Hawk told him. "This isn't your business."

"You're wrong. Nicole thinks she's plenty tough, but we both know that's not true. You don't do serious relationships. Nicole is the relationship type."

Hawk wanted to rewind the last few minutes and get a do-over. Or be the hell out of the house before Raoul came home. This was not happening.

For one thing, he'd done nothing wrong. Where did Raoul get off judging him? Second, how did the kid know so much about Nicole?

An ugly, dark emotion blossomed inside of him. One that had Hawk curling his fingers into fists. He forced himself to relax as soon as he realized what he was doing, but the totally unreasonable suspicion wouldn't go away.

Why did Raoul care so much? Was there something going on?

Even as he asked the questions, he knew he was being unfair to both Raoul and Nicole. She wasn't interested in a teenager and Raoul was crazy about Brittany. But the jealousy felt primal. He wanted to take on Raoul, to beat the crap out of him, then pound on his own chest and proclaim himself the winner. What the hell was wrong with him?

"Don't assume the worst about me," Hawk said at last. "I'm not playing with Nicole." Not the way Raoul thought. They had a deal, which had been her idea. He was the innocent party here.

"I've seen how the women look at you," Raoul said. "How available they are. What you did before didn't matter, but this does. She does. Think long and hard before you take any of them up on their offers."

"Or what?"

"You don't want to know."

Did the kid really think he could take him? Hawk would have laughed if he hadn't been so damn pissed off. "Where do you get off lecturing to me? What I do in my personal life is my business."

"Nicole is my friend. She's taken care of me

when she didn't have to. I'm not going to let anyone hurt her. Not even you."

Normally Hawk enjoyed a good challenge, but this time there couldn't be any winners. He was angry and frustrated with nowhere to put it.

He swore under his breath, then pushed past the kid, shoving Raoul harder than he needed.

"I don't need this crap," he muttered as he walked to his truck. "Go to hell."

Raoul didn't say anything. He didn't have to. In some way, he'd already won.

CHAPTER FOURTEEN

NICOLE WAS ACTUALLY looking forward to the game Friday night. Both she and Hawk had been busy, so she hadn't had a chance to see him or speak with him in a couple of days. Not that she wasn't still tingling. The man could work some serious miracles on her body and he was welcome to hone his skills anytime he wanted. She was so impressed, she was actually starting to think that if she'd known him a few months ago, when she'd had her surgeries, he could have cut her healing time in half.

She was still smiling at the memory as she walked into the stadium.

"Hey, Nicole," one of the kids called.

Nicole sort of recognized her from the group that hung out at the house. There were a few regulars she knew and some that just stopped by every now and then. Eventually she would know them all. She waved as she made her way up to where most of the parents sat.

"Nicole! How's it going?" Barbara asked.

"We're going to win tonight," Dylan, father of Aaron and Kyle, told her.

"I can feel it, too," she said with a laugh.

There were more greetings. She settled by Missy and Greg, a quiet couple with two boys on the team.

From her bleacher seat, she could see the whole field. She looked around until she saw Hawk, then hoped her smile didn't give away her quivery insides.

Their deal had been for him to get the sex he wanted and her to get a chance to show people she wasn't a pity party of one. But she had a feeling she'd gotten the better part of the arrangement, because the sex certainly worked for her in a big way. Maybe tonight after pizza they could...

She caught sight of Raoul and remembered that inviting Hawk by after hours was no longer an option. Still, they were going to have to figure out something. She didn't want to go weeks between encounters again.

Speaking of encounters, she saw Hawk on the field. When he looked toward the stands, she waved. He didn't wave back. Nicole frowned. She would have sworn he'd seen her, but then he looked right past her. Of course, she was a long way from the field and it would be easy for him to miss her. Not that he'd ever missed her before.

A few minutes later Raoul spotted her. She half expected him to tell Hawk where she was, but he didn't. Which was odd. Then Brittany bounced over to her boyfriend. Raoul said something and she looked up toward the stands. When she caught sight of Nicole, she waved her pom-poms and hurried over to her dad.

Anticipation tightened Nicole's stomach. She tried not to smile, but it was as effective as trying to ignore the sun. She shimmied in her seat and told herself to act cool. Which turned out to be good advice.

Brittany spoke to Hawk, pointed toward the bleachers. Hawk glanced Nicole's way once, then turned his back and walked away.

Nicole felt as if she'd been hit in the stomach. Her chest hurt and it was hard to breathe. Humiliation washed over her. Hawk had just rejected her— totally and publicly.

Heat burned her cheeks. She pretended to look for something in her purse so she could look down and let her hair hide her face.

What had just happened? Why had he done that? Dismissed her that way? Just a couple of days ago, they'd been laughing and making love in her bed. They hadn't seen each other since or even spoken on the phone. So what could have gone wrong?

A thousand possibilities flashed through her brain. He hadn't had as good a time as she'd thought. He'd met someone else. He was tired of pretending. He was repulsed by knowing she'd been stupid enough to marry Drew.

She felt sick and desperately wanted to run away. Unfortunately she was trapped by the crowd and the fact that she always drove kids to the pizza place. If she ducked out now, her absence would be noticed. For some reason, she didn't want Hawk to know he'd hurt her.

So she raised her head and refused to let anyone see that she'd been humiliated and emotionally kicked in the gut. She was so grateful that Missy and Greg weren't big talkers. When the game started, she did her best to pay attention, ignoring how the seconds crawled by.

She hadn't realized how many times Hawk looked her way during his time on the field until he began to ignore her completely. Even though there was no way anyone would notice the difference, she still felt exposed and ashamed. As if she'd done something wrong. Finally the whistle blew and the players lined up to shake hands. Which was usually her cue to go down to the field.

Nicole hesitated. Should she just leave? No, she told herself. She would go down and figure out what had happened. It was the mature thing to do. It would strengthen her character and make her a better person. Then when she got home, she would go upstairs and throw up.

She let the crowd push ahead, then went through the gate and onto the field. Several parents crowded around Hawk, wanting to talk to him about how the game had gone. Nicole had to glance at the scoreboard to figure out if they'd won or not. When life went by in slow motion, it was tough to keep score.

She waited until there was a lull in conversation, then stepped forward.

"Hi," she said, going for a light, easy tone. Until she knew otherwise, she was going to pretend nothing was wrong.

"Hi," Hawk said, not looking at her.

She waited, but he didn't say anything. Then, just when she was going to ask him what was wrong with him, Annie, one of the slutty mothers, strolled up and put both hands on Hawk's chest.

"So I should just wait for you in the parking lot?" she asked, the lights from the field glinting off her impressive diamond wedding set.

"That's right. I'll send the kids to you."

She smiled into his eyes. "Thanks for asking me to stay tonight, Hawk. I'm really looking forward…to everything."

"Me, too."

It was as if he'd slapped her, then reached into her chest and pulled out her heart. This could not be happening. Okay, sure, she and Hawk weren't actually dating, dating. Not in the traditional sense, but they had a deal and they were having sex and she would never in a million years have believed he was the kind of man to not only go back on his word but also be deliberately cruel.

That's what got her the most. He was doing this on purpose, as if wanting to exact the most amount of pain. And damn him, it was working.

She turned and hurried off the field. She fought the tears in her eyes, refusing to give in and show weakness until she was by herself. Her to-do list was getting longer. As soon as she got home, she was going to throw up, cry and, oh, yeah, walk the dog.

She'd nearly made it to her car when she felt someone touch her arm. She looked up and saw Raoul standing next to her.

"I'm sorry," he said, his voice low, his expression tight with guilt and pain. "This is my fault."

"What are you talking about?"

"Coach. The way he's acting. It's my fault."

Nicole ignored the fresh wave of embarrassment as she realized there had been witnesses to Hawk's rejection. "Raoul, you have nothing to do with what's going on."

"That's not true. I saw him, the other night. When he was leaving."

And the hits just kept on coming, Nicole thought, wondering if she was going to have a permanent blush.

"I, ah, told him he shouldn't hurt you." Raoul traced a pattern on the parking lot with his spikes. "That you were someone special and that he didn't get to play any games."

He'd defended her? Raoul had stood up to his coach to defend *her?*

Now the need to cry was even stronger, but the reason was totally different.

She hugged him. "I'm twenty-eight years old. I've been married. I can take care of myself."

"I didn't want him to hurt you."

"I know. Thank you for that."

"I'm sorry Coach is being an ass."

Nicole stepped away. Everything was clear now, including how she was going to handle the situation. "Me, too. Thanks for telling me this, Raoul. And for what you did. It was sweet, but unnecessary."

He shrugged, looking both uncomfortable and proud.

She pointed to the entrance to the locker room. "Go shower and get changed. I'm going to have a little conversation with Hawk."

"Yes, ma'am."

He jogged off.

Filled with purpose and energy, Nicole marched back toward the stadium.

Knowing what had happened was both better and worse, she thought, letting her anger build up so it would peak right when she needed it. While she now knew why Hawk was acting the way he was, it made her like him a whole lot less.

She stepped onto the field. Most of the parents and players were gone, including Annie. She marched right up to Hawk, stuck her index finger in his chest and said, "We have to talk."

"This isn't a good time for me."

"You think I give a shit?"

Hawk narrowed his gaze. "What's your problem?"

"Apparently you are. You're acting like a two-year-old, pouting because something didn't go your way. I couldn't figure out what was wrong because the last time I saw you, I had a great time. But rather than discuss anything with me, or pretend to be an adult, you sulked and tried to make me feel bad with that surgically enhanced bimbo."

"Annie is a very nice woman."

"I can only imagine." She poked him again. "Raoul was looking out for me. It was totally unnecessary of him, but still really sweet and kind and as this is the guy dating your seventeen-year-old daughter, you should be doing cartwheels. If he's willing to face you down to look out for me, imagine what he would do for the girl he loves. He's a hell of a guy and there's a tiny chance you're part of the reason. But do you see that? No. You're far more upset about the fact that he stood up to you so your overinflated male ego is all bruised and broken. Poor Hawk. Your star player is more interested in acting like a man than kissing your ass. You should be proud of him instead of pouting."

Hawk's gaze turned icy. "Are you done?"

"Just about. I thought you were different. I thought you were special. You walked away from a dream career to take care of your daughter. You work with these kids, not because you need the money, but because you want to help. At least that's what you tell people. But the truth is, all of this is about you. About how you look and how much the world worships you. As soon as things don't go your way, you're not interested in the game anymore. You don't want to play and you sure don't want to play fair. I thought you were someone I wanted to know, but if this is who you really are, I don't even want to pretend to date you. Go to hell, Hawk."

She turned and walked away.

She thought he might have a scathing comeback but there was only silence. She was so mad, she was shaking. She also felt sick inside, like she'd just lost something important.

It wasn't supposed to be like this, she told herself as she climbed into her car. It wasn't supposed to hurt. But it did. All of it. It hurt really bad.

THE LAST THING Hawk wanted to do was hang out with his players, but there weren't a lot of options. He drove to the pizza place and walked inside, only to be greeted by the crowd.

He faked his way through a few short conversations, then glanced at his watch and wondered how long until he could duck out. An hour? Maybe two. Until then, he was stuck.

"Hi, Hawk."

The low, sultry voice made his skin crawl. Annie. She was here because he'd invited her. Because he was an idiot, and now he was stuck with her.

"I've saved us a table," she said, pointing to a small booth in the corner. One that would seat two. She'd already told him her husband was out of town and that the house was empty and a very lonely place.

He knew better than to encourage women like her. He wasn't interested and he sure as hell wasn't going to spend time with a married woman. He'd reacted. Nicole had been right—he'd been pouting.

The reality of how he'd acted crashed in on him. He felt humiliated and stupid and in desperate need of a do-over. But life was like football…the clock only counted down. He couldn't take back the plays he'd made, he could only deal with the consequences.

He looked Annie square in the eye. "I had a fight with my girlfriend. I was using you to make her feel bad. I acted totally inappropriately. I'm sorry."

Annie blinked at him. "You're kidding."

"No. I'm telling you the truth. Hey, if you were in my position, aren't you the one you'd pick?"

It was one part shameless flattery and two parts truth. He hoped it was the right combination.

Annie flipped her long, dark hair over her shoulder and then smoothed the front of her tight sweater. "Okay, yeah. I'd pick me, too." She sighed. "You're really seeing someone?"

"Her name is Nicole. You can ask Brittany."

Annie sighed. "Oh, well. I had a feeling it was too good to be true. I'll let you off this time, Hawk, but don't make that mistake again, or I'll expect you to make good on your promises."

"You have my word."

She sauntered away.

Hawk glanced around the pizza place until he spotted Raoul, then walked over to speak with him.

"I owe you," he told the kid. "You were looking out for Nicole and I respect that. Keep doing the right thing, no matter what anyone else says."

Raoul looked him in the eye. "Even you, Coach?"

"Even me."

They shook hands. Hawk knew Nicole had been right. He was grateful Raoul was dating his daughter. He knew Raoul would take care of her. Which meant he'd mended all his bridges except one.

He glanced at his watch. He was stuck here for the next couple of hours. Or was he?

He turned back to Raoul. "Can you handle things here for a little while?"

"Sure, Coach."

"I'll be back."

He hurried to his truck and started the engine. The need to talk to Nicole pushed everything else from his brain.

He drove fast enough to get a ticket, but got lucky and wasn't caught. Less than twenty minutes later he was pounding on her door.

"Nicole, come on. It's me. Open up. I know you're in there."

Finally he heard footsteps. "Go away," she yelled through the door.

"Nicole, I know you don't want to see me, but this is important."

She didn't say anything.

He pounded on the door again. "I was wrong, okay? I was a jerk. I've known Raoul for years now and he's known you for a couple of months and he stood up to me because of you. I wasn't expecting that. I didn't realize he'd become a man. He challenged me. He was willing to take me on. It's not supposed to be like that."

The front door opened. Nicole stood in front of him, her face streaked with tears. "Sure it is. The alpha male of the pack always has to fight for his spot. It's the circle of life."

She looked both beautiful and miserable and he regretted that he'd made her cry. "Do you wish he'd kicked my ass?"

"Yes." She sniffed. "Big-time."

"I'm sorry," he said and pulled her close. "I'm so sorry. I suck at this relationship thing. The last time I had to get to know a girl, I was fifteen. It was easier not to screw up."

He hugged her and kissed her. "Nicole, I'm really sorry."

She swallowed, then nodded. "I know you were just reacting. Besides, this isn't a real relationship. We have a deal, remember?"

He stared into her blue eyes. A deal? Sure, that's how things had started, but now?

"I'm not in it for the deal," he said. "I'm in it for you."

She sniffed. "Yeah?"

"Yeah, and I have fifty kids waiting for me at the pizza place."

"Oh, sure. Say something like that and take off. Typical guy." But she didn't sound mad anymore.

"Come with me?"

She stepped back. "I can't. I look terrible."

"You look fine. Streaky, but women know how to fix that sort of thing with a little, I don't know, powder or something."

She smiled. "Okay. Give me five minutes."

"I'll wait."

She turned away.

He grabbed her arm and pulled her against him, then kissed her again. "I'm sorry," he murmured, his mouth against hers.

"I got that."

She looked into his eyes and smiled.

It was a soft I-forgive-you smile that made his breath hitch and the world go silent. Because in that moment, there was nothing he wanted more.

NICOLE BENT OVER the textbook. "I don't like any math problem that starts with two cars traveling toward each other. Why does it have to be cars?"

"Sometimes it's trains," Raoul said.

She rolled her eyes. "That doesn't make it better. Okay, two cars driving toward each other. Car A is going thirty miles per hour. Car B is going forty miles per hour. They begin a mile apart. Where on the one-mile track will they meet and what is the time, assuming it is now 2:00 p.m.?"

Nicole looked at him. "Is this a joke?"

"No."

"I was afraid of that."

She picked up the book and flipped back a couple of chapters, hoping to get a hint of how to work the problem. She kept turning back the pages until she reached the front cover.

"Do you want my book from last year?" he asked, grinning at her. "Or my books from middle school?"

"Do you want my help?"

"Maybe not."

She handed him his textbook. "This is not my thing. I'm sorry, but I was a business major in college. We had a special calculus class. Dummy calculus, according to our instructor. We were mocked by the real calculus students, but I learned to live with that." She stared at the problem again.

"You're going to have to convert the miles to feet. And I guess convert the miles per hour to feet per minute. Then write an equation with maybe distance as a function of time for each car. Which gives you time in common. You can solve for time. Does that sound right?"

He picked up his pencil. "I'll let you know."

"If it's not, I've exhausted all my higher math knowledge. Seriously, after this, we'll have to discuss the revolutionary war."

Raoul sighed. "I'd rather work on math than history."

"Typical guy. What do you want to study in college?"

"You mean aside from football?"

"Uh-huh."

"I don't know. I'd like to work in business. Advertising."

"Excuses to have expensive lunches with clients?"

He grinned. "I'd be good at that."

"Especially if the clients were women."

He laughed. The humor faded. "First I have to get into college."

"Is there any doubt?" She pointed at the textbook on the kitchen table. "This isn't dummy math, Raoul. You're taking hard classes and getting good grades."

"I guess I meant I have to get my ride lined up."

"Ah, the football scholarship."

"That's the only way I'll make it to a good school."

Because there wasn't any money. Of course there were grants and loans but she understood why Raoul would want a scholarship if one were available.

She wanted to say she'd seen him play and he was brilliant. That of course he'd get a football scholarship, but what did she know?

"What does Coach say?"

"That I've got a shot. That I should listen to everything they say and then he'll help me make the right choice if I want."

"The colleges come to you?"

"Recruiters. They're contacting me."

"You meet with them?"

"They want to take me to dinner or to a Seahawks game. That kind of stuff."

Gee, all she'd gotten from the University of Washington was an application and later a letter of acceptance.

"So do they give you gifts?" she asked eagerly.

"They're not supposed to."

"If they offer chocolate, say yes."

He laughed. "They don't offer chocolate. It's football."

"So you're more likely to, say, get half a cow."

"Right."

"I don't have the freezer space for that."

"They want to take me to nice places and tell me how great their school is, talk about the program, the perks, that sort of thing."

"Sounds like fun."

He picked up his pencil, then put it down. "I guess. I'm kind of nervous."

"Don't be. You're the talent, Raoul. You're what they're looking for. You are their reason for living."

He didn't smile. Instead he ducked his head and said, "There's a guy coming in next week. He wants to take me to dinner. Would you come with me? To the dinner?" He glanced at her, then looked away. "I don't know what I'm supposed to be asking, so I thought you could help with that."

Nicole was stunned and flattered. "Shouldn't Hawk go with you?"

"He is. But I want you there, too."

Warmth spread through her. She touched his arm. "I would be honored to help in any way I can."

NICOLE PARKED in the garage and pulled out her Nordstrom's bag. She'd had a great afternoon of shopping with Claire. They'd started with brunch at The Cheesecake Factory, then had shopped for a killer dress for the recruiter dinner. Nicole wanted to make Raoul proud and Hawk whimper. While there was now a sizable balance on her credit card, she'd accomplished her mission. Life was good.

She carried her bag inside and found Raoul standing by the back door. She'd noticed Brittany's car out front, but didn't see the girl anywhere.

"Hi," she said. "I bought an amazing dress. It's…"

She paused. Raoul looked uneasy, in a trying-to-act-casual sort of way.

"What's going on?" she asked.

"Nothing."

"Where's Brittany?"

"In the bathroom."

She swore under her breath. "Were you two having sex? Raoul, we've talked about this. Not in my house. Hawk will kill both of you. You're too young and this is not something I want to deal with."

She hadn't even thought about leaving them alone. Should she have to? Was it her job to monitor them every second?

He flushed. "We didn't have sex. I swear. She's just in the bathroom. With all her clothes on."

As if on cue, water rushed down the pipes from the upstairs bathroom. The sound of footsteps clattered on the stairs.

Raoul muttered something Nicole didn't quite catch. It almost sounded like a prayer. Then Brittany burst into the kitchen. She looked both happy and terrified and there was something in her hand. Something white and plastic and sort of Popsicle-stick shaped. She held it out in front of her.

"Look," she said, glancing between Raoul and Nicole.

Nicole felt the floor shift. Blood turned solid in her veins, and she couldn't breathe.

"I wasn't sure," Brittany continued. "I'd sort of guessed because I haven't been feeling good. Now we know for sure." She turned to Raoul. "I'm pregnant. We're going to have a baby."

CHAPTER FIFTEEN

NICOLE STOOD in the center of the kitchen, waiting for the shift in the universe to stop and everything to return to the way it was. Her mind raced in four hundred different directions and she wasn't sure speech was possible. Even more astonishing than the news was the way Raoul and Brittany looked at each other with an impossible combination of love and hope and certainty. Hello, they were talking about a baby.

"You're sure?" Nicole asked, then shook her head as she eyed the stick in Brittany's hand. "Never mind. Stupid question. How far along are you?"

"About six weeks. Maybe seven."

Back before Raoul was living here, Nicole thought, sure it must have happened while Raoul was staying in the abandoned building. Who knows how much time they'd spent alone together with no one to disturb them.

Brittany rushed to Raoul and snuggled close. "This is going to be great," she said. "Just like we talked about."

Nicole fought against the need to shake her head. There was no way she'd just heard that. "Great?" she asked, her voice slightly strangled. "Great? On what planet?"

Brittany gave her a comforting smile. "We have it all figured out. You don't have to be worried. We're good."

"You're pregnant. You're still in high school. Nothing about that falls under the definition of good." Nicole sucked in a breath in an effort to keep from getting shrill.

"We'll be fine. Nicole, I promise, it's okay. Look, my parents did this and everything turned out fine. They were young and in love and they were totally happy. Raoul and I are going to be the same way. You've seen him play. He'll get a scholarship to college for sure. We'll get to be together, like a real family."

Family, huh? Maybe they could move into Cinderella's castle, next door to the talking mushrooms but in front of the magic forest. "You can't have thought this through."

"We're getting married," Raoul said, standing tall and putting his arm around his girlfriend.

Nicole tried to ignore her bone-crushing disappointment. Not him, too. He couldn't honestly think this was going to turn out well.

"Brittany's not eighteen."

The teenage girl flicked away that reality with her wrist. "I will be in the spring, but my dad will give me permission. It'll be fine. I'll have the baby next summer, which is perfect. Then I can move to college with Raoul and stay home with our child."

"Supported by?"

"Different people. It happened for Mom and Dad. The boosters, the alumni, they take care of their athletes. Dad talks about it all the time. We'll have a cute little house and I'll learn to cook. I've kind of been starting with you, Nicole. It'll be so much fun."

Nicole grabbed on to her patience with both hands. "Have you had any experience with children or babies? Do you know how much work it's going to be?"

"Oh, sure. It'll be hard at times, but we love each other. Raoul and I only want to be together."

"That's not going to happen. He's going to be practicing every day, and studying. He'll be going to class and traveling to games while you're home with a colicky baby, far from your family and your friends."

"I'll go on the road trips."

"Who will take care of the baby during all this?"

"I don't know. Someone. Or we'll take the baby with us."

"You know they cry, right? Sometimes all night long. Raoul will need to sleep so he can play or go to class, which means it's all up to you."

Brittany glared at her. "You're just trying to be mean and I don't know why. I know it works. My parents made it work. They said it was wonderful and you're trying to ruin all that. I guess you don't know what it's really like to be in love."

The well-timed verbal slap hit the mark. Nicole took a step back. Maybe Brittany was right. It wasn't as if she'd been desperately in love with Drew and before him, the men in her life had been rare as Bigfoot sightings.

Still, she knew in her gut this was a disaster in the making. No one wants to get pregnant at seventeen and give up her future.

"What about you going to college?" she asked, keeping her voice low. "What about your dreams?"

"I'll go back later, after Raoul makes it to the NFL. We'll be rich. Or my dad will pay for it. I'll get my degree. I still want that."

Talk about entitlement, Nicole thought grimly. She turned to Raoul. "Is this what *you* want? Honestly?"

He nodded. "I love Brittany."

Meaning he would stand by her no matter what. Nicole had to respect that, if nothing else.

She told herself that at least there was still time. No decisions had to be made this minute. Maybe one of them would get a minor head injury and rediscover common sense.

Brittany smiled at him, then looked at Nicole. "I know you're having a hard time with this, but please be happy for us. I know it's all going to work out."

"Sure."

"I need to get home." She kissed Raoul and started for the door. On the way she dropped the pregnancy stick in the trash. "Oh. I left the rest of the kit upstairs."

"Don't worry about it."

"Okay. Thanks." She paused, then looked back at Nicole. "My dad doesn't know. Can you please not tell him? I want the news to come from us."

Nicole held up both hands. "I won't say a word."

It wasn't a conversation she was excited about having with Hawk. Not when all she could think to say was, "I told you so."

AFTER DINNER Nicole went up to Raoul's room. The door was open, but she still knocked before entering.

He sat up on his bed, reading Julius Caesar.

"I remember having to get through that," she said, pointing at the slim paperback. "Then they test you on the material because reading it wasn't enough torture."

He smiled. "You want to talk about Brittany being pregnant."

"You're saying I'm not subtle?" She stepped into the room and turned the desk chair toward him, then sat down.

"I'm worried," she said. "This is a huge deal. I want to make sure you understand what you're getting into."

"Brittany is pregnant. I'll take care of my responsibilities."

"Which sounds great, but how? We'll ignore the fact that after Hawk finds out, he's going to kill you."

Raoul shifted on the bed. "Coach won't be happy."

"You think? So assuming you make it out of that conversation alive, then what?"

"I get a scholarship and play football."

If only it were going to be that simple. "What if that goes badly? You blow out a shoulder or a knee? You take a bad hit and you're out for the season, or worse, permanently. Then what?"

"Then I'll get a job and support Brittany and the baby."

"Doing what?" She held up a hand. "Raoul, I know this all seems possible and you can make it work, but it's not the only option. Doing the right thing doesn't mean putting your future in danger. Brittany is convinced everything is going to work out perfectly, but you and I live in the real world. We know things can go wrong. There are countless wonderful couples out there who are emotionally and financially prepared to have children."

"I'm not giving my baby away."

As soon as he spoke, she realized what she'd said. He was a boy who had never had a home. He would never willingly turn his back on any family he had.

"Of course. I'm sorry. I should have realized."

That for him, there were no other options. Raoul wasn't that upset about the baby because to him it meant finally belonging. He wouldn't lose Brittany or the baby, or so he thought.

"I'm sure everything will work out," she said.

"You're not sure. You think it's a mistake."

She stood. "Maybe, but what I think doesn't matter. You know she's not mature enough to handle this well, right?"

He hesitated, then nodded slowly. "I know, but I am. We're going to be a family."

Which in the end was what mattered.

She left him and went into her room and closed the door. It was only then that she realized yet another woman in her world was pregnant. Claire, Jesse, the dog and now Brittany. It seemed like everyone was having a baby but her.

"JUST BE GRATEFUL my ex-husband was totally inept," Nicole muttered as she finished tying Raoul's tie. "So I learned how to do this sort of thing." She adjusted it, then stepped back so he could look at himself in the mirror. "I'm one of three girls. This was not supposed to be in my life-skill set."

"Thank you." He smoothed the front of his shirt. "Do I look okay? I feel stupid."

"You look good. Very *GQ*."

Hawk had taken him shopping the previous day after school and bought him slacks, a couple of dress shirts and a sport coat. The items would be getting a lot of use during the next few weeks as college recruiters came calling.

Now Raoul looked uneasy in his new clothes. "I don't know," he muttered.

"Hey, listen up. Who's the best?"

"What?"

"This is a pep talk. Who's the best?"

"I am."

He grumbled the words more than spoke them.

She put her hands on her hips. "Excuse me? I want a little enthusiasm or I'm not going."

His eyes widened. "You have to go. I'm not walking into that restaurant all alone. I won't know what to say. Look, Nicole, I'm just some kid. I've never been anywhere or done anything. I'm not like you. You know, sophisticated."

If he hadn't been so sincere, she would have laughed. Her? Sophisticated? Surely he meant her world-traveling, piano-playing sister. Claire had been all over the world. Nicole's claim to fame was a trip to New York several years ago. They'd seen *The Lion King* on Broadway, which was just so sophisticated.

"You're going to do fine because you're the one being courted. The colleges all want you to lead their winning teams. You're going to have your pick. They know it and you need to know it. Let him do all the talking. If the conversation stalls, Hawk or I will pick up the slack. You're the talent. For the night, just pretend you're Lance Armstrong."

"He's a cyclist."

"Then insert the name of your favorite pro football player into the sentence. You're the man. Now let's get going. There's going to be traffic. You can spend the drive telling me how pretty I look. I'll find it relaxing and you'll be distracted."

Raoul laughed, which was good. Things had been a little strained between them for the past couple of days. Ever since she'd found out that Brittany was pregnant. As she hadn't heard a giant primal scream coming from the west, she assumed Hawk didn't know yet. She wasn't looking forward to *that* conversation.

BUCHANAN'S was an elegant steak house near the downtown shopping district. The food was excellent, the portions generous and they were practically revered for their wine list. Not that Nicole was going to get much wine that night. Not only did she have to worry about driving home, but the whole point was to pay attention so Raoul found out as much as possible so he could make a smart decision when it came to his college selection.

She used the valet to park her car, then walked into the restaurant with Raoul. Hawk was already by the reception desk, talking to a middle-aged man in a great suit.

Nicole hadn't expected to feel anything but the normal tingles when she saw him, so she was left practically gasping when a wave of emotion swept through her. This wasn't about sex, although she wouldn't say no to that, but the feelings were so much bigger.

What was wrong with her? Did she have a fever? Had she eaten one too many cupcakes at work? Did she need to start exercising? Well, maybe not that. But what?

Before she could decide, Hawk looked up and saw her. He smiled, a big, wide smile that made her thighs start to tremble.

"Here they are. Walt, this is the star player I was telling you about."

Hawk introduced everyone, using the title of "friend of the family" to describe her. They all shook hands and were quickly shown to a quiet booth on the side of the restaurant.

Walt launched into a speech about the college. "We take our football very seriously," he said, smiling at Raoul. "You're a talented quarterback and that's the position we're most focused on this year. Our college is in a small town where everyone supports our team. You won't be able to walk around at the local Dairy Queen without someone wanting to tell you what a good job you're doing. You ever lived in a small town, Raoul?"

"I've been in Seattle all my life."

Walt leaned toward him. "There's nothing like it. We all look out for each other. It's like one big family. Personal relationships matter and you can't get that in a big city. Let me tell you a little bit about our football program."

By the time dinner was over, Nicole found herself wanting to move more than halfway across the country to live in the beautiful campus housing. Walt made it all sound perfect.

His presentation was impressive. In addition to the usual brochures, he had a mini movie he played on a DVD player. He bought everyone the most expensive steak on the menu, kept them laughing with funny jokes and charmed with just enough sincerity to keep Nicole from getting suspicious.

She tuned out the talk on team building. The number of backs or halfbacks or whatever-backs wasn't her thing. What she did get was that this could be a very difficult decision.

When dinner was finished, Walt shook hands with them all and returned to the hotel. Hawk patted Raoul on the shoulder. "We'll talk about this more tomorrow. Why don't you wait in the restaurant so I can say good-night to my girl."

Raoul smiled and stepped back inside.

"You two seemed to have made up," Nicole said, figuring that was a safer topic than addressing the "my girl" part of the statement.

"We have an understanding," Hawk told her, pulling her close to the building, then kissing her.

"Does this mean my curfew got extended?"

"Not exactly."

That made her laugh. "He's still willing to take you on, huh?"

"Let's say I'm not pushing it. You're right. He's a good kid. I respect that."

Nicole was suddenly fighting against a crushing

tide of guilt. Brittany hadn't told Hawk about the baby. When she did, it would change everything, especially Hawk's relationship with his star player.

Should she tell him now? Give him some kind of warning? Was it her place? Her business?

She was torn. Not only had she promised Raoul and Brittany that she would keep the information quiet, Hawk had made it clear that he was the experienced parent while she was just a pretender. It had pissed her off at the time and it was kind of making her want to keep quiet now.

Was that bad? She was willing to accept immature, but bad was different.

Before she could decide, he said, "Thanks for coming tonight. Having a family member along keeps these things more low-key."

"I'm not exactly a family member."

"You're the closest he has."

Which was really sad. "I care about him. He has to make a tough decision. It's going to change his life forever. Whatever he decides, he shouldn't have to do it alone."

Hawk tucked her hair behind her ears, then touched her cheek. "You're amazing. You took him in, you're looking out for him. How many people would do that?"

She felt embarrassed. "It's not that big a deal. It just sort of happened."

"To you. I meant what I said before."

She had no idea what he was talking about. "When?"

"At your place. I'm done with the deal. I want us to date because we want to date. Not to prove anything. I want to be with you, Nicole."

Her heart pounded so loudly, she wouldn't have been able to hear him if he'd kept talking. Hope and need and happiness bubbled up inside of her.

"I'd like that, too," she said, hoping she didn't sound as eager as she felt.

He smiled, then kissed her. "So we're dating."

"Uh-huh."

"Exclusively."

That made her laugh. "Yes, which means no dates for you with football moms."

"Not a problem. You're the one that I want."

Magic words, she thought with a sigh. Amazing words.

He kissed her again, his mouth pressing against hers as he claimed her with his tongue. She yielded to him, wanting more, needing him as much as she needed to breathe. Then a car drove by and she was aware of where they were and how late it was.

She pulled back. "I need to get Raoul home."

"Brittany's waiting for me. But I'll see you soon."

It sounded a whole lot more like a statement than a question, which she liked.

He stuck his head in the restaurant and motioned

for Raoul. Together they walked to the valet, who quickly collected their cars. Hawk held her door open.

"I'll give you a call tomorrow."

"I'd like that."

She drove home, doing her best not to spontaneously giggle with delight.

NICOLE DUMPED the spaghetti into the serving bowl and Raoul carried it over to the table.

"How many more recruiting dinners do you have lined up?" she asked as she opened the refrigerator and pulled out the salad.

"Three, including UCLA and Ohio."

"Good schools. I don't know how you're going to decide."

It was like teenage-boy heaven. All these colleges wanting to sign him. They had great organizations, offered an outstanding education and as many perks as the rules would allow. How was he supposed to figure out which one was the best?

"I'm making a chart," Raoul told her as he poured himself a giant glass of milk. "Coach said that was a good place to start. Make a list of all the things that are important to me and rank the school that way. Like they do with cars in *Car and Driver.*"

"My favorite magazine," she teased.

"I'll show it to you."

"Promises like that shouldn't be made lightly."

He grinned. "I want to be at a school where they're going to play me. Time on the field is everything."

Because it was hard to impress anyone from the bench. "Got that. But you also need a team with depth."

He raised his eyebrows.

"I've been doing some reading," she admitted. "I can see we're going to be on this topic for a while, so I want to be informed."

"Impressive."

"I know."

"Brittany's making a chart, too. What she likes about the schools and doesn't like."

Nicole's good mood popped like a punctured balloon. Brittany's input shouldn't matter, but there was no point in saying that. Raoul wouldn't listen.

"When are you going to tell Hawk?" she asked. "He needs to know. I was okay keeping your secret before, but it's starting to bother me."

The need for him to know had gotten worse after he'd talked to her about dating for real. Now she felt as if she were keeping secrets from someone she was supposed to be loyal to.

"Soon."

"According to Brittany, this is all total happiness, so why wait?"

Raoul looked at her. "I know you don't agree with what we're doing, but our minds are made up. Brittany and I are going to have a baby. That means we'll be together."

"I know. You keep telling me."

"But you're mad."

"I'm not mad. I'm disappointed. Raoul, you're both so young. I know it seems like everything is going to be fine, but what if it isn't? You don't have a backup plan."

"I love her, Nicole. Love doesn't come with backup plans or guarantees. You have to take it on faith. I want to be with her. I want to see her smile every day. I want to hear her voice and have her tell me what I've done to make her happy. I want to go to sleep, feeling her heart beating against mine. I want her to be the mother of my children. I want to experience everything in life, with her, because being with her is the best part of my day."

It was an amazing speech, Nicole thought, stunned both by the words and the emotion behind them. At that moment Raoul wasn't a teenager or some kid who needed a place to stay. He was a man in love with a woman.

"Okay," she said quietly. "I get it. I'll stop pushing."

Probably because what he'd said had made her realize something about herself. She, too, was in love with someone amazing. A caring, sexy man who made her heart beat faster every time he was around. A smart, funny guy who made her want to believe in possibilities and hope and love. A man who might still be in love with his late wife, whose daughter was pregnant and from whom she'd been keeping a really big secret.

Lucky, lucky her.

CHAPTER SIXTEEN

HAWK SCROLLED through the Web site. He wanted to plan a weekend away with Nicole after football season ended.

Somewhere nice, he thought, checking out different hotels. But he didn't want to spend the whole time driving. He had other things on his mind. Maybe Portland. It was only three hours away and there were plenty of good restaurants. Or they could head down to the Oregon wine country and do some tasting.

In the other direction, there was Bellingham, close to the Canadian border. He'd heard one of the teachers talking about a small hotel with a spa. Now he wasn't into the whole mud wrap, massage thing, but Nicole might be and he wanted to make her happy.

San Francisco was only a couple of hours away by plane. Still, there was wait time at the airport, time he could spend with Nicole in bed.

"Daddy, can I talk to you?"

"Hmmm? Sure." Hawk motioned his daughter

into his study but didn't turn his attention away from the computer.

Should he ask Nicole first or surprise her? He wanted the trip to be a surprise, but women didn't always take that sort of thing really well. She might need to make special arrangements. Raoul could take care of himself and the dog, but what about Nicole's business? Yeah, he would have to tell her.

What if he could find a place with a private hot tub? Now that was some quality time he could get behind.

"Daddy, are you listening?"

"What? Sure, honey. Go on."

He forced his attention away from the computer and looked at his daughter. Brittany stood in the doorway to his office.

"Like I was saying, I've been thinking a lot about Mom and what you two went through."

What? When? "Uh-huh."

"You had a very special relationship," Brittany continued.

He still had no idea what this was all about. "We both loved you a lot. You know that, right?"

"Sure. I've always felt special, Daddy. Like I'm a part of something really important."

"Good." His attention strayed back to the screen.

"That's why I'm excited about following in your footsteps."

Footsteps? He clicked on a link.

"You know. With the baby and all."

Baby?

Hawk's gaze narrowed down to a single point of light. He heard a rushing sound, followed by the thundering of his heart. It was as if he suddenly weighed ten thousand pounds. He could barely move his head. He managed to turn so he could see his daughter.

"Baby?"

She paused, then licked her lips. "Uh-huh." Her smile trembled at the corners. "Are you excited? I'm excited, Daddy, and Raoul is, too. Now let me explain. We're going to be fine. We have it all worked out. We'll do what you and Mom did. Raoul will get a full scholarship to college and I'll move there, too. It'll be great. I'm excited about being a mom. A little scared, but excited. Raoul's really happy. And he's going to pick a good school. One I'll like, too."

Hawk heard the words, at least he thought he did. But none of them made sense. Was it a language thing? Had she suddenly started speaking Polish or something?

"You're pregnant?" he demanded, slowly rising to his feet, feeling the heat of anger matched only by his sense of betrayal.

She took a step back. "Daddy, don't be mad. It's no big deal."

Nothing made sense. How could this be happening? "No big deal? You said you weren't having sex with Raoul."

She flushed and stared at the floor. "Yes, well, we were. Sort of."

"Sort of? Not if you're pregnant. If you're having a baby, you weren't going halfway. Goddammit all to hell, Brittany, how could you do this?"

She looked at him, her eyes filling with tears. "Daddy, don't yell at me."

"What else am I supposed to do? Congratulate you? You're only seventeen. You're still in high school. You're supposed to be smarter than this. You lied to me—you've been running around behind my back."

"Like you told your parents when you were having sex with Mom?"

He wasn't going there. "This is about you. I can't believe it. Even if you were willing to be that dumb, I can't believe Raoul went along with it."

"Why wouldn't he? We love each other. We're getting married."

"The hell you are. You're seventeen. You're not doing anything but going to your room."

"What? You can't send me to my room."

"Watch me. You're going there right now and you're going to stay there."

She started to cry. "Daddy, no. Why don't you understand? This is what we want."

"You're too young to know what you want and apparently you're too young to have any judgment. I expected better of you, Brittany."

"That's how I feel about you. You're being horrible."

Too little, too late, he thought, knowing he

wasn't feeling it all now, knowing it was going to get worse. Pregnant? This was a disaster. What about her future? What about college? A kid would screw up everything. How had this happened?

He shook his head. He knew all too well how it had happened. He'd been there, done that, bought the T-shirt. Or bag of diapers.

"I'm going to kill him," he muttered.

Brittany grabbed his arm. "Daddy, no. I want to marry Raoul."

"No way. Just so we're clear. You are going to your room and you're going to stay there. You are not to see Raoul or talk to him or text with him. You'll have no contact. The only time you'll leave this house is when I drive you to and from school. You won't see your friends, nothing."

She glared at him. "Locking me up isn't going to make me any less pregnant. I hate you."

"You're not my favorite person right now, either."

"Nicole wasn't anything like this," she yelled as she stomped toward the stairs. "She didn't scream or anything."

Everything went cold and dark. Hawk fought to not put his fist through a wall.

"Nicole knows?"

Brittany ignored him and ran up the stairs. He followed her and caught her just as she entered her bedroom. He grabbed the door before she could slam it.

"Nicole knows?" he asked again.

Brittany stared at him with all the loathing a seventeen-year-old could generate. "Yes, she knows."

"For how long?"

"About a week."

He released the door and his daughter slammed it.

A week? Nicole had known and not said anything? She'd gone to that dinner, had listened to him say he wanted to date her and all the damn time she'd known his daughter was pregnant and hadn't said a word?

THE NIGHT WAS COOL and clear. Nicole sat out on the front steps, staring at the stars in the sky. She was feeling restless and emotionally on edge and knew the cause. Jesse.

She missed her sister. Jesse might lie, steal the family cake recipe and sleep with Nicole's husband, but she was still her sister.

Raoul stepped out onto the porch. "You okay?" he asked. "You've been out here a long time."

She smiled at him. "I'm the grown-up. I'm supposed to worry about you."

"You've been quiet a lot lately."

"I've been thinking about Jesse."

Raoul knew the basics of what had happened. "Still no word?"

"None. She's not going to get in touch with me. Why would she? I made it really clear I wanted her gone."

"But you didn't?"

"I don't know what I wanted. I guess I wanted her to be different." Like that was going to happen.

"You could go after her," he said.

"I've thought about that. I can't decide. Should I let her grow up on her own? Is it better to let her see what life is really about? Then I remember she's my baby sister and she's pregnant and maybe this is all too much." There was a child to think of. Nicole's niece or nephew. There was a connection. She just didn't know where her responsibilities started and stopped or how much more pain her heart could handle.

"Sometimes people have to find their own bottom," he said.

She shook her head. "Don't you dare get all twelve-step on me."

"I won't."

He moved to the other end of the step and sat down. Sheila followed him, her movements slow. At her last checkup the vet had said it was just a matter of days until she had her puppies. Nicole already had plenty of towels and newspaper on hand.

"I won't know if I'm doing the right thing until it's too late. And if letting her go is the wrong decision, how do I fix it?"

"Why is she your responsibility?" he asked.

"Because she always has been. Even when I resented everything about her, I took care of her. I raised her. I wish I'd done a better job."

"You were a kid yourself."

"Still, I'm the reason she is how she is."

"Not necessarily. Maybe she was just born that way."

"That would be nice," Nicole said, resting her forearms on her knees. "Then it wouldn't be my fault."

"It's not now."

"It feels like it is." She looked at him. "Sometimes you're very wise."

"Growing up on the street does that."

"Then be smart about Brittany and the baby."

"Get off me about that."

"I'm not sure I can. I know you love her, but jeez, Raoul. Get a clue."

Sheila lay down, then got up and walked over to Nicole.

"What's the matter, baby?" she asked, stroking the dog's heaving sides. "Is it close to your time?"

Sheila didn't answer. Raoul's eyes widened. "Is she going to have her puppies?"

"I don't know. The vet said—"

A truck screamed around the corner and slammed to a stop in front of her house. Hawk jumped out of the vehicle and stalked toward the house.

She could tell by the way he moved that he was more than angry.

"Get inside," Nicole told Raoul as she scrambled to her feet.

"What?"

"Get inside now. I'll deal with this."

"I'm not afraid of him."

"Then you're an idiot. You have a future that depends on you still being alive. Get in the house."

But it was too late. Hawk took the stairs two at a time, grabbed Raoul by the front of his shirt and pulled him to his feet.

"What the fuck were you thinking, sleeping with my daughter? I'm going to kill you. You got that? When I'm done there will be nothing left. The biggest piece of you won't even fill an envelope."

He vibrated with fury.

Nicole pushed between them, but Hawk wouldn't let go of Raoul's shirt.

"Stop it," she yelled. "Just stop it. Hawk, take a step back, now. I mean it."

Sheila whined and moved closer to Nicole. Hawk ignored them both.

"This is between me and him. Back off, Nicole. You and I will talk about what you did later."

"Let's talk about it now," she said, knowing she needed to distract Hawk before he did something they would all regret. "I knew. That's what you mean, right? I knew Brittany was pregnant and I didn't tell you."

He released Raoul and turned on her. At least she knew she wasn't in any physical danger. She willed Raoul to run, but the kid was too honorable. He just stood there.

Hawk's eyes blazed with fury. "How could you not tell me? She's my daughter. I had the right to know."

"Believe me, I'm not happy about any of this, but I found out she was pregnant and they asked me not to say anything. I agreed to keep quiet until Brittany could tell you herself."

"Where do you get off doing that?"

She understood that he was angry and that none of this seemed fair, but she felt a little temper of her own stirring.

"You're the all-knowing parent," she told him. "You're the one with the special bond with your daughter. I told you they were probably sleeping together, but did you listen? Was it possible I was right? Of course not. Because I don't have children of my own, I'm not privy to the secret and special code."

His gaze narrowed. "This is a hell of a time to throw that in my face."

"You can't have it both ways. Either I'm one of you or I'm not. Besides, why are you so upset? Brittany is only trying to relive your perfect life. You've told her and told her that this is exactly how things were for you and Serena. You've practically carved it in a gold tablet. I said it might not be a good idea to paint the past so damned perfect, but once again, I was wrong. You knew it all. So here's the result. She's pregnant and now there's a really big problem."

"There's no problem," Raoul said. "I love your daughter, Coach, and I want to marry her."

Nicole groaned. The kid was not helping.

"I'll kill him," Hawk muttered. "Get him away from me."

Nicole pointed to the front door. "Go inside. I'll deal with this."

"I don't need you to fight my battles."

She wanted to scream. "You're all so stubborn and convinced you're right. None of you are willing to look at anything rationally." She pointed at Hawk. "You were so determined to teach your daughter a fairy tale. Why? So what if it was hard? You and Serena loved each other and you had a great marriage. Isn't that what matters?"

Hawk started to speak. "Shut up," she snapped. "I'm not done." She turned on Raoul. "And you've bought into the fairy tale. Yes, you've had a hard life and you don't want to give up your child, but you're setting yourself up to fail. You're not being realistic."

Sheila whined again and pushed her nose into Nicole's leg. Nicole glanced down at her. "This is not a good time." The dog whimpered and walked to the front door.

Just then another car came tearing around the corner. Brittany parked behind her father's truck. Nicole groaned when she saw the coupe was overflowing with what looked like a lot of personal belongings.

Hawk swore. "I told you to stay in your room. What are you doing here?"

"I hate you, Daddy. You're mean and I'm never going to forgive you."

Nicole closed her eyes and prayed this wasn't what she thought. Apparently God was busy.

"I'm moving in with Nicole and Raoul," the teenager announced. "Raoul loves me and Nicole might not get it, either, but at least she's willing to listen."

"You will get your butt back home this minute," Hawk told her.

"No, I won't, and unless you're going to drag me there by my hair, you can't make me."

"I can and I will. You're not seeing Raoul again. Do you understand me?"

"Barn door? Meet horse," Nicole muttered.

Hawk turned to her. "You're not helping."

"How surprising."

Brittany climbed out of her car. "Daddy, you don't understand and until you do, I don't want anything to do with you."

"You can't stay here," Hawk told her. "I won't allow it."

"You don't love me. If you did, you'd be happy for me."

"Happy that you're throwing your life away? Oh, yeah, this is great. All my dreams have come true."

Raoul stepped toward Hawk. "You won't talk to her that way."

"What are you going to do about it, kid? Take me on. You think you can win?"

"Yes."

"Stop it," Nicole snapped. "Neither of you are helping."

Sheila whined again.

Nicole moved between Raoul and Hawk. "There is a lot to consider here and no good solution is going to come from beating the crap out of each other. Besides, if anyone gets to be violent tonight, it's me."

"There's nothing to consider," Brittany said, sounding whiny and stubborn. "Raoul and I are getting married and we're going to be very happy together."

"You're not getting married," Hawk growled. "You're still seventeen."

"Why not?" Brittany asked, pushing Nicole aside and standing up to her father. "What's the big deal? You did it and it was fine. Or were you lying? Why are you so upset, Daddy?"

Nicole saw the trapped look in Hawk's eyes. While she was annoyed for how he'd ignored her before, she couldn't help but feel sorry for him now. Besides, she loved the man.

She took a deep breath. "We all need a little time and space. Brittany can stay, but only until everyone cools off."

Brittany stuck her tongue out at her father.

"That was so mature," Nicole muttered and held

up her hand before Hawk could explode. "In Jesse's room. If I catch either of you trying to share bed space, you're both out. Is that clear?"

The teenagers looked at each other, then reluctantly nodded. Nicole moved in front of Raoul.

"I want you to look me in the eye and give me your word," she said.

He drew in a breath. "I give you my word I will not sleep with Brittany under your roof."

"Raoul!" Brittany stamped her foot.

"We have to do the right thing."

"I'm not giving my permission for this," Hawk muttered. "Brittany needs to come home."

"What are the odds of that happening?" Nicole asked.

"You're saying I can't control my daughter?" he demanded, then shook his head. "Don't answer that."

"I won't." She touched his arm. "At least we'll know where they are. Raoul gave me his word. I believe him. Do you?"

Hawk nodded slowly.

"You two, go upstairs," Nicole said. "You can get Brittany's stuff later. Raoul, see if Sheila's hungry."

The kids went inside.

Nicole waited until they'd left, then turned to Hawk.

"This is all your fault," he muttered.

She glared at him. "How is that possible? Brittany got pregnant on your watch."

"You shouldn't have gotten involved."

"In what? Their lives? Raoul was living in an abandoned building. Was that okay? I'm thinking it's where all the trouble started."

"I don't want this," he said, not looking at her. "Any of it."

Did that *any of it* include them? The night got very cold.

"Hawk," she began, but he shook his head.

"I can't talk about this now. You wanted them, you got them. I need to think."

He walked toward his truck.

"Wait," she yelled. "You can't just walk away."

"Why not? It's done."

Was he crazy? They hadn't even begun.

She started to go after him when the front door burst open.

"Hurry," Raoul called. "It's Sheila. She's having her puppies."

"THE CIRCLE OF LIFE is a whole lot messier than I'd realized," Nicole said several hours later as Sheila licked her sleeping puppies. The birth had gone smoothly and now there were three tiny, blind newborns nestled against their mother.

Sheila had handled it all like a pro, asking for nothing more than a little company as she delivered her litter. She'd allowed Nicole to move her to a clean bed and had accepted a light meal.

Raoul and Brittany huddled together on the side of the box Nicole had prepared.

"You did good," Raoul told his dog. Sheila looked up, her eyes half-closed. She thumped her tail once, then was still.

"You have babies," Brittany whispered. "That was totally incredible."

Nicole had to agree.

She looked at the teenagers sitting across from her on the floor. Were they even ready for the responsibility they were facing? Did it matter? One way or the other, in about eight months it would be here.

CHAPTER SEVENTEEN

HAWK WAITED UNTIL the next afternoon to return to Nicole's house. He figured everyone could use the time to calm down. He ignored the fact that the person who probably needed the time most was himself.

He hadn't slept the previous night—he'd barely stopped pacing. He couldn't shake the anger and sense of betrayal directed toward everyone involved.

Brittany had lied to him. She'd looked him in the eye and flat-out lied. How was that possible? They'd always been close. He'd given up his career to be with her when they lost Serena. She'd always seemed like she had it together, but that wasn't true. And if she'd lied about sleeping with Raoul, what else had she lied about?

He couldn't think about Raoul without wanting to strangle the kid. Being Brittany's boyfriend was one thing, but sleeping with her was something else. Still, he knew he couldn't talk to Raoul until he could imagine the conversation without wanting to beat the shit out of the kid.

Strangely the one who bugged him the most was Nicole. She'd known and hadn't told him. What the hell was up with that? She was the adult in the situation. She should have handled things better. Okay, sure, they'd asked her not to say anything, but so what? He was Brittany's father and he had the right to know.

He pulled up in front of Nicole's house and stared at the structure. What he didn't want to admit was the person he was most angry with was himself. This had happened on his watch. He'd always prided himself on being a father who was involved, who knew the truth. He'd secretly pitied those parents who weren't as cool, as involved. But it had all been a giant joke on him. Where had he screwed up?

When he couldn't find an answer, he left the car and walked up to the front door. Nicole opened before he could knock.

She looked tired and apprehensive. Despite the raging emotions inside of him, he found himself wanting to pull her close and hold her. He wasn't sure if the action was supposed to make her feel better or him.

"I figured you'd drop by," she said, stepping back to let him in. "You missed the big excitement. Sheila had her puppies."

"How many?"

"Three. Two girls and a boy."

He nodded, then glanced toward the stairs. "I want to talk to Brittany."

"I figured. Are you going to yell at her?"

"Probably."

Nicole sighed. "Not a great way to start the conversation. You might try listening."

"She has nothing to say that I want to hear."

"Then why talk at all?"

He didn't have an answer for that. Nicole shrugged, then headed upstairs. A few minutes later, she returned, without Brittany.

"She's refusing to come out."

"What did you tell her?" he demanded.

Nicole's expression hardened. "Absolutely nothing, but please, feel free not to believe me. Go up and yell through the door. She'll tell you herself."

She turned away, then faced him again. "I swear, if I thought I was strong enough, I'd shake you. You do know that I'm on your side, right? Does it occur to you that I understand a little of what you're feeling? I'm not the enemy here. I am not in favor of them getting married. They're both too young and unprepared. I don't even know if they should keep the baby. But hey, go ahead. Yell at me. I'm an easy target."

He felt stupid and ineffectual. It wasn't a comfortable combination. "I'm sorry," he muttered. "I didn't expect any of this. She told me she and Raoul weren't having sex."

"And you believed her?"

He nodded. "She's never lied to be before. I thought she'd tell me."

"Not a smart assumption."

"I know."

She sighed. "So you're done yelling at me?"

"Yeah."

"Good."

She still looked annoyed, but he had a feeling they were going to be okay.

She was nothing like Serena, who had always deferred to him. Nicole did things her way and didn't take any crap from anyone. He kind of liked that.

She led the way into the living room and pointed at the sectional. "Have a seat. This is going to take a while."

He shook his head and paced to the window. "At least I'm done having kids. I always told myself I was glad I'd had my family early and this only reinforces my opinion."

Nicole smiled a wicked smile that had him bracing himself. "What?" he asked.

"You're going to have to learn to like kids a little." She paused. "You're going to be a grandfather."

He swore under his breath, walked to the sofa and sat down. He could feel his hair turning white as he considered what her words meant. "My baby is having a baby. How is that possible?"

"Your mom didn't have that talk with you?"

"This is not funny."

"You're going to be a grandfather, Hawk. It's a little funny."

He ignored that. Brittany pregnant? He'd heard the words before, but this was the first time he understood what they meant. She would be a mother. She would have responsibilities for the rest of her life. Everything had changed.

"I can't do this," he muttered.

"You don't have a choice."

Simple words that reminded him of another time and another conversation much like this one. Only he had been the optimistic, slightly defiant, terrified teenager.

"My dad died when I was pretty young," he said. "I don't remember much about him except he always made my mother cry and she was a strong woman. She raised me herself, teaching me that I had to work for what I wanted and how important it was to dream big. She was always proud of me. The only time I disappointed her was when I told her Serena was pregnant."

He still remembered the way she'd looked so sad, as if all her hopes and expectations had been crushed. He'd been determined to prove to her that he hadn't screwed up entirely.

"We made it without asking her for anything," he said quietly. "I wanted that more than anything." Proving himself to her had meant a lot. Did his opinion matter as much to Brittany?

"Where did I go wrong?" he asked.

Nicole sighed. "I don't have an answer. I want to say you trusted her too much, but maybe it would have happened no matter what. It's what teenagers do. At least some of them. Jesse discovered boys when she was about fifteen. I was horrified, but short of chaining her up in her room, I couldn't stop her. I tried curfews, grounding her, phoning the parents of all of her friends to find out if she was really where she said. But she found a way."

She leaned back on the cushion. "I can't tell you the exact moment things went wrong and believe me, I've tried to look. I wanted her to have everything she wanted but our definitions of that were different."

"My mom would be really disappointed by this," he said. "I don't know what would hurt her more. That Brittany screwed up or that I didn't stop her."

"Were you listening?" Nicole asked. "How were you supposed to stop her? You had no reason not to trust her."

"I should have known."

"Beating yourself up doesn't solve the problem."

"Meaning don't make it about me."

"Something like that."

He barely knew the questions, which meant he wasn't going to find answers anytime soon.

"You're probably going to tell me not to go up there and break in her bedroom door so she has to talk to me."

"Yes."

He looked at the ceiling. He'd never not been able to talk to Brittany. They'd always been able to work out their problems. Why did this have to be different?

"I'm still pissed as hell at Raoul," he muttered, "but I'm losing energy for killing him."

"I'm sure he'll be excited to know that."

He leaned forward and rested his forearms on his thighs. "I don't know what to do."

"You don't have to do anything right now. Give it a little more time."

Walking away went against everything he believed, but short of physically dragging Brittany home, did he have a choice?

"I'll give her another day," he said. "Then she's going to have to face me."

"That seems fair."

He stood and walked to the door. "You doing okay?"

"No, but I'll survive. Sheila's puppies are a good distraction."

"More babies."

She nodded. "Just to be clear. As soon as she's done nursing, I'm getting her fixed."

NICOLE HAD BEEN DEALING with a headache on and off since Brittany had walked out with the stick that told the world she was having a baby. Now she popped a couple more ibuprofen with a big glass of water, all the while wondering if chocolate or ice cream would make the better chaser.

"I need a vacation," she muttered, thinking that doing her quarterly taxes for the bakery had never looked so good. Math might not be her thing, but she understood it and it never talked back, slammed doors or glared at her.

She went upstairs and knocked on Brittany's door. "He's gone," she called. "You can come out now."

Brittany pulled her door open. Tears streaked her face. "He left? He didn't try to talk to me?"

"You said you weren't going to speak to him. He believed you. Kind of the way he did when you told him you weren't sleeping with Raoul."

Brittany folded her arms across her chest. "You can't talk to me like that."

"It's my house, honey. I can talk to you any way I want. I'm cutting you some slack because this all just happened, but the next time your father comes over, you *will* speak to him."

"Not if I don't want to."

Raoul stepped into the hallway. At least he was following the rules and staying out of Brittany's room…as far as she knew. Nicole wasn't sure she trusted either of them right now.

"Brittany," he said gently. "Nicole is helping us."

Brittany didn't look convinced. "You're telling me what to do."

"Yes. Mostly because you're a minor and hey, this is still my house."

"I don't like all these rules."

"You're free to go home."

Tears spilled down Brittany's cheeks. "I thought you liked me."

"Liking you has nothing to do with this situation.

You're pregnant. That means it's time to grow up and part of that is having a rational adultlike conversation with your father."

"He's going to yell at me."

"Something you deserve."

Brittany turned to Raoul. "Make her stop being mean."

Raoul looked helpless.

Nicole felt sorry for him. If they went through with the marriage, he was going to have a tough road dealing with Daddy's little girl. Would having a child help Brittany grow up or would she be one of the drama-queen mothers, insisting on always being the center of the universe? If only they didn't have to find out.

HAWK WAS WAITING in the backyard of his house, with the barbecue going and a bottle of white wine chilling on ice. Nicole pushed the gate open.

"Is it safe to enter?" she asked, crossing toward him.

"I invited *you.*"

"I thought maybe it was a trap."

He'd called about an hour ago and asked if she wanted to join him for dinner. She'd been surprised, but had accepted. If nothing else, they had a few things to talk about.

"No trap," he said as he pulled her against him and kissed her.

Despite everything, she melted into his embrace,

getting lost in the feel of his mouth against hers. Lips pressed as heat built. Passion ignited, making her both weak and impossibly strong. The fire between them promised to heal or at least allow them to forget for the moment.

It had never been like this for her before. The speed with which he turned her on. How much she wanted him, wanted them together.

She buried her fingers in his hair and let herself lean on him. His muscles were hard, as was his erection. He dropped his hands to her rear and squeezed.

Wanting escalated into something alive and undeniable. She forgot whatever she'd been planning to say and instead slipped her hands under his polo shirt so she could touch bare skin. He was strong and tempting and everything she'd ever wanted. Their breath mingled as his tongue stroked hers, arousing with every touch.

He released her long enough to turn off the barbecue, then nudge her toward the back door of the house. When they were inside, he grabbed the hem of her T-shirt and pulled it over her head. Even as they kissed and she sucked his lower lip, he unfastened her bra and tossed it away. Then he touched her curves and she was lost.

His hands were everywhere. On her breasts, her sides, her back. He shoved her jeans down and pushed his fingers between her legs. She was already hot and wet and surged against his touch.

He found her center immediately and began to rub it. Tension pulled at her muscles. They kissed over and over while he circled and brushed, then plunged his fingers inside of her. It wasn't enough. It would never be enough, she thought frantically. She needed all of him.

Even as she pulsed her hips and felt herself getting closer, she reached between them and unfastened his jeans. He moved them both backward until she felt the back of the kitchen table against her thighs. He eased her onto the hard surface. She pushed off the rest of her clothes, slid back and parted her legs.

Hawk pushed down his jeans and briefs and thrust into her. She arched back, bracing herself with her arms. Her eyes fluttered closed.

He moved in and out of her, taking her higher and higher. One of his hands still rubbed her center, while the other played with her breasts. The room was silent except for the sound of their breathing and her gasps as she got closer and closer to her orgasm.

"Hawk," she breathed and wrapped her legs around his hips. "Harder."

She meant all of it. His touch, the way he filled her over and over again. Harder and faster, taking her until she had no choice but to get lost in a convulsion of pleasure and liquid release.

He followed immediately, groaning her name and shuddering. Then they were still.

After a couple of steadying breaths, she began to be aware of the fact that she was naked…on his kitchen table. She opened her eyes and found him watching her.

"You eat breakfast here," she said.

He smiled. "I know."

"You might want to clean it before tomorrow morning."

He laughed and kissed her. "You're amazing."

"So I've heard. It's been in all the papers. I'm thinking of getting cards printed up."

He brushed her hair off her face. "Thank you."

"For?"

"Everything."

She sighed and knew she could do this with him forever. Not just the sex, but all of it. Looking into his eyes, being close, sharing. Her stomach growled.

He grinned. "Not eating much these days?"

"It's been a little stressful."

"How about salmon?"

"Sounds good."

He stepped back and she slid to the floor. He helped her find her clothes, then opened the wine while she dressed. All he'd had to do was refasten his jeans and pull up the zipper. Men had it so easy. Not that she was complaining.

AFTER DINNER, Nicole curled up next to Hawk on the sofa.

"We should probably fight now," she told him.

"Is that next on our list?"

"We have a lot to talk about."

"Brittany."

"Mostly." She put her hand on his thigh. "Your daughter is spoiled and a little immature."

"I know."

That surprised her. "I thought you'd deny it."

"I want to, but I can't. I didn't set out for her to be that way. Serena did a better job with balance than I did. Once she was gone, it was just Brittany and me. Sometimes I did what was easy rather than what was right."

His admission was unexpected. "So you're saying it's all your fault?"

"Part of it is my fault. She's not a bad kid."

"I agree, but she's used to getting her way and Raoul loves her enough to go along with what she says." She risked the good mood and said, "I don't think they should get married."

"I agree, but once she turns eighteen, I can't stop her from doing anything."

Nicole wasn't so sure. If Hawk got serious about being honest with Brittany, that might change things. Threatening Raoul wouldn't work—he was too honorable.

"This is all a mess," she said. "You're going to have to take one of the puppies to help make up for putting me through this."

"I'll take the boy."

"Of course. I'm not even surprised."

She sat up and reached for the bottle of wine. As she moved, she caught sight of the porcelain rabbits on the coffee table and the aging silk flower arrangement. This was still Serena's house and no amount of sex on the kitchen table was going to change that. Her ghost was a tangible presence everywhere. Was that on purpose?

"Have you brought a lot of women here?" she asked.

Hawk frowned. "What?"

"Other women. You've had a couple of serious relationships since you lost Serena. Did you bring any of your lady friends here?"

"First, I don't call them my lady friends. Second, I've been careful about who I introduce to Brittany. But yes, one or two have been over. Why?"

"I just wondered."

She wasn't comfortable simply asking her questions. Like did he keep this house this way because he was a guy and it never occurred to him to paint and box up some of the memories, or was he trying to warn off all who entered? Did he like this still being Serena's house?

Under other circumstances, she wouldn't much care about the answers, but she was in love with Hawk so they mattered a lot. Had she fallen for a wonderful man only to lose him to a ghost, or was there a chance?

"I told Brittany she doesn't get to pout much longer," Nicole said, choosing safety over knowledge and changing the subject. "She's going to have to talk to you the next time you come over."

He leaned back and rubbed the bridge of his nose. "When did everything change? She used to be my little girl. I used to be her world. That's all gone."

"She's growing up."

"I don't want to lose her."

"She's not lost. It's just different."

"I don't like different."

"You don't get to pick."

"What am I supposed to say to her?" he asked.

"That you love her and you'll work it out."

"I want to beat the crap out of Raoul."

"Sorry, no. It took both of them to do this."

"She's my daughter."

Which said everything, Nicole thought. Brittany was family and she mattered more than anything.

She was surprised at the ache in her chest, then realized the cause. She wanted someone to feel that way about her. She wanted to be loved. And not just by anyone, but by Hawk.

An impossible situation, she thought. Was that just like her or what?

"I should be getting back," she said. "I don't want to leave them alone late at night."

"The damage has been done."

"I know, but I'm responsible. I can't help myself. It's like a disease. One day I'm going to learn to embrace my inner control freak."

"I like your inner control freak."

He walked her to her car and kissed her. The familiar need rose up inside but she ignored it. As much as she would like nothing more than intimate time with Hawk, she really did want to get home.

"Rain check?" she asked.

He nipped her earlobe. "Sure. This is Seattle. It rains all the time."

"No, a rain check works the other way. When it's not raining."

"I don't care about the weather."

She laughed and then got in her car. He watched her pull away. She knew because she was looking at him in the mirror.

He was a good guy, she thought, wondering what would happen now. Did anyone stand a chance against the memories Serena had left behind? Sure Hawk had wanted to date, but that wasn't the same as falling in love. He'd already experienced everything he wanted—why would he want to do it again?

She told herself not to go there. That they were just at the beginning of their journey. She shouldn't borrow trouble.

She managed to work in a couple more clichés before she pulled into her garage, turned off the car, then walked into the house. It was quiet and dark, but it was also nearly ten so she expected that. She didn't turn on any lights on her way to check on Sheila, so she almost didn't see the piece of notebook paper on the kitchen table. Once she spotted it, she flipped on the lights.

She picked up the note and read it, then read it again before letting the paper fall to the floor. She blindly reached for the phone. She was too stunned to know what to think. This couldn't be happening.

Hawk picked up on the first ring.

"They're gone," she said. "They ran off together. They have a fake ID for Brittany and they're going to get married."

CHAPTER EIGHTEEN

NICOLE RACED through the house, looking for clues. Most of Raoul's stuff was still in his room, but much of Brittany's was gone. Suitcases were missing from the basement and while Raoul's car was still parked in front of the house, Brittany's was nowhere to be seen.

"At least they took the newer, more reliable vehicle," Nicole muttered to herself as she ran outside and stood impatiently on the porch. She'd already called Hawk and knew he would be over any second.

Sure enough, his truck rounded the corner and screeched to a stop behind Raoul's car.

"Did you know about this?" he yelled as he got out of the truck and jogged down the front path.

She blinked. "What? No. Are you serious? You're asking me if I knew they were running away together? As if I'd keep that from you?"

"Why not? You didn't tell me Brittany was pregnant."

She was both outraged and aware he had a point. "That was different."

"How?"

"It just was. *When* you found out wasn't going to change the facts. She asked me to let her be the one to give you the information. I didn't agree, but I went along with it. I would never go along with this plan."

"So you would have told me because you don't like what they're doing, but if you'd approved, you would have kept it quiet."

He was furious. She could see the anger in his eyes, but she couldn't figure out why she was the bad guy. "You tell me I don't know what I'm doing and at the same time, complain that I'm not acting responsibly. You have to pick, Hawk. Either I'm on your team or I'm not."

"You let her go."

"I didn't."

"You let her go the way you let Jesse go."

She felt as if she'd been slapped. "You have no right to compare these situations. For one thing, Jesse is my sister, not my daughter, and for another, she's over twenty-one. Brittany is only seventeen."

"We have to find them."

He walked past her and went into the house. Nicole trailed after him, feeling hurt and confused. They'd just spent an amazing few hours together. How could he have held her and touched her and made love with her, then turn on her like this?

He walked through the house, as if they were still there and somehow Nicole had missed them.

When he walked into the kitchen, she handed him the note.

"Not that it matters," she said, "but this was waiting here when I got back."

"And you didn't know."

She sighed. "No matter how many times you ask me that question, I'm not changing my answer."

He walked to the phone, picked it up and dialed 9-1-1. "My seventeen-year-old daughter is missing. I need to speak to the police."

NICOLE'S HOUSE was overrun within the hour. There were police everywhere, asking questions, going over Brittany and Raoul's rooms, taking notes and making calls. Nicole knew Hawk had called in more than a few favors to get this much action so fast.

She made coffee while Hawk told the officers everything he knew. The note was examined and options discussed.

"She's going to marry him," Hawk said during a lull in questioning.

Nicole poured him more coffee. "She can't. She's underage. Using a fake ID isn't going to make the marriage legal. I'm surprised Raoul didn't already think of that."

"Maybe they both did," Hawk muttered. "Maybe they're hoping that a fake marriage will convince me to let them get married for real."

"So tell them no."

He looked at her, then away, making her wonder how often he refused his daughter anything. He saw her as the problem, maybe because he couldn't see the real one…himself. Nicole thought maybe she'd been too hard on Jesse, but Hawk was guilty of being too easy on Brittany. It turns out either mistake caused disastrous consequences.

"They're not going to look for Raoul," Hawk told her. "He's over eighteen and has left willingly. There's nothing they can do. Brittany is underage, so she can't just disappear." He lowered his voice. "I told them she was pregnant. They want to know if I want to press charges against Raoul for sleeping with her."

Nicole stared at him, waiting for him to say he wouldn't. When he was silent, she moved closer to the table and glared at him.

"Don't even think about it," she told him, her body shaking with anger. "He was seventeen when this whole thing started. He's her boyfriend, not some child abuser and you know it. He was just doing what teenagers have been doing since the beginning of time, including you. That boy is not to blame and he's not the problem."

"Meaning Brittany is?" Hawk asked, coming to his feet.

"No. I didn't mean that. Everything is a mess and it all has to change, starting with your past. Be honest with her and with yourself. Your life with Serena wasn't perfect. Brittany deserves to know that."

His gaze narrowed. "You leave my wife out of it."

Wife. Why did he have to say it like that? "I'm not saying she was the devil, Hawk. I'm saying she was human. That there were times when the marriage was great and times when each of you hated the other. It was two people who loved each other living together in reality. With good times and bad times. Little birds didn't show up in the morning to sing and help you dress. It was life, not a fantasy. But you've been unwilling to let Brittany see any of that, so now she assumes that she's going to relive something magical."

"You don't know what you're talking about," he said as he turned away and walked out of the kitchen.

NICOLE AND HAWK avoided each other for the rest of the night. After the police left, she went into her room and closed the door. She wasn't sure where he slept, but he was still there in the morning.

She walked into the kitchen and found him pouring fresh coffee. They looked at each other. She was hoping for some hint of reconciliation or compromise in his gaze, but it was like staring at a stranger.

"I have to get to school," he said. "You'll let me know if you hear anything?"

She nodded.

"I'll do the same." He took another drink of coffee, then he left.

Nicole sank onto one of the kitchen chairs and wondered how everything had gotten so messed up. Then she reached for the phone and dialed a familiar number.

"What are you doing after you drop off Amy at school?" she asked her sister.

"Coming to see you," Claire said.

"Good answer."

FORTY MINUTES LATER Claire was stretched out on the sectional, her feet propped up as she rested her hand on her growing belly.

"I don't get it," Claire said, then sipped her herbal tea. "Why is Hawk mad at you?"

"Because I'm an easy target. Because he can't seem to blame himself or Brittany or circumstances. Because he can't see reality." Nicole leaned back in the club chair and sighed. "Can I pick 'em or what?"

"It's not that bad."

"His daughter is pregnant and not speaking to him. The boy who got her pregnant is living with me. Hawk thinks I knew about them running away and didn't tell him and he pointed out I let Jesse go without a fight. Why wouldn't I do the same with them?"

"Because it's not the same," Claire said. "Are you sure you like this guy? He sounds like a real jerk."

"He's not. He's a worried father."

"You're making excuses for him. That can only mean one thing."

"I know."

"You like him."

Nicole looked at her sister. "I'm in love with him."

Claire grinned. "If I could jump up easily, I would. Really? That's so great."

"No, it's not. It's a mess and makes the disaster that was my marriage to Drew look positively successful by comparison."

"I don't believe that."

Nicole didn't snap at her sister, even though that was her first instinct. For one thing, Claire genuinely loved her and there weren't enough people with that attribute hanging around her world. For another, Claire led with her heart. She believed the best of people, no matter what. She'd been surprisingly sheltered in her life. Nicole was the cynic in the family.

"Whatever happens with Brittany, Hawk's going to blame me," Nicole said. "Because it can't be his precious daughter's fault or even his own."

"When this gets resolved, and it will, you two can move on."

Nicole shook her head. "He's still in love with his late wife. She's been gone about five years and their house is exactly how she left it. Her stuff is everywhere. It's like she went to get milk and will be home any second. I wouldn't expect him to pretend she didn't exist, but there should have been some changes after all this time."

"People deal with grief differently."

Nicole clenched her jaw. "You are the most annoying person on the planet. Stop acting like the middle child."

"I would be a great middle child."

"We're twins. We're a team. Take my side."

"Hawk is a big fat poophead."

Nicole couldn't help laughing. "Oh, he's going to run scared now. You're calling him a poophead."

"I learned that from Amy."

The mention of Wyatt's daughter reminded Nicole of Brittany and her humor faded. "I don't actually care about any of this," she admitted. "What kills me is Hawk's attitude. He can't or won't see the truth. I would be willing to accept the problems if he saw them, too. But that's not his style."

"You love him. You're going to have to figure something out."

"I guess."

"Nicole, falling in love is a big deal."

"It's less of one when the guy in question isn't interested."

"Is that what you think?"

"I don't know. He likes me. He wants me in bed."

"That's a start."

"I'm not sure it's enough of one." She sighed. "I

married Drew for all the wrong reasons. I knew I was in a rut. I had so much responsibility all the time. I never got a chance to be a kid. Not really. Drew was the opposite of that. He couldn't take responsibility for anything. I saw a flake and thought he was a free spirit. I saw an inability to commit to anything and thought it was spontaneity. I thought he'd be good for me."

"And he broke your heart."

"That's the problem. He didn't. When he proposed, I accepted, not because I loved him more than anything, but because I didn't think anyone else would ask. I didn't want to die alone."

Claire had always been the emotionally sensitive one of the sisters and her eyes filled up with tears. "Oh, Nicole. I wish you'd called me and talked to me."

"I hated you then, remember?"

Claire dismissed that reality with a flick of her fingers. "Still, I would have listened."

Nicole didn't bother pointing out she wouldn't have called. "I knew the marriage was a mistake within the first couple of months, but I was too proud to say anything or do anything. So we stayed together. By the time he slept with Jesse, I was emotionally divorced already. It still hurt, but I was so much more angry at her than him. That says something."

"I know. So it's different with Hawk?"

Nicole thought about the sexy, stubborn, difficult, amazing man she'd gotten to know over the past few months.

"More than different. Hawk makes me crazy in the best way possible. I just have to be around him and I can't catch my breath. He makes me laugh, we talk about stuff. He's fun and responsible. He cares so much about his kids and yet he has an ego the size of the *Titanic*. He's…"

"Perfect."

"No, but he's perfect for me."

Claire clutched her tea. "I'm going to cry again."

"That's getting really boring."

"You try being pregnant. The hormones are a nightmare. Sometimes I feel like a character in a horror movie. My point is, you'll get through this. The situation with Brittany will be resolved and then you and Hawk can get back to being in love."

It hurt to think the truth, let alone say it, but Nicole wasn't going to lie to herself. "He's not in love. He likes me, but I'm no Serena."

"Does he want a replacement for her?"

"I don't think he wants anything romantically. In his mind, he's had it all. A wife, a kid, a great career. He's not interested in more children and he's not looking to get serious." He was everything she wanted and nothing she could have.

"Maybe he'll change his mind."

"Maybe." Nicole wasn't holding her breath for the possibility.

"You can't give up hope."

Nicole shook her head. "*You* can't give up hope. I'm very comfortable with the process."

"You're going to walk away?"

"I'm going to see how this plays out. That's all I can do."

NICOLE HAD a restless day. She ended up cleaning bathrooms, which only went to show how bad things were. She hated cleaning bathrooms. But it beat wandering from room to room, wondering what was happening with Raoul and Brittany and wishing Hawk would call and say he wasn't mad at her anymore.

Wanting to hear from him was so pathetic, she told herself. She was a totally self-sufficient, self-actualized woman. She'd been successfully running the family business since she was a teenager. She didn't need Hawk's approval. So what if he was blaming her rather than taking responsibility himself? She didn't care.

Except she did. She cared a lot and she missed him. She also missed Raoul, which was weird. The kid had only been living with her for a month or so. Even Sheila seemed to be moping a little.

Rather than indulge in self-pity, Nicole collected cleaning supplies and attacked Raoul's bathroom. She made the tub sparkle, the shower doors streak-free, then started tidying up the long counter. There was a half-open box of condoms just behind the cup dispenser. She shook the box.

"Should have used them every time," she murmured. That would have solved a lot of problems.

Of course condoms weren't a hundred percent effective. So they might have always used them.

Nicole stared at the box. Condoms failed. She and Hawk used condoms. Except for that last time. Not that she could be pregnant. It was the wrong time of the month. She was sure of it.

Panic was a funny thing. Sometimes it came in big rushes, but sometimes it started so small it was hard to recognize the feeling. Sometimes it was nothing more than a flicker that grew and grew until it filled the room and made it impossible to breathe.

The phone rang.

Nicole jumped then ran to her bedroom.

"Hello?"

"It's Raoul."

Relief was instant and sweet. "Where are you? Are you okay? What's going on? Did you try to get married? Did you consider that using a fake ID invalidates the marriage? When are you coming home?"

There was a slight pause, then he said, "That's a lot of questions."

"Answer them in any order. No. Start with telling me if you're okay."

"I'm okay. We both are. We're not married, we didn't try." He paused again. "There's no baby."

Nicole sank onto her bed. "You're sure?"

"Yeah. She got her period. Brittany isn't pregnant."

Thank God, Nicole thought. "Are you okay with that? Is she?"

"We're good. She was a little upset at first, but now she's better. I'm…" He cleared his throat. "I started thinking about what you said before. About something going wrong. Me busting up my knee or something. I got scared. I'm glad there's no baby. Is that bad?"

"Of course not. You're still in high school. Why would you want to take on that kind of responsibility?"

"I still want a family."

A place to belong, she thought, recognizing the longing in his voice.

"I'm your family," she said. "I miss you. So does Sheila. This is your home, Raoul."

"Still?"

"You mean because you took off in the night and didn't give me any warning except a crappy note?"

"I'm sorry about that. I wanted to tell you but Brittany was afraid you'd try to stop us."

"She's a smart girl." Spoiled, but smart. "You're still welcome to live here. Although we're going to have a long talk about the rules. There will be some new ones. When are you coming home?"

"Today. Brittany's on her cell phone with her

dad. They seem to be getting along again. She'll be moving back home."

That was a relief, Nicole thought. "She'll be happier there," is what she said, followed by, "Drive safely."

"I will."

"Good."

"I would have done it," he said. "I would have taken care of her and the baby."

"I know."

"I'm glad I don't have to right now."

"Me, too."

"Thanks, Nicole. You've been great. I couldn't have gotten through this without you."

She felt all warm and squishy inside. Having Raoul around was like having a better version of Jesse home.

"Hurry back," she said.

"We will. Bye."

She hung up. It was a good ending to what could have been a disaster. Brittany moving back with her dad was also a plus. Let Hawk deal with his little princess. She had enough on her plate right now.

She put down the phone and walked into the hallway. On the top shelf of the linen closet was the pregnancy kit Brittany had left. There were still two tests left inside.

Nicole thought about the condoms and how her luck had been running lately, then she carried the box into her bathroom.

Ten minutes later, she stared at the plastic stick.

There was still a baby, she thought, unable to believe the news. It just wasn't the one everyone thought.

CHAPTER NINETEEN

HAWK STOOD by the garage as his daughter drove her car inside. He'd always prided himself on being in control but he'd never had to struggle so hard to keep it all together. Relief battled with anger. He wanted to hold Brittany close to prove to himself that she was all right, then he wanted to lock her in her room for the next hundred and fifty years. She'd scared the hell out of him.

She climbed out of her car and walked toward him. Her expression was wary, as if she wasn't sure how mad he was going to be. Indecision pulled at her mouth. No doubt she was trying to figure out the best way to play him.

Nicole had been right about him taking the easy way out with Brittany. He hadn't wanted to hear that truth and he'd taken a lot of his temper out on the messenger, but he'd been unable to escape reality. Somewhere in the past few years, Brittany had turned into a spoiled brat.

"Oh, Daddy, I'm so happy to see you," she said, rushing toward him. "I missed you, Daddy. I missed you so much."

So she'd decided to play the loving daughter game. He accepted her hug, patted her back, then led the way into the house. When they were in the kitchen, she walked to the refrigerator and pulled out a can of soda.

"I feel really bad about worrying you," she said as she popped the top. "I should have called sooner. Raoul and I hadn't planned to run away. It just sort of happened. We were talking and then we were packing and then we were gone."

She paused and smiled, blinking her eyes. "It was very immature of me."

Did she really think he was that stupid? Hawk shook his head. He already knew the answer to that. Of course she did or she wouldn't be working the program so hard.

"It was a spontaneous decision to run off?" he asked.

She sipped. "Uh-huh."

"You just happened to have a fake ID in your back pocket?"

Her eyes widened. "Um, no. It was just lying around."

"A fake ID in your name with your picture on it."

"I don't know where that came from."

Better to play innocent than come up with a crappy lie, he thought.

"Either you got it or Raoul got it," he continued. "I'm guessing it has to be Raoul. You'd never do anything like that, would you?"

Her eyes widened even more. "No, Daddy." Her smile trembled a little at the corners.

"It's illegal. Getting a minor a fake ID. The police know about it. I should probably warn Nicole they'll be by to arrest him. Damn. We're going into the play-offs, too. If Raoul has to miss games because he's in jail, we'll never win. It's his senior year, too. If he doesn't play, the colleges are going to forget about him. But hey, he earned it, right? He screwed up and now he has to face the consequences."

Brittany's face crumbled. She put her soda on the counter and reached out for him. "Daddy, no. Don't talk like that. Raoul can't go to jail."

"Sorry, Brittany. He has to learn his lesson."

"No. That's not fair."

The tears fell faster. Normally Hawk would do anything to make her stop crying, but not this time. He felt oddly detached from the moment. She was his daughter and he would always love her, but he was tired of her calling the shots.

He turned to walk out of the kitchen. Brittany followed him, then grabbed his arm. "It was me," she said, sobbing and gasping for breath. "It was me. I got the fake ID. It was my idea to use it so we could get married. Raoul didn't want to. He's really sweet, Daddy. He worships you. He would never do anything to hurt you or me."

Hawk did his best not to think about Raoul sleeping with his daughter. While he would consider that crossing the line, Raoul and Brittany wouldn't see it that way.

"You lied to me," he said, his voice low.

"I know. I know. I'm so sorry. I just thought…I wanted to get married. I wanted to start my life with Raoul. I wanted us to be happy and a family. Just like you and Mom."

He put his arm around his daughter and led her into the family room. When she was settled on the sofa, he sat on the coffee table in front of her and took one of her hands in his.

"I loved your mom more than anything," he said slowly. "I still remember the first time I saw her. She was laughing and the sound cut through me. I knew she was the one, that we would always be together, that I would marry her. There was never a question. She knew, too."

Brittany wiped away her tears. "Just like me and Raoul."

He ignored that. "We got together and fell in love. We had plans. Then she turned up pregnant."

"I know this part."

"No, you don't. You know what we told you. Your mom and I were worried that if you knew the truth, you'd feel you weren't wanted, weren't loved. I don't know if it was the right decision, but it's the one we made. You've only heard half the story, Brittany. There's more I need to tell you."

"Like what?"

"Like how your mom cried every night for six

months because her parents turned their backs on her. How after we were married, we hardly ever saw each other. We were living in my room at my mom's house, both working two jobs to save as much money as possible because once I went to Oklahoma and started playing football, there wouldn't be any time for me to work."

Brittany shifted in her seat. "But that was only for a few weeks. Then you were together."

"Then I was at practice or in class. Your mom was alone in a strange city where she didn't know anyone. She was given a job as a receptionist, but she was the youngest person there. She had nothing in common with the other women who were single and going out all the time. She went home to an empty house and waited for me to come home. She spent four years waiting."

"But then she had me."

"Yeah, she had a baby. So now she was alone and responsible for an infant. She had no friends, no one to call. Her own mother didn't speak to her for over a year."

"But what about the alumni? You said they helped."

"They did. They brought casseroles and sometimes babysat. They gave us names of doctors and helped with the bills. They made it possible, but it was never easy. There were times your mom and I fought so much we made you cry. There were weeks we hated each other and if we'd had the money, we would have gotten divorced a hundred times over."

Tears filled Brittany's eyes again. "Daddy, no."

He squeezed her fingers. "We worked it out. We realized we loved each other and we were going to have to try harder. Then I signed with the NFL and we were able to move back here. Life got easier. You started school and Serena and I could finally spend some time together. We made it, but just barely."

"I thought it was different. I thought it was a fairy tale."

"I know. Maybe that was a mistake."

Nicole had been right. He and Serena had paved the way to this disaster. They'd practically illustrated a manual on how to screw up a life.

"There's no baby," Brittany whispered. "I was sad before, but maybe it's a good thing. I guess I should go on birth control, Dad."

Not a conversation he wanted to have.

"You'll have plenty of time to think about how you want to handle that," he said. "You already have an appointment with your doctor in two weeks."

She pulled back her hand. "Dad! That's so embarrassing."

"So's getting pregnant at seventeen. Not that I see that happening again anytime soon."

"What do you mean?"

"You won't be going out with Raoul for a while."

She glared at him. "You can't make me break up with him. He's my boyfriend and I love him."

"I'm sure you do, but this isn't about him. This is about you. You lied to me about your relationship. You moved out, you ran off, you got a fake ID. I've always trusted you and given you a lot of freedom. Obviously you're not mature enough to handle it."

"What?"

He stood. "You're grounded, Brittany. You won't be dating anyone for a while. You'll go to school, then sit in my office and do homework until I'm ready to leave."

"That's crazy. I'll drive myself home."

"I'm taking away your car."

"What? You can't!" She shrieked loud enough to injure the neighborhood dogs. "Daddy, no!"

"No car for a month. You're grounded for six weeks. The last two weeks are to test your ability to be responsible. If you can't handle it, you'll lose the car completely until you're eighteen. For now I'm letting you keep your cell phone and Internet privileges, but let me be clear. They are privileges. I can take them away, too."

She pushed past him, turned and glared. "You can't do this."

"I can and I have."

"It's not fair. I wasn't that bad."

"You were that bad and worse. I worried so much about how you felt after your mom died. I wanted to make things easy for you and I did. Too easy.

You're spoiled, Brittany. If something doesn't change, you're going to become the kind of person no one likes. I don't want that. I want to be proud of you again."

She began to cry again. "Daddy, don't."

He wasn't sure what she wanted him to stop, but he didn't care. He walked past her and entered the kitchen. Her car keys were lying on the counter. He pocketed them.

Brittany ran into the kitchen. "You can't do this. You can't treat me like a child."

"You're acting like one."

"This is so unfair. I hate you."

"Right now, you're not my favorite person, either. I love you, Brittany, but you've crossed the line."

She turned and raced out of the room. He heard her footsteps on the stairs, followed by the sound of her slamming her door. When there was silence, he leaned against the counter and wondered how the hell he was going to get through the next month.

It would be hard. There were more laws to lay down and Brittany wasn't going to take any of it well. He was fighting uphill—he should have done this years ago. But with luck, he could still turn her around.

He walked into his study, but couldn't sit. He felt too restless. Something was still wrong and he couldn't figure out what it was. He felt uncomfortable. Like he didn't fit in his skin anymore.

Brittany was back, he'd done the father thing. Everything was right. What did he have that was…

Nicole, he thought. He needed to talk to Nicole. They'd fought and he'd hurt her. She'd only been telling him the truth, saying what he needed to hear. He respected that, and he missed her.

He walked upstairs and knocked on Brittany's door.

"Go away," she yelled.

"Keep talking like that and you'll lose your phone."

There were a couple of seconds of silence followed by her opening her bedroom door.

Her face was pale and streaked with tears. "Okay," she said, then sniffed.

His knee-jerk reaction was to tell her not to worry, that they could put this all behind them. But he knew that would be a mistake.

"I'm going to see Nicole," he said. "I'll be gone a while."

"You're leaving? Now? After ripping my life apart and destroying me?"

Good to know Brittany hadn't lost her flair for the dramatic. "Just wanted you to know I was gone. I'm taking your car keys with me, so don't think you can sneak out. I expect you to stay up here and think about what you did wrong."

"Daddy, no. You can't leave. Not now." More tears slid down her cheeks. "Don't. Don't go to Nicole."

"Why not? I want to spend time with her."

"If I can't go out, you can't go out."

He folded his arms across his chest. "You didn't just say that."

She swallowed. "Sorry. No. I didn't mean that. It's just I don't want you to be gone right now. You hurt me."

"I punished you. There's a difference."

"But, Daddy…" Her voice was a high-pitched whine. One that grated on his last nerve.

"What's the real problem here?"

"I don't know. It's just… How much do you like her?"

Interesting question. "I like her a lot."

Brittany's eyes widened. "You mean, like it's serious?"

"Yes." More than serious, he thought. "She's very important to me."

"But you said you were just dating. You said it didn't matter."

"That was before." When they'd had a deal. But the deal had turned out to be real.

"You're not supposed to be with anyone but Mom. You promised."

"I will always love Serena, but it's been five years, Brittany. I'm allowed to have a life."

"No, you're not. You're my dad. You can't care about someone more than me. Is that it? Do you love her? Do you?"

Did he? Love? He'd never thought about that.

He'd always had fun with women, but he didn't get involved. Not seriously. Love.

"I don't know," he admitted, turning the idea over in his mind. Love?

"I hate you," Brittany screamed. "I hate you and I hate her."

Her door slammed. Hawk ignored the sound and his daughter's tantrum.

Why hadn't he seen it before? How important Nicole had become to him? How much he looked forward to seeing her? How he counted on her and trusted her and needed her in his life?

Love. Who would have guessed it was possible?

"I'M SO EXCITED," Claire said, grabbing Nicole by the arms and bouncing up and down. "This is wonderful and amazing. How did it happen?"

Nicole wasn't in the mood to bounce. She pulled back and walked into the kitchen. "The usual way."

"You're pregnant." Claire sounded far too happy.

"I know. I'm the one who told you."

"You should be happier. Pregnant. That means a baby."

"I'm clear on the biological ramifications of the event."

Claire shook her head. "Why aren't you more excited? I thought you wanted a family."

"I do."

"Now you and Hawk can get married."

Nicole ignored the stab of pain that ripped

through her. If only. But that wasn't going to be happening.

"It's a new century," she said. "Getting married because the girl gets pregnant is no longer required."

"But you really like Hawk. Actually, you love him."

"So not the point."

"Why?"

Nicole crossed to the freezer and pulled out two pints of Ben & Jerry's. She really hated to share her stash, but Claire wasn't going to simply sit by and watch her eat ice cream alone. It was unnatural.

"There are complications," she said setting the cartons on the table and grabbing spoons. "I'm not sure Hawk is over his late wife. His house is a shrine to Serena. He has this vision in his mind about her and no mortal woman can measure up."

"You can handle that."

"There's more." Nicole sat across from her sister and picked up one of the pints. "He has a spoiled princess of a daughter who isn't going to deal with any of this well."

"Brittany will be graduating in June and leaving for college. She's a short-term problem."

Possibly. But there was still one more thing.

Nicole waited until Claire had swallowed before saying, "Hawk and I weren't really going out. I made a deal with him to be my pretend boyfriend. I was tired of everyone feeling sorry for me because of Jesse and Drew. He was coming on to me, so I traded him sex in return for pretending to date me. We're not really going out."

Claire dropped her spoon. "You lied about your relationship?"

"Yes."

"To me?"

"Yes."

Claire's face got all scrunchy, like she'd just been hit in the stomach. Nicole felt sick.

"It's not what you think," she said quickly. "Everyone seemed overly concerned. I hated that. And Drew was showing up every fifteen minutes telling me I had to take him back because no one else would ever want me. I felt completely undesirable. Then I met Hawk and he was interested in sex, which isn't exactly a love match, but he's hunky and appealing and I thought it would be better to make people think we were together."

"You lied to me."

"I know. It was wrong. I'm sorry."

Claire nodded slowly. "I guess I've been a bad sister, if you thought you had to trick me."

Nicole felt herself shrinking. "Don't go there. You're taking it wrong. This is all about me. You've been great and patient and I appreciate that."

"You hate me."

Nicole wanted to pound her head against the table. "This isn't about you," she yelled. "Don't you see? This is about me feeling like crap about my life. I was humiliated by what happened and then you found Wyatt and you're so damn happy. It was really annoying. And you were worried and Wyatt was worried and I couldn't stand it."

Claire licked her spoon. "Was the sex good?"

"Amazing."

"That's something."

Nicole took a deep breath. "Are you still mad?"

"I'll get over it. Tell me about Hawk."

"There's nothing to say. We had sex, I got pregnant."

"You fell in love with him."

"Yeah, that, too. Not very smart, huh?"

"You can't control your heart."

"Right now I can't control anything in my life."

"What do you want from Hawk?" Claire asked.

"A happy ending. But I'm not fooling myself. I know that's not going to happen."

"It might."

"Unlikely," Nicole muttered. "He doesn't want more children. He never gets involved. His life is complete. He doesn't need me."

"On the surface."

"Have I ever mentioned how your ongoing optimism gets on my nerves?"

"Everything gets on your nerves."

That was true.

"Are you happy about the baby?" Claire asked.

Nicole felt the need to touch her stomach, as if that would connect her to the child growing inside.

"Sort of. How crazy is that? Like I need more responsibility in my life."

"Oh, please. You love responsibility. You always have."

Nicole glared at her. "You have no idea what you're talking about."

"I know a lot more than you think. You thrive on responsibility. Why else would you have kept the bakery? You could have sold it years ago, taken the money and done something else with your life. It's in a great location. Just the land has to be worth a couple million. So you're there because you want to be there. You love Jesse, so as much as she bugged you, you never wanted to get rid of her. Even now. With all she's done, you miss her. It will be the same with the baby. You'll eat up the responsibility."

Nicole didn't know if she should be impressed by Claire's insights or totally pissed off.

"It's kind of cool that we're all pregnant," Claire said. "The three Keyes sisters. The timing is pretty amazing."

"So's the fact that none of us are married," Nicole said, not wanting to think about Jesse pregnant and gone. "Although you're engaged, so you're almost married."

Claire squeezed her arm. "You're having a baby. Aren't you excited?"

Despite everything, Nicole smiled. "I am. I'm also terrified."

"Me, too. The mom thing. What if I don't know how?"

"You know. You lead with your heart. Sometimes that's very annoying."

"You know, too. You've had practice."

"I didn't do a great job with Jesse."

"You did. She created a lot of the problems herself. Plus, you were just a kid."

Nicole nodded slowly. "I miss her. I keep wanting to go find her."

"And then what?"

Nicole didn't have an answer for that. "My head tells me I have to let her go. My heart says she'll never make it on her own. I don't know which one is right."

Claire squeezed her arm again. "You'll figure it out."

"I hope so."

RAOUL ARRIVED a few minutes after Claire left. Nicole hugged him hard, then hit the back of his head.

"Don't run off again. You scared me."

"I know. I'm sorry."

"Sheila missed you. I had to explain to the puppies where you were. I won't cover for you again."

"You won't have to."

They stood smiling at each other. Nicole felt as if some of the weight had been lifted from her shoulders.

"Go unpack," she said. "If you're lucky, I'll cook dinner later."

"I'd like that."

He carried his duffel bag upstairs.

She watched him go. Life would be a whole lot easier if he would stop seeing Brittany, but she doubted her luck was that good. She would guess it was just a matter of time until Hawk's daughter showed up, so she might as well cook enough for three.

She headed into the kitchen, then made a detour to the front door when the bell rang. She half expected to see Brittany on her doorstep, but instead found herself staring at Drew.

This was so not how she wanted to spend her evening.

"Hi, Nicole," he said. "May I please come in for a few minutes?"

Her instinct was to say no. She wasn't in the mood for his rants right now. But it would probably be faster to let him say whatever he wanted and then get him the hell out of here.

She stepped back to let him enter. He closed the door behind him and gave her a tentative smile.

"You're looking good," he said as he shoved his hands into his pockets, then pulled them out again. "Better than good. Great. Really great."

"Is this about money?" she asked. "Do you need a loan?"

"No. It's not about money. It's about…" He

looked into her eyes. "I'm sorry. I'm here to tell you that I was wrong about, you know, everything. I hurt you. You were great to me, Nicole. I never appreciated you the way I should have. I'm sorry about what happened with Jesse. I take full responsibility for that."

Her first thought was that he was on drugs. Her second was that he'd had his body hijacked by some kind of space alien.

"I don't know what to say," she admitted.

"Then let me talk. I still love you, Nicole. I've never stopped loving you. I know coming on to Jesse the way I did was totally wrong. I was messed up in the head. But I'm clear now and I know what I want. I want you. I want us back together, the way it used to be."

An apology at last. He was taking responsibility. While she appreciated it, she knew it was too little too late.

"The divorce will be final in a couple of weeks," she said.

"We can get married again. It will be great."

She studied him, his blue eyes, the way his smile was slightly lopsided. At one time she'd done her best to convince herself he was the one.

"Why?" she asked, curious rather than angry. "Why do you want to be with me?"

He frowned. "Because I love you."

"Do you like me?"

"Sure."

"What do you like about me?"

"I don't understand."

She shrugged. "We don't have very much in common. You like to party and it's not really my thing. You enjoy going out every night and I like staying in. I'm sort of a morning person and you're a night owl. You never liked that I work at the bakery, I don't really like your friends. We don't have very much in common, Drew."

He looked at the floor, then back at her. "I'm at my best when I'm with you."

Which was kind of sweet and still all about him. "Maybe you should try being your best on your own."

"But…"

"Drew, you don't really love me. I'm not sure you like me all that much. You weren't happy married to me. Were you? Really?"

He slowly shook his head.

"We're not in love," she told him. "It's over. I think you need to go find someone who likes what you like, who understands you."

"I guess." He looked at her. "But you loved me. You know, before, right?"

She thought about how she felt about Hawk. It was so different, so powerful, so unlike anything she'd felt before. That was love. Really deep, lasting love. But there was no win in hurting Drew and that's all the truth would do.

"I loved you," she lied.

"Well that's something." He gave her a small smile. "I guess I should go."

She moved around him and opened the door. "Goodbye, Drew."

He leaned in and kissed her cheek. "Bye, Nicole."

And then he was gone.

She leaned against the closed door. Life was nothing if not interesting.

She'd barely gotten halfway across the room when there was another knock. Nicole sighed. She was just going to have to get mean. She didn't want to hurt Drew, but the situation was getting out of hand.

She turned around, crossed to the door and pulled it open. But instead of Drew, Hawk stood on her porch.

Her body reacted as it always did, with heat and longing. Her heart fluttered. She wanted to throw herself at him, to kiss him and then take him to bed. None of which was going to happen.

"What do you want to blame me for this time?" she asked.

"Nothing. Do I do it that often?"

"More than I would like," she muttered, stepping back and letting him in. "I take it Brittany got home."

"A couple of hours ago. We had a talk. How are you? Are you okay?"

"I'm fine."

He cupped her face and kissed her. "Brittany's grounded. I took her car away from her."

Nicole didn't know what to say. "That's a good thing?"

"You were right about me not acting like her parent. I didn't take responsibility and I didn't make her take responsibility. I kept hearing your voice in my head, Nicole. The one telling me the right thing to do. That's what's happened. When I wasn't paying attention, you crawled inside of me. I never thought I'd care about anyone again. But I do. I love you."

He stood there looking so hopeful and proud. Nicole told herself she should be happy—that this was everything she'd ever wanted. Only she knew it wasn't going to be that easy. She didn't know what had brought Hawk to this point, but she had a bad feeling it wasn't reality.

She desperately wanted to believe, to hope, to have this be the moment her dreams came true. But she wasn't comfortable taking that leap of faith. Not with her heart on the line.

"You don't love me," she said as she pulled back. "You can't possibly have room in your life or your house."

"What does my house have to do with anything?"

"It's a shrine to Serena. I know she was your wife and you loved her, but it's been what, five years? Six? Nothing has changed. You've never moved on. You still use her to keep everyone at bay and when that doesn't work, you use Brittany. You're happy just being on a team of two. There's no room for anyone else, Hawk, and you don't want there to be. You're trading on your looks and your charm."

He glared at her. "If you're not interested, just say so."

"I wish I wasn't, but I am. This isn't about me trying to hurt you or be mean."

"The hell it isn't. I love you."

The words cut so deeply because she wanted to believe them so much.

"Do you?" she asked. "Seriously? You love me? Are you sure? Are we getting serious now? Are you proposing?"

He took a slight step back. "I want us to get serious."

"How serious? What about a family? Do you want kids with me?"

He took another step back. "It seems early to be having that conversation."

"I guess. I just wondered where you saw this going."

She waited, hoping she wasn't reading the look of panic correctly, even though she knew she was.

"I don't know what you want," he told her. "I care about you. Isn't that enough for now?"

It was as if he wanted to be rewarded for suddenly realizing she was more than a convenience. Talk about special, she thought with a sigh. She might as well get it all out there right now.

"I'm pregnant," she said, staring into his eyes as she spoke. "We're having a baby."

She held her breath, hoping she was wrong, desperate for him to be happy. She wanted to see him smile, then laugh. She wanted him to say that they would work everything out now that they were having a baby together. She wanted him to know the truth and *then* tell her he loved her.

Instead he turned and walked away.

CHAPTER TWENTY

NICOLE SAT CURLED UP on the sofa, eating ice cream. She really wanted wine or a margarita, but that was out of the question, thanks to her pregnancy.

"You'd better be worth it," she told her stomach as she scooped up another spoonful.

She felt empty inside. Drained and not even hurt. She suspected she was still numb and the pain would come later. Then she would have to deal with the reality of carrying Hawk's child, loving him and knowing he didn't or wouldn't love her back. But until then, there was the smooth escape of a sugar rush.

"Nicole?"

Nicole ignored the high-pitched shrill call of her name.

Brittany raced in through the kitchen and into the great room. "How could you do this to me?"

Nicole didn't even look at her. "I have no idea what you're talking about."

"You're pregnant!" Brittany yelled. "You had sex with my dad! I thought you were my friend. How could you do this?"

"Aren't you grounded?" Nicole asked, still concentrating on the ice cream and ignoring most of what Brittany said. Right now there wasn't room for a teenage drama queen in her life. "Aren't you supposed to be at home in your room?"

"That isn't your business."

"That would be a yes," Nicole said conversationally. "I also heard your dad took your car away from you. I'm going to take a stab here and say he didn't tell you about the baby. Which means someone else told you."

She was guessing Hawk was going to take a few hours to absorb the news. No way he would have dumped this information on Brittany. No one else knew except…

She raised her head and saw Raoul hovering behind Brittany. Apparently he'd heard the conversation she'd had with Hawk.

That pain she did feel. It felt a lot like betrayal. She looked at him. "You told her?"

Raoul shuffled his feet. "I had to do something."

"And you thought letting her know was a good idea?"

"Not anymore."

"Don't talk about me like I'm not here!" Brittany stamped her foot. "I hate this. I hate all of it. My dad was never mad at me before he met you. You've changed everything. I didn't think you would do this. He doesn't love you. I know he doesn't. I want you to know that. You're not going to take him away from me. He loves me best."

"Brittany, stop it," Raoul told her. He grabbed her arm and tried to pull her out of the kitchen. "Don't talk to Nicole like that. You don't want to do this."

She jerked free of him. "Don't tell me what to do." She spun around and faced Nicole. "I'll never forgive you."

"Back at you."

"What?"

"There's nothing like a crisis to bring out a person's character. I'm not impressed with yours. Good thing you didn't get married, Raoul. Trust me, you wouldn't want to face this every day for the next thirty years."

"You bitch!" Brittany yelled.

Raoul stepped between them. "That's enough," he told his girlfriend. "You don't get to talk to her that way."

"You will not take her side."

"I will. She's been good to me. She took me in and Sheila."

"But you love me."

"I do, but I respect Nicole and you should, too."

There was a quiet dignity in his words, a maturity Nicole didn't expect. His defense of her soothed the wound of betrayal. She watched them, wondering who would blink first.

Brittany squared her shoulders. "I'd like you to take me home, now."

"All right."

She walked out of the kitchen. Raoul looked at Nicole.

"I keep screwing up. I'm sorry."

"Don't be. I'm not doing any better myself. Life is nothing if not interesting."

"Are you happy about the baby?"

She put down her spoon and covered the ice cream. "I am. Despite everything."

"Good. I'm glad. Hawk will come around."

Nicole didn't want to talk about that. "You'd better get Brittany home before her dad finds out she's gone. I doubt he's in a mood to be patient with her."

"Yeah, I know." He hesitated. "You said stuff like this shows a person's true character. You're doing great."

If only… "Not for long. I'm planning a breakdown for later in the day."

"I'll be around if you need me."

"Thanks, but I'll get through it." By herself. She was good at that.

Raoul left and she was alone in the house.

The silence didn't bother her that much. She curled up on the sofa and flipped channels. There had to be something on to distract her from her earlier conversation with Hawk and his reaction to her pregnancy. Something to help her stay numb.

But the pain was there, creeping closer. She'd allowed herself to hope and then she'd fallen in love and then she'd been unable to protect herself. Sure, this wasn't what either of them would have chosen, but if he really loved her, he would have wanted to at least talk about the pregnancy. He wouldn't have run for the hills. He wouldn't have made it so clear how much he still loved Serena.

HAWK STOOD in the middle of his living room, seeing it for the first time in years. Everything was exactly as it had been when Serena had still been alive. The paint on the walls, the furniture, the pictures. Even the damn ceramic rabbits he'd always hated.

He crossed to the fireplace and fingered the pictures there. So many of them. Brittany, Serena, wedding pictures and vacation pictures. There were more in the hallway and going up the stairs. Serena's presence was still tangible in the house, as if she'd lived here until yesterday.

Hawk hadn't meant that to happen. He loved Serena; he would always love her, but he'd never meant to build a shrine to her. He'd never meant to use her to put his life on hold or keep people away.

Nicole was right…he'd been getting by on good looks and charm. His relationships had never gone anywhere before. Most of them had ended after he'd brought the woman in question to his house. Now he knew why.

At the time he hadn't been interested enough to figure it out. But what if Nicole had left?

He didn't want to think about that. Didn't want to think about losing her. He'd meant what he said. He loved her. Not that she was likely to believe him.

Brittany ran into the house. "Daddy, Daddy, where are you?"

"In here," he called.

She raced toward him and threw herself at him. "Oh, Daddy, it was so horrible. Raoul heard you and Nicole talking and he told me about the baby. Daddy, tell me it's not true. Tell me you didn't do that with her. Daddy, you can't have another child. You can't."

A baby. He'd ignored that part of what Nicole had said, had pushed it from his mind. It had been too much to deal with. A baby? Now?

He looked at his teenage daughter, the little girl he'd loved so much. Loved and failed.

"You're grounded. You weren't supposed to leave your room."

"Oh, please." She rolled her eyes. "Nicole is pregnant and you want to talk about me being grounded?"

"Where did you go?" And then he got it. "You went over there, didn't you?"

"I had to talk to her. I had to find out if it was true. I told her it didn't matter, that you'd never want to be with her or have another child. It's disgusting."

Hawk had been annoyed with his daughter

before. And disappointed. But he'd never been truly angry. "Nicole has been nothing but kind and supportive of you. Even when you were running off with Raoul, she was understanding. And this is how you thank her?" Hawk pushed her away.

Brittany stared at him. "Why are you looking at me like that?"

"Because you're a selfish, thoughtless person and not at all who I thought my daughter would be. I'm angry and ashamed of how you've acted."

She blushed and tears filled her eyes. "You can't mean that," she whispered.

"I absolutely do. Hand over your phone."

"What?"

He grabbed her purse and pulled out her cell phone.

"Daddy, no! You can't take it. This is crazy."

"You're right. This is crazy. I've screwed things up, but I'm going to fix them. Let me be clear, Brittany. You're my daughter. My child. You are not an equal or an adult. You're spoiled and immature."

"Takes one to know one," she said, practically spitting the words. Apparently her embarrassment had been short-lived.

"You're right. I haven't been on my best game, either. But that's going to change, starting right now. We're both going to grow up. I think I'm going to have an easier job of it, but I'm willing to be wrong."

"I hate you." Tears spilled onto her cheeks.

"I'm okay with that."

"I'll never forgive you."

"Not a problem."

She fled the room and thundered upstairs. Her cell phone began to ring. Hawk turned it off.

He'd screwed up royally. With Brittany and with Nicole. He needed his daughter to figure out her responsibility in all this, and he had to make things right with Nicole. But how? How to convince her that he'd been surprised by the news, not angry.

A baby. They were having a baby.

He'd never thought about having more children, but why not? She would be a great mom and he would know more than he had with Brittany. Besides, he loved Nicole and wanted to be with her. If she loved him, then they could be a family together.

But how to convince her he meant what he said? How to show her that he was the right man? How to win her back forever?

THE LAST THING Nicole wanted to do was go to a football game. But it was the last game of the season and Raoul had wanted her to see him play.

They'd spent more time together this past week. With Brittany grounded, he'd been home every night and they'd spent quiet evenings reading or watching TV. It was like having a baby brother around and Nicole knew she would miss Raoul when he went off to college.

As she settled on the bleacher seat, she thought about how much her life had changed in the past couple of months. She'd lost Jesse and she still couldn't decide if that was a good thing or not. Her heart cried out for Nicole to find her sister and bring her home. Her gut and her head said Jesse had to figure it out on her own.

There were other changes, too. Raoul and Sheila. Nicole had never thought of getting a dog, but she liked the company. Now she was going to have a baby.

Even though her child was probably the size of a pea, Nicole was still excited. She ignored the fear that said she'd totally messed up with her sister. After all, she'd been a kid herself. She knew a lot more now. She wanted to have a baby, be a family. While she'd never seen herself as a single mother, she wasn't worried about being on her own. She was more than capable. Not to mention the fact that she had a great support system in place.

She hadn't heard from Hawk in a couple of days. She knew she would eventually. Even if the thought of another child horrified him, he wasn't the type of guy to walk away from his responsibilities. So he would want to work out a sensible arrangement. It was too bad that he couldn't be enough in love with her to put his past behind him and live in the present.

But he wasn't. She appreciated that he'd been willing to say he loved her. That meant something. He just didn't love her enough to want it all.

Several of the parents called to her. She waved, but didn't try to talk to anyone. She would simply get through the game then go home. It hurt to be here. It hurt to try not to look at the field and then have her gaze shift that way so that she could see Hawk.

She wondered how long it would be until she could see him and not feel that painful combination of need and longing. The sexual draw was as strong as ever, but even worse was the love that welled up inside of her. She'd fallen for yet another disaster of a man and didn't seem to be in any hurry to get over him.

Maybe she should give up on romantic love. She could fill her life with other things. Oh, but she would miss him.

She shifted her attention to the guys on the field and easily found Raoul. He looked up and waved. He was too far away for her to be sure he was smiling, but she sensed he was. He felt responsible for her, now that she was pregnant. Crazy but true, and she adored him for it.

"Nicole?"

Nicole turned and saw Brittany standing next to her. Nicole went on alert, not sure what the teenager intended. But instead of screaming, Brittany sat down and ducked her head.

"I'm sorry," she murmured in a low voice. "About how I acted before. My dad says I'm not very mature, and I guess he's right. I've had a lot of time to think while I've been grounded, and Raoul's been yelling at me about how I hurt you."

She raised her gaze. "I'm sorry. I didn't want to do that. I just wanted to act out. I still do, but I'm trying not to."

Nicole didn't know what to say. While she appreciated the apology, she didn't totally trust it. "It was a lot to take in," she said carefully.

Brittany smiled. "I know. First me, then you. I still don't like thinking about my dad doing, you know, that."

"I get it. Parental relationships should not happen in the open."

"Yeah. But I want us to stay friends. Raoul was right. You've been really great to me and I'm sorry for how I acted."

Nicole knew the apology was a big deal. "Thanks for saying that. I appreciate it."

"Are we still friends?"

Nicole wasn't sure, but she nodded. Brittany would always be dramatic, but Nicole wasn't going to escape her any more easily than she would escape Hawk.

The teenager leaned toward her. "You're having my baby brother or sister. It's kinda cool. Maybe when I come home from college, I can babysit or something."

"Sure." Nicole wouldn't hold her breath for that to happen, but it was nice that Brittany was interested instead of screaming.

"He really likes you," Brittany confided. "It freaked me out at first, but it's been a long time. Since my mom died. I guess when I'm gone, he's going to need someone."

It was a peace offering, however lacking in graciousness. Nicole took it in the spirit in which it was meant. "Thanks."

Hawk "needing someone" wasn't what she wanted to hear. She wanted him to tell her he was desperately in love with her. That she mattered, that she was the best part of his day. He didn't have to claim to love her more than he'd loved Serena. The other woman would always be a part of him. She knew he wouldn't be the man she loved without that important relationship. But she wanted to hear that he could love her as much. Just differently. That he wanted to grow old with her, have a family with her. She wanted to be more than a convenience or a good time.

None of which she said to Brittany. "Thanks for telling me all this," she murmured instead.

"Okay. I gotta get down to the field for the game. See ya."

Nicole watched her go. She felt her gaze slip to Hawk again, who was watching her. He waved and she waved back. Which meant what? She didn't have an answer.

The game started a few minutes later. Hawk's guys easily scored three touchdowns in the first two quarters. Five seconds before halftime, the score was twenty-one to ten. The guys were getting ready to leave the field when the band started a fanfare that quickly turned into the wedding march.

Nicole frowned. What on earth? Then the crowd gasped.

"Nicole, look!"

She stared at the reader board and saw it had changed from the score to a message.

"Nicole, marry me."

Her body froze. This was not happening. She wanted to bolt, but she couldn't seem to move. Then she looked down at the field and saw Hawk grinning up at her as if this was the coolest thing in the world.

Just like that? He proposed in public? No conversation, no apology for ducking out on her, no talk about the reality of their situation and how they were going to deal with the complications of her life and his life and the life they'd created together? Just a proposal, because hey, if he was willing to marry her, everything had to be okay?

She hadn't thought the pain could get worse, but it did. If he'd really loved her, he would have talked to her. Didn't he understand how much she needed to hear the words and believe them?

She could feel him watching her. Actually, she could feel everyone watching her. Heat climbed her cheeks. She just wanted to disappear.

Instead she grabbed her purse and stood, then walked out of the stadium. She went directly to her car and drove away.

CHAPTER TWENTY-ONE

NICOLE RETURNED HOME from what felt like an endless day at the bakery only to find she could barely move inside her house. There were wall-to-wall football players. They were polite, eating enough for five times their number and oddly protective of her.

In the time it took her to cross from the back door to the doorway between the kitchen and the great room, she'd been relieved of the small bag she was carrying, asked how she was feeling twice and had an offer to go put gas in her car.

"I'm fine," she told them all.

"Yes, ma'am. We know," a boy named Kenny said. "We'll be quiet. You won't even know we're here."

There were at least ten of them. She was going to know.

"There are cookies in the pantry," she said. "And a big box of frozen mini tacos that are pretty good in the microwave. Help yourself."

Thank goodness for Costco, she thought as she

made her way through the football players and climbed the stairs. Before Raoul had moved in, she'd never seen the point of buying for four hundred. Now she understood.

She closed the door of the bedroom and walked over to the bed. She knew why the guys were there. It was Wednesday and they'd been hanging out at her house every afternoon this week. They would leave when Raoul got home from working at the bakery. For some reason, he didn't think she should be alone. It was sweet in a way. He was trying to take care of her.

He was going to be an extraordinary man, she told herself. One day he would find someone equally amazing and they would have a marriage that millions would envy. Including her. Because her love life was still floating in the toilet.

She loved Hawk enough to both be furious and feel bad for him. His move had been totally dumb. Why would she agree to marry him when they hadn't even talked about the baby or how they felt about each other? His announcement that he loved her had been overshadowed by his bolt for freedom when she'd mentioned her pregnancy.

But she did feel bad that he'd been publicly humiliated. He was a guy with a big ego. Maybe too big. Maybe he couldn't recover from what had happened.

Better to know now, she told herself. If he couldn't handle the reality of a relationship, she needed to know that. But thinking the words didn't erase the knot in her stomach.

She curled up on her side and pulled her knees to her chest. She kept waiting for him to show up and convince her he meant it. But he'd managed to keep his distance now for four days.

A couple of hours later, someone knocked on her bedroom door.

"I'm home," Raoul called. "The guys are gone."

She stood and crossed to let him in. "You can't keep doing that. Your friends need to get their own lives. I'm perfectly capable of taking care of myself."

He ignored that and instead held out a large, thick envelope with the University of Washington logo in the corner. "They're making a really good offer," he said. "They'll want me to live on campus the first year, but I'll still be close and I can come back anytime you need me."

He was only eighteen. This wasn't his baby and she was only the person who'd given him a place to stay. But Raoul was loyal and responsible and he wanted to make sure she was taken care of.

"I don't know if I should slap you or hug you," she said, settling on putting her hands on her hips. "Either way, you are not putting your dreams on hold because I'm pregnant."

"I'm still playing ball. They have a good team and they're in a good conference. This is an offer I need to consider."

"You are not picking a college based on the fact that I'm pregnant. I'm the grown-up here. I'll be fine."

"I want to be sure."

Which was too sweet. "Raoul, I was born to take care of the world. I accept it. You need to consider all your offers and make your decision based on what is best for you. Pretend I don't exist."

"I can't. You've been there for me."

"We'll talk about this later," she said. "Okay?"

He nodded.

She was more touched than she could say and in more pain than she wanted him to know. While she knew he was speaking from the heart and she would always remember this moment, she also understood why he was worried. He didn't think Hawk was going to come through. She had a bad feeling he was right.

CLAIRE'S STOMACH had grown since the last time Hawk had seen her at that dinner at her house. He hadn't paid attention to the changes pregnant women went through since Serena had been carrying Brittany, and that was a long time ago. Now he found himself wanting to ask how Claire was feeling and when she was due. It just wasn't natural.

But then nothing had been right for a while now. He missed Nicole more than he'd ever missed anyone. He was also angry and humiliated by the way she'd left him hanging out there.

It had taken him a couple of days to cool down and try to see things from her point of view. But the embarrassment still burned.

"I don't know what to do," he told Claire as she led him into her living room.

"Which is why I agreed to see you," Nicole's sister said. She motioned for him to sit on the sofa, while she took one of the chairs opposite. "I heard about what happened on Friday at the game. Did you really think it was a good idea?"

"Obviously or I wouldn't have done it. I wanted her to know I was serious."

Claire stared at him for a long time. He could see a lot of Nicole in her sister, although Nicole was much prettier.

"You took off like your butt was on fire when she told you she was pregnant," Claire said. She didn't sound amused.

Hawk resisted the need to squirm. "I wasn't expecting it. I needed time to figure out what was going on."

"Telling a woman you love her then running for the hills isn't exactly the kind of demonstration we're looking for."

"It was a lot to take in. I didn't have any warning." He leaned forward and stared at Claire. "I didn't expect to fall in love with her, okay? I loved Serena and when she died I figured I was done with love. I dated some, but I never seemed to get serious. I didn't see the point. No one got to me the way Nicole does."

He paused to remember their first meeting. "She's so damn tough on the outside. Smart and mouthy. She'd rather eat glass than let anyone think she's got a vulnerable side, but she also has the biggest heart I've ever seen. She's kind and generous and she'll get in my face when she thinks I'm wrong. God, I love her."

He rested his forearms on his thighs. "But I don't know how to tell her that. I don't know how to make it right. I pulled what I thought was this big romantic gesture and it blew up in my face."

Claire's expression softened. "Hawk, I hate to break it to you, but nothing about what you did was romantic. It wasn't about Nicole and her needs. It was about you and your ego. You didn't just want to propose, you wanted to be the star. That's not the way to win most women and it's sure not the way to win Nicole."

"I know that now," he muttered. "What is the way?"

"Tell her what you told me. Tell her why you love her. Tell her that she's special and you've never known anyone like her. Tell her you love her more than anyone in the world."

He started to say he couldn't love her that way. That Brittany would always have a special place in his heart. Only his feelings for his daughter had nothing to do with his feelings for Nicole. They were totally different relationships.

"I don't want to lose her," he said slowly. "I can't."

"You shouldn't. I think she needs you as much as you need her. The trick is going to be getting her to admit it."

Hawk thanked her and left. He wanted to see Nicole, but instead he drove home and went into his study where he made a list of all the possible ways he could win Nicole.

BRITTANY STOPPED by after school on Wednesday.

"I can't stay long," she said as she walked into the house and smiled at Nicole. "I'm still grounded, which is a total drag. My dad really didn't like the whole fake ID thing. I think it's because it's easier to deal with than me having sex with Raoul. Is that a dad thing?"

Nicole was surprised to see the teen. "Um, I'm sure it is."

Brittany handed over the basket she was carrying. "This is for you. Kind of an apology for everything." She sighed. "I'm doing a lot of apologizing lately and I'm getting really good at it. I'm not sure that's an improvement or not. I think I'm supposed to get to the place where I don't have to apologize. Oh, my dad took me shopping for all this. I didn't sneak out. In fact, it was kind of his idea."

Nicole didn't know what to think. She still hadn't heard from Hawk and it hurt more than she could say. If he'd really meant his proposal, wouldn't he have tried to get in touch with her? Except she was the one who had rejected him, so maybe it was up to her. The problem was, she didn't know what she wanted and she was terrified about putting herself on the line and admitting her feelings. Which meant they were both trapped in silence until one of them managed to make the first move.

Brittany set the basket on the sofa. "Well, open it."

Nicole settled on the couch and pulled off the ribbon holding on the tinted plastic.

Inside were a couple of books on pregnancy, a stuffed bear, a receiving blanket, baby wipes, a baby-naming book, a gift certificate for ten hours of babysitting from Brittany, a rubber duck and a rattle.

Small presents, silly presents, but so thoughtful.

"This was really sweet," she said, fighting a rush of emotion. "Thank you."

"You're welcome." Brittany grinned. "I liked buying the baby stuff. My dad told me a lot about when I was little, which was cool. He's excited, too, about having more kids. He told me."

The teen hesitated. "I know my mom and dad really loved each other and it's hard for me to think of my dad marrying again. But he's a really great guy and he deserves someone special. Someone like you, Nicole."

Which was great to hear, but did the message come from Brittany or Hawk and, if it was Hawk, what on earth was he doing sending it through his daughter?

"Thanks," Nicole told her. "That means a lot."

"We're changing stuff at the house. Painting and getting some new furniture. Dad's had me pack up a lot of the pictures. I'm keeping most of them to help me remember my mom. It's kind of hard, but it's good, too. You know? Making changes. Dad says it's time for us to move on."

"I'm glad," Nicole said, hoping the moving on meant moving toward her. Was that what Hawk wanted her to think? And if it was, why wasn't he telling her himself?

THE KEY TO WINNING a game was the details, Hawk thought as he diagramed out his strategy. Practice the basics, the essential skills that the other team would take for granted. Want it more than anyone else, put in the time and have a plan for success.

He picked up the phone. It was time for the first play of the game.

FLOWERS ARRIVED at the bakery Thursday morning. Beautiful starburst lilies with pink and white roses. The card said, "I can't stop thinking about you."

Nicole touched the perfect petals and, for the first time since the previous Friday, felt herself relax. She hadn't driven him away, rejecting his proposal like that. Which was good. Did he understand why it hadn't been enough? Did he really love her?

She stared at the phone, wanting to call him and

ask, but she wasn't ready to talk to him. Not until she was sure.

At eleven, a real estate agent called.

"Ms. Keyes? I'm Geralyn Wilder. I have some material I'd like to send you."

Nicole stared at the phone. "Okay, I think you have the wrong person. I'm not looking for a new house."

"Mr. Eric Hawkins was very clear. He said for me to find the perfect house for a family. One close to your business and his school, with plenty of bedrooms and a big lot. I have a few listings I'd like to drop by. Will you be available tomorrow morning?"

"I guess," Nicole said, not sure how to take the information. A big house perfect for a family sounded good to her. She pressed a hand to her chest and decided maybe, just maybe, it was okay to hope.

Chocolate was delivered at one, followed by a short man with a crew cut at two.

"Ms. Keyes, I'm Don Addison. May we speak privately?"

Nicole was more than a little nervous as she led Mr. Addison into her office. He shut the door.

"I'm a private detective, hired by Mr. Hawkins. He came to me a couple of days ago and told me about your sister. That she's moved away. As she's well over eighteen, she has a perfect right to do that, but family members worry about each other. I've found her."

Nicole sank onto her chair. "You found Jesse?"

"Yes. Mr. Hawkins made it clear. If you don't want to know, I'll walk away. It's up to you."

Nicole didn't know what to think. She'd been so torn about Jesse. About letting her go versus going after her. The old battle between head and heart.

"Tell me," she whispered.

He handed her a folder. "She made it as far as Spokane. She's working in a bar. The owner seems to have taken her under his wing. He's older, a well-liked member of the community. There's nothing romantic or sexual between them. He appears to be acting like a surrogate father. Her health is good. She recently saw a doctor about her pregnancy and all appears normal."

She didn't ask how he knew that or got access to Jesse's medical records. What did it matter? What was important was her sister was okay. She'd managed to find a place for herself, which was all Nicole could have asked for.

"Thank you so much for this," she said, hugging the file close to her chest.

"You're welcome. Mr. Hawkins has prepaid for quarterly reports. Would you like me to deliver them to you directly?"

Nicole nodded.

The man excused himself and left.

She looked at the clock and saw it was still early in the afternoon. Hawk would be at the high school, practicing for the play-offs.

She thought about the flowers, the house, and most important, the report on Jesse. Hawk had more than proved he knew her and understood what was important to her.

She grabbed her car keys and hurried out of the bakery.

Fifteen minutes later she walked toward the football field. Hawk stood with his players, a clipboard in his hands. He blew his whistle and the guys formed two lines.

She moved to the side of the field, prepared to wait until he could take a break, but when Hawk looked up and saw her, he literally dropped everything onto the grass and started toward her. Nicole hurried toward him and they met by the fence.

"I'm sorry," she said, while at the same time he said, "I screwed up."

"You didn't," she told him.

"I shouldn't have proposed like that. I didn't get it. We had to talk because I ran off when you told me about the baby. It's not that I don't want more kids. I was just surprised."

She stared into his dark eyes, telling herself the love burning there had to be good news. "Are you sure? You said before you didn't want another family."

"That was because of Brittany. This is different. I love you, Nicole. I want to have kids with you. I want to love you forever. I want us to be together. I want to make you happy."

"You do."

"I haven't, but I will."

She put her hands on his shoulders. "You found Jesse for me."

"I wanted to show you how much you mattered to me. I knew you were torn up about what to do. It was a risk. You could have been mad."

"She's okay. Did he tell you? She's okay. I needed to know that."

Hawk cupped her jaw and kissed her. "God, I love you. Do you believe me? I love you, Nicole. Not just because you're beautiful or great in bed. But because you get in my face and tell me the truth. You never back down. You're loyal and tough and soft and giving. I never want to spend another night apart from you. I love you and I want to marry you."

The words washed over her like a warm, healing rain. "I love you, too."

He stared at her, hope bright and alive in his gaze. "Are you sure?"

"Very sure. I think I've been in love with you from the first minute you walked into my bakery. You were just so damned hot."

"I know."

She laughed. "You have the biggest ego of anyone I know."

He leaned close. "That's not all that's big."

She leaned against him and he held her tight. Held her as if he would never let her go.

"We have complications," she said. "I don't think Raoul and Brittany should be living under the same roof."

"I'm not waiting to marry you. Unless you want me to."

She eyed him. "So I'm in charge?"

He looked uncomfortable, but nodded.

She grinned. "You're so lying."

"You can try to be in charge. Maybe I'll like it."

That made her laugh again.

"I'm never letting you go," he told her. "We'll figure it out."

Then he kissed her. A long, slow, sexy kiss that made her blood heat and her toes curl. Somewhere in the background, she heard the hoots and applause from the players.

"Ignore them," Hawk murmured against her mouth. "Let 'em get their own girl."

* * * * *

Don't miss Jesse's story in
SWEET TROUBLE
Available September 2008
from SUSAN MALLERY
and HQN Books!

Turn the page for your sneak preview...

DESPITE THE PROMISES of several famous poets and a couple of tear-jerker country songs, Jesse Keyes discovered it *was* possible to go home again, which was just her bad luck. Not that she could blame anyone for her current circumstances—she'd decided to return to Seattle all on her own. Well, okay, maybe she'd had a little help from the cute guy in her life.

She glanced in the rearview mirror and smiled at her four-year-old son.

"Guess what?" she asked.

His dark eyes brightened as he grinned at her. "Are we there yet?"

"We're here!"

Gabe clapped his hands. "I like here."

They were in town for the summer or however long it took to get her past in order and her future set. Give or take a week.

Jesse put the car in Park, then got out and opened the rear passenger door. She unbuckled Gabe from his car seat and helped him out of the car. He stood next to her and stared at the four-story building.

"We're staying here?" he asked, his voice low with awe. "Really?"

The extended-stay hotel was modest at best—a local place. Jesse didn't have the money for one of those fancy national chains. But the room came with a kitchen and the online reviews had said it was clean, which was what mattered to her. Once she had an idea of how long they were staying, she would look into renting a furnished apartment in the university district. It was summer, which meant empty rooms while the students were away, and cheap rent.

But to Gabe, who'd never been in a hotel in his life, their temporary shelter was exciting and new.

"Really," she said, taking his hand. "Want me to get a room on the top floor?"

His eyes widened. "Can we?" he breathed.

It would mean more stairs for her, but she would feel safer up top. "That's what I asked for."

"Cool!"

Thirty minutes later they were testing the bounce in the two double beds as Gabe tried to decide which one he wanted. She unpacked the single suitcase she'd carried up the three flights of stairs. She really had to think about starting to work out again. Her heart was *still* racing from the climb.

"We're going out for dinner," she said. "How about spaghetti?"

Gabe flung himself at her, wrapping both his arms around her thighs and squeezing as hard as he could. She stroked his soft brown hair.

"Thank you, Mommy," he whispered. Because eating his favorite food ever out in a restaurant was a rare treat.

Jesse wondered if she should feel guilty for not cooking her first night in Seattle, then decided she would beat herself up later. Right now she was tired. It had been a five-hour drive from Spokane, and she'd worked well past midnight the previous evening, wanting to earn every last tip she could. Money was going to be tight while she was in Seattle.

"You're welcome." She dropped to her knees so she was at eye level with him. "I think you'll really like this place. It's called the Old Spaghetti Factory." A perfect, kid-friendly restaurant. No one would care if Gabe made a mess and she could have a glass of wine and pretend that everything was all right.

"Do I meet my daddy tomorrow?"

Jesse's heart raced again, and this time it had nothing to do with taking the stairs. "Probably not tomorrow, but soon."

Gabe bit his lower lip. "I love my daddy."

"I know you do."

Or at least the idea of having a father. Her son was the reason she'd decided to face all the ghosts in her past and come home. He'd started asking questions about his father a year ago. Why didn't he have a daddy? Where was his daddy? Why didn't his daddy want to be with him?

Jesse had debated lying, simply saying that Matt

was dead. But five years ago, when she'd left Seattle, she'd vowed to live her life differently. No more lies. No more screwing up. She'd worked hard to grow up, to make a life she was proud of, to raise a son on her own, to be honest, no matter what.

Which meant telling Gabe the truth. That Matt didn't know about him, but maybe it was time to change that.

She didn't allow herself to think about meeting Matt. She couldn't. Not and keep breathing. So for now, there was only her son smiling at her and the love she felt for him. The rest would take care of itself. At least she hoped it would.

Because it wasn't just Matt she had to face. There was Claire, the older sister she'd never really known, and Nicole, the older sister who probably still hated her guts. Talk about a homecoming.

But she would deal with that tomorrow. Tonight there was the promise of spaghetti, then a rousing evening of cartoons and quality time with the best part of her life.

"Are you ready?" she asked as she grabbed her purse, then held out her arms to pick up Gabe.

He jumped into her embrace—loving and trusting—as if she would never hurt him, never let him down. Because she never would—no matter what. At least she'd gotten that part right.

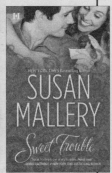

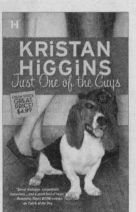

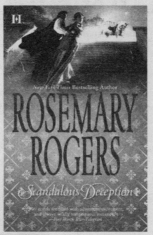

REQUEST YOUR
FREE BOOKS!

2 FREE NOVELS
FROM THE ROMANCE/SUSPENSE
COLLECTION PLUS 2 FREE GIFTS!

YES! Please send me 2 FREE novels from the Romance/Suspense Collection and my 2 FREE gifts (gifts are worth about $10). After receiving them, if I don't wish to receive any more books, I can return the shipping statement marked "cancel." If I don't cancel, I will receive 4 brand-new novels every month and be billed just $5.49 per book in the U.S. or $5.99 per book in Canada, plus 25¢ shipping and handling per book plus applicable taxes, if any*. That's a savings of at least 20% off the cover price! I understand that accepting the 2 free books and gifts places me under no obligation to buy anything. I can always return a shipment and cancel at any time. Even if I never buy another book from the Reader Service, the two free books and gifts are mine to keep forever.

185 MDN EF5Y 385 MDN EF6C

Name	(PLEASE PRINT)

Address	Apt. #

City	State/Prov.	Zip/Postal Code

Signature (if under 18, a parent or guardian must sign)

Mail to **The Reader Service:**
IN U.S.A.: P.O. Box 1867, Buffalo, NY 14240-1867
IN CANADA: P.O. Box 609, Fort Erie, Ontario L2A 5X3

Not valid to current subscribers to the Romance Collection,
the Suspense Collection or the Romance/Suspense Collection.

**Want to try two free books from another line?
Call 1-800-873-8635 or visit www.morefreebooks.com.**

* Terms and prices subject to change without notice. N.Y. residents add applicable sales tax. Canadian residents will be charged applicable provincial taxes and GST. Offer not valid in Quebec. This offer is limited to one order per household. All orders subject to approval. Credit or debit balances in a customer's account(s) may be offset by any other outstanding balance owed by or to the customer. Please allow 4 to 6 weeks for delivery. Offer available while quantities last.

Your Privacy: Harlequin is committed to protecting your privacy. Our Privacy Policy is available online at www.eHarlequin.com or upon request from the Reader Service. From time to time we make our lists of customers available to reputable third parties who may have a product or service of interest to you. If you would prefer we not share your name and address, please check here. ☐

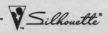

SPECIAL EDITION™

NEW YORK TIMES
BESTSELLING AUTHOR

DIANA PALMER

A brand-new Long, Tall Texans novel

HEART OF STONE

Feeling unwanted and unloved, Keely returns
to Jacobsville and to Boone Sinclair, a rancher
troubled by his own past. Boone has always
seemed reserved, but now Keely discovers a
sensuality with him that quickly turns to love. Can
they each see past their own scars to let love in?

*Available September 2008
wherever you buy books.*

SUSAN
MALLERY

77297	SWEET TALK	___ $6.99 U.S. ___	$6.99 CAN.
77205	ACCIDENTALLY YOURS	___ $6.99 U.S. ___	$8.50 CAN.
77210	TEMPTING	___ $6.99 U.S. ___	$8.50 CAN.
77176	SIZZLING	___ $6.99 U.S. ___	$8.50 CAN
77117	IRRESISTIBLE	___ $6.99 U.S. ___	$8.50 CAN
77056	DELICIOUS	___ $6.99 U.S. ___	$8.50 CAN..

(limited quantities available)

TOTAL AMOUNT	$ _____
POSTAGE & HANDLING	$ _____
($1.00 FOR 1 BOOK, 50¢ for each additional)	
APPLICABLE TAXES*	$ _____
TOTAL PAYABLE	$ _____

(check or money order—please do not send cash)

To order, complete this form and send it, along with a check or money order for the total above, payable to HQN Books, to: **In the U.S.:** 3010 Walden Avenue, P.O. Box 9077, Buffalo, NY 14269-9077; **In Canada:** P.O. Box 636, Fort Erie, Ontario, L2A 5X3.

Name: _____
Address: _____ City: _____
State/Prov.: _____ Zip/Postal Code: _____
Account Number (if applicable): _____

075 CSAS

*New York residents remit applicable sales taxes.
*Canadian residents remit applicable GST and provincial taxes.

HQN™

We *are* romance™

www.HQNBooks.com

PHSM0808BL